# A Vain Thing

# A VAIN THING

four novellas by
Tom Wayman

TURNSTONE PRESS

Turnstone Press
Artspace Building
018-100 Arthur Street
Winnipeg, MB
R3B 1H3 Canada
www.TurnstonePress.com

Turnstone Press gratefully acknowledges the assistance of the Canada Council
for the Arts, the Manitoba Arts Council, the Government of Canada through
the Book Publishing Industry Development Program, and the Government of
Manitoba through the Department of Culture, Heritage and Tourism, Arts
Branch, for our publishing activities.

The names, characters, locations and events portrayed in these stories are
entirely fictional. Any references to historical figures and actual locations,
or descriptions of landscapes, are for fictional purposes only and are not
intended to represent reality. Any accuracy is coincidental and unintended by
the author.

Cover design: Jamis Paulson
Interior design: Sharon Caseburg
Cover image: Jeremy Addington
Edited by: Wayne Tefs
Printed and bound in Canada by Friesens for Turnstone Press.

Library and Archives Canada Cataloguing in Publication

Wayman, Tom, 1945-
    A vain thing / Tom Wayman.

ISBN 978-0-88801-328-6

    I. Title.

PS8595.A9V33 2007          C813'.54          C2007-905851-5

*Why do the nations so furiously rage together,
and why do the people imagine a vain thing?*

G.F. Handel, *Messiah* (after Psalm 2:1-2)

# CONTENTS

# A Vain Thing

VANITY is an old song, one of humanity's most ancient. Species, race, nation, our own personal attributes and our creative and other endeavours can be construed to be evidence of our individual importance, attractiveness, fitness to control others and decree truths. Despite ours being a planet of competing vanities, each with its accompanying delusions, art gets constructed, love flourishes and sometimes triumphs, societies more or less function. The wonder of it is what I mean these tales to convey.

# The Nations

# Djakarta Now

Two young dudes have the occupants of the shiny Mercedes absolutely freaking. We're stopped at a light at Clark Drive en route to the press conference and I'm reviewing my briefing notes and not paying attention. Adam, who is driving the van, yanks my sleeve and points to our left. "Check this out," he grins. The Muscle in the back seat—three from the bodyguard pool, only one of whom I'd met before—are also digging the action and chuckling.

The guys at the Mercedes—mid-twenties, I'd say, with jeans, ball caps, one with a Hoyas bulldog jacket and the other a tattered-looking sweatshirt—must have been in the crosswalk when they scoped the car's inhabitants. In the driver's seat is a young Honger woman, wearing a fashionable power business suit, swivelled away from her side window and frantically jabbering into a cell phone. In the back seat an elderly couple—also in expensive-looking garb, probably Miz Bizness' aged parents—are desperately clutching each other.

One of the young guys has crouched down with his face at the level of the rear side window. He's alternately pointing the first finger of his right hand toward the old folks and then flashing them the "D" sign as vehemently as he can: first finger of his left hand raised, with the thumb and first finger of his right hand joined to the vertical digit to make the curve of the letter. The two-handed D is jerked toward the couple with all the emphasis you use shooting someone your middle finger if you really mean it. D for Djakarta: what you bastards got coming to you, unless you get the fuck out of our country. The kid is yelling at Mom and Pop Gook, but I can't hear a distinct word over the noise of engines idling around us. I can imagine, though.

His pal is flashing the same D sign at the woman behind the wheel, except he's flipping out. One second he's draped half on top of the car, knocking on the sunroof window and showing the D through there. Next second he's pounding on the driver's side window. Then suddenly he's sprawled across the hood, hammering on the windshield like a crazy fool, alternating between a rain of blows and jabbing seven or eight good Ds into the faces on the other side. As he rolls off the hood, he clutches one of the wipers for support and "accidentally" bends it all to shit.

I glance around at the other vehicles waiting patiently like us for the light to change, occasionally gunning their motors. The usual East End mix of drivers: whites, East Indians, dusky folks of some indeterminate description—Filipinos?—and of course lots and lots of Orientals. Their eyes either are observing the boys busy at the Mercedes or are carefully gazing elsewhere. Nobody appears anything other than bored or indifferent.

Then I hear shouts from somewhere behind us, and suddenly the back doors of our van are open and the cabin fills with the damp spring air—it rained most of the night. The Muscle are standing out on the pavement to the left of the van.

I can't see too clearly from the right-hand seat, but Adam keeps me posted. A boom-car back down the line—a beat-up Firebird or IROC—packed with a bunch of what Adam speculates are young Vietnamese-Chinkies, has disgorged four or five guys who look like they might be interested in interfering with the fun the boys in the crosswalk are having. Before the Boats can thread their way forward through the traffic, however, the wall of Muscle has materialized up ahead to block their path. No question who they are, beefy as hell with the big red DN on their jackets. The Muscle have put their sunglasses on; they don't look like anybody you'd want to mess with. The Boats stay in a milling clump alongside their car—smart move.

The emergence of my people from the van distracts the pair in the crosswalk. Once they see the lettering on our van they start toward us, waving their arms and hooting gleefully.

"Alright, alright!"

"Hey, DN! Yeah!"

The duo are obviously still pumped by their little political dem-onstration. As the shorter of the two dudes passes in front of the Hongmobile, he takes out the passenger side headlight with the back of his boot. Glass all over the bumper.

Then the two must recognize me in the passenger's seat, because the next second they've dashed around and are cavorting to the right of the van at my window. Huge gap-toothed smirks and laughter, a high-five slapped to each other. This near to them, I can see both sport thin scraggly beards. The skin below their eyes is too weathered for what you'd expect on a young person. On their pitted cheeks grog-blossoms are poised to flower, as though to indicate where the blows of life have smashed them in the face.

The boys are plenty stoked. "It's Bryan."

"Bry-an! Bry-an!"

"We're with you, man."

I switch the window down. "Gentlemen," I say sternly. "I see you're having yourselves a good D."

That cracks them up. "Hey, a good D to you, too, buddy."

"Yeah: have a nice D! Yee-haw."

"Keep pushing, Bryan. Don't let up on the fuckers."

Supporters. Voters. I flash them some teeth, put my hand out, and we shake vigorously.

"Geez, it's a real honour to meet you, man."

"Way to go, Bryan. We're for you. A hundred per cent. Two hundred."

The light changes. "Thanks, men," I declare. The lane of traffic to our left begins flowing; the Mercedes screeches through the intersection the second it can.

The Muscle climb into the rear seat and settle themselves. Some brave honks float up the line from behind us. One more round of hand-shakes insisted on by the boys and they split for the curb. Adam steers us across Clark Drive.

I turn around to compliment the Muscle on their professional han-dling of the situation. "No problem, Bryan," one of them replies. Nobody smiles, but they're not paid to smile. They appear pleased, though; everybody can use a little praise. "An ounce of prevention," the stockiest of the Muscle pronounces sagely. I'm a bit taken aback that any of them would quote that hoary bit of wisdom, but I nod and resume scanning my notes. People tend to be surprising; that's what's endlessly interesting about them.

The Crip has arranged for the media to assemble at a conference room in some swanky new hotel in the Howe Street financial district. Don't ask me how he does it, and on such short notice. The event we are supposed to be responding to only occurred about midnight. Less than ten hours later, The Crip's team had all the arrangements made, TV, radio and the papers notified, and a statement in my hands to base my remarks on. Adam and a few others on the Council and around the office laugh at Bruce—The Crip—when he's not around. Bruce is solemn and serious and definitely gimped: one arm a flipper and two-count-'em-two hearing aids. Yet any success we're enjoying is in no small part due to Bruce and his eye for details, and his willingness to put in the hours. You'll never see Adam hauling his fat ass out of bed in the middle of the night to seize an opportunity to make some political hay. If it was up to Adam, we'd still be calling press confer-ences in some rinky-dink East Van community centre. And the only coverage we'd receive would be when the community centre board cancels our booking at the last minute in some clumsy and prob-ably illegal way, and we're burning up our time and energy protesting that instead of getting on with the job. "Don't sweat the small stuff" is Adam's motto. I've noticed that's the handy excuse many people adopt for not paying attention, and for goofing up nearly every task they're assigned.

The Crip may not be much for strategy, but that's the Suits' job, in any case. At least The Crip doesn't shoot off his face embarrassingly at Council meetings, like Adam does. Talk about lowering the tone of a discussion. Lard-butt Adam doesn't know it but his days on Council are numbered. And The Crip has a kind of genius for tactics when it comes to publicity—which is exactly the skill he's paid to have.

When the van pulls into the unloading zone of the hotel, a dozen more Muscle are lined up to escort me inside. I no longer have any idea how many people we've hired as Muscle; security work falls under The Crip's direction. I can remember when I knew all the guys personally. Those days are definitely history. When The Crip first proposed we develop a regular security squad—this was after somebody torched our storefront on Fourth east of Burrard—I was dubious. The Crip had a hard-on for the Black Muslim's Fruit of Islam bodyguards, and had made quite a pitch to Council for us to adopt the same: he had photos, news clips, recruitment criteria, budget. Lots of jokes among the original Council members about Fruit of the Loom. But in terms of optics, the Muscle—officially, the DN Security Service—paid off like a damn. "Television is about conflict," The Crip always says. Without question, any group of these guys look like Conflict personified. Once they emerged onto the scene, our coverage soared like crazy. Our poll numbers began to lift along with it.

Sure enough, as I step out of the van, TV lights blaze on, with the Muscle keeping the camera crews back as we proceed toward the hotel doors. Three or four nice-looking girls break through—or are allowed to, or are paid to; you never know with The Crip. I duly scribble some autographs. I once read where Elvis' manager at the start paid teenyboppers to scream and faint and mob the King. I asked Bruce if he had arranged the same for me, when these babes first started to demand my signature each time I appeared in public. More than just beautiful ladies show up, but inevitably some major honeys, too. "You're a good-looking guy, Bryan," was The Crip's reply. "You didn't answer my question," I pointed out, but he just smiled his annoying little smile.

I guess the ladies' true motivation doesn't really matter at this point, except the scene pisses off Marcie. I insist that a politician kissing babes is no different than a politician kissing babies, except Marcie has no sense of humour about some things. I've told her it's all about image, and staged, and entirely the fault of The Crip—except, I call him Bruce around Marcie. She doesn't see nicknames as a guy thing, but an affront to human decency. Hey, I know for a fact that those on the inside refer to me as The Mouth rather than their glorious Leader. But Marcie won't hear Bruce referred to by any other name. I also mentioned to her once that Bruce said I'm a handsome dog, and asked if she agreed. I mean, I look awfully hunky in the official portraits, if I do say so; of course, that's what the image consultants are retained for. But I wanted to learn from Marcie if *she* thought I was good-looking. She just smiled the same irritating smile The Crip produces. I couldn't believe I'd get this at work and on the home front, too. Okay, not at home, exactly, since The Big M and I don't live together. When I pressed her about my handsome quotient, she looked me up and down and said, "You always look handsome to me, dear," in this mocking tone. Then she laughed. I couldn't judge whether she was trying to needle me or what. And I couldn't get her to be serious about my question.

But at the hotel I sign the bits of paper waved in front of me, and one of the ladies with a bodacious set of assets steals a kiss. The TV guys love it.

Then we flow on through the big doors into the hotel lobby and here's The Crip. He's even managed to round up a half-dozen other members of the Council, including Andrew, obviously representing the Suits, and Priscilla, the legal beagle of our group, a tough-faced and tough-minded lady lawyer of the matching-gloves-and-handbag sort. Behind them are five or six more Muscle: these guys are becoming a regular army.

So it's handshakes all around for more footage and still photos, and then I'm escorted into the conference centre auditorium. The Crip has outdone himself again—lots of banners and a couple of huge portraits of yours truly on the wall behind the podium. I'm still not used to the sight of me in a tie. For months after the decision that a suit-and-tie for me was better optics for us, I hated the relentless choking pressure of the damn knot around my throat. Now I'm so accustomed to a tie— even if I haven't adjusted to suddenly encountering photos of myself wearing one—that I'd feel naked presiding at an official function without wrapping a strip of cloth around my neck. When we were handed the first set of photos with me in a suit, to select the official PR portrait, I asked Marcie what she thought. She inspected them all and smiled. She refused to pick. When I inquired why she wouldn't help, she said, "Nothing's wrong with any of them. But they're not you, Bryan."

I sneak a word with Bruce as we stride toward the front of the hall.

Any late-breaking developments I should know about? Then we are up on the dais taking our seats. The room is nearly full, with the sides of the hall closest to the front crammed with cameras and sound booms and the rest of the TV paraphernalia. I recall when we were ecstatic if even a solitary reporter from a community give-away paper came to hear what we said.

A thirty-ish woman staffer from The Crip's group rises to the podium and begins in a confident, firm voice to introduce the members of Council perched in the row of chairs behind her. Then: "And now, with a statement from Democracy Now concerning last night's events, here's the Leader of our party and your next provincial premier, Bryan Packard."

Nobody applauds, since this is media and not a rally, but she gives the intro with the same verve and rising intonation as if she had been speaking to an auditorium full of thousands of enthusiastic party members. She probably had the same public speaking training that the Suits and The Crip insisted I take. I grip the edges of the podium and scope around the room, drinking it in, letting everybody have a good squint at the source of all wisdom. The Pause that Focuses the Audience, as the instructor labelled it.

Not that a breathless hush ever falls over *this* audience. The media boys and girls at such gatherings regard my initial remarks merely as the preliminary bout. The main event is the questions the reporters want to ask. And there's barely a friendly in the bunch. We're aiming to play to the audience at home. The mission is to figure out how to get our message across to the folks on the other side of the media screen by any means possible—humour, witty catchphrases, or outrageous statements that everybody knows are true but nobody else will utter. At this precise instant, I'm the sharp end of the entire project. The Council, the Suits, The Crip, the Muscle, the office staffers, and the Action Faction—authorized or not—all function to put me here in front of these mics and lenses. The whole edifice balances for these minutes on my shoulders, or more exactly, on my brain and tongue. This is what they pay me the big bucks for.

I'm joking about the money, but I am making half again what I earned pulling boards and running the trim saw and taking those MBA courses at night. If you don't already loathe Hongers, try taking a night business course. Look up the word "aggressive" in a dictionary, and you'll see a photo of about 90 per cent of your classmates. The hallowed corridors of Uhlman's Technological College, Inc. is where in fact I first saw a notice about a DN rally. I attended out of curiosity, and now I'm the number one man. Naturally, the party has been through about a thousand changes since its bush-league days when I met up with them. Otherwise I wouldn't have stuck around.

I recognize several reporters in the hall—upturned faces of columnists and news hounds who have interviewed me plenty of times. Some strategically placed clusters of Muscle are scattered amid the chairs in case of trouble, while the rest are posted on either side of each exit and in a line behind the row of us on the dais. I glance a last time at my notes, breathe, and we're off.

About eleven-thirty last night four goofs swacked on something-or-other burst into a Chinky nightclub, the Good Luck Bunny, upstairs on Broadway near Oak Street. Ordinarily, no big deal, right? Either some internal dispute of the Hong Kong triads, or gang versus gang among the Boats. Except in this case, the bad guys were indisputably honkeys. In the process of flashing guns around and robbing the patrons, they punched and kicked a few worthy Oriental souls and conked at least one on the head with a weapon. They also fondled a few Suzy Wongs found on the premises. In fact, as the perpetrators escaped through the kitchen and down some back stairs, they took one of the ladies with them as a hostage. And they managed to plug some master of kung fu who intended to bravely Bruce Lee them into submission. A witness got the licence number of the car, and when the cops eventually checked out the owner's apartment they found the hostage none the worse for wear except that she had been tied up and sexually assaulted. The accused wasn't home himself, but the boys in blue claimed to have discovered a fair bit of Djakarta Now literature in the living room.

Since the apartment was the abode of a guy who fell into the classification of "known to police," they zipped over to a house in Burnaby owned by an associate of his they had on file and encountered the suspect vehicle parked at the curb. By this time it was about two A.M. The SWAT team came crashing through the windows and doors and found all four of the alleged criminals snoozing peacefully, tuckered out after their night's work. Rounded 'em up without firing a shot. But again there were Djakarta Now posters and leaflets everyplace, and also one of the four was a card-carrying Democracy Now member.

Of course at the podium I don't recap the events with such flippancy, but rather with great solemnity, as befits a prospective first minister of a great province. I give an extra fillip to the heinous sex-crime angle, since both the media and we are aware that sex doesn't hurt sales of papers and airtime. As The Crip astutely noticed, this little caper in the wee smalls was perfect for us. I pronounce our usual Dire Warning, now reinforced by this latest outrage against peaceful people enjoying themselves of an evening with a little harmless boozing, stuffing their faces and lurching around a dance floor.

"As we have stated on many occasions, British Columbia faces an unprecedented crisis. Current immigration policies have brought us to a crossroads. The citizens of this province can choose either democracy, or another Djakarta. We of the Democracy Now party believe democracy is the better choice."

In case anybody out there hasn't been paying attention to what DN has been yammering for the past eighteen months, I sketch out the Djakarta scenario one more time. Repeat, repeat, repeat is The Crip's mantra as Communications Director. "We're working to be heard over a howl of media static," he is fond of reminding us. His idea is that people's ears are stuffed with celebrity news noise, sports news noise, bogus how-to-get-rich news noise. We're asking people to pay attention to what's happening to *them*, what's happening here at *home*, not the latest in the lives of richies in Hollywood or New York or London—or Toronto or even the ritzy hillsides of West Van. To enable what we're saying to register with anybody through the static, we have to keep sending our message over and over. Eventually bits and pieces become discernible above the prevailing crackle and roar. The Crip claims the technique got a bad rap when the Nazis called it The Big Lie. His view is that The Big Lie now is the silence about how people are hurting from government decisions, from imposed changes in our society. "Our tactic is The Big Truth," he says. Sounds right to me.

Our continual repetition seems to be working with the public, though I could see certain reporters roll their eyes when I tick off the Djakarta facts. Hundreds, maybe thousands, of ethnic Chinese shot, beaten and burned to death in May 1998 in Indonesia's capital city.

Hundreds more assaulted and raped. Homes, stores, entire malls looted and torched. The police and army at best doing nothing, at worst egging the citizens on or even joining in themselves. All this furor aimed against only 3 per cent of Indonesia's population, but a group that somehow managed to control two-thirds of the retail trade. The Crip's staff keep downloading more exquisite details of the carnage off the websites that various Indonesian protest groups and human rights watchdogs still maintain in broken English and constantly update nearly a decade later. Our Communications team had a great fresh tidbit for me to toss into the old stew, given the sex-crime nature of the previous night's activities. You never know with The Crip: he might have had this little delight for a while and was just saving it up, or maybe it really was new. But it fit perfectly. According to one website, families of some women who were raped have only recently begun receiving in the mail graphic photographs of the rape in progress, thereby forcing everybody to relive the trauma.

That gem gets the room stone quiet. Four or five hacks, among those I could see lounging in their seats just waiting for me to finish so they can air their opinions thinly disguised as questions, even stop chewing gum for a minute. How does The Crip do it?

"No person, no family—no matter what harm their ethnic compatriots may have inflicted on a society—should be forced to endure such evil," I intone. "Yet the head-in-the-sand policies of our other political parties are driving British Columbia inevitably toward such a catastrophe, toward another Djakarta. Events such as the tragedy last night prove this. We believe British Columbians do not want a violent resolution to our current predicament. British Columbians do demand relief—and speedily—from the problems that threaten to overwhelm the peace and stability of our province. Democracy Now offers the only viable alternative to the horrors of a Djakarta."

Winding up my opening statement: "When I form the next government, we will provide the citizens of BC with a return to the peaceful social fabric they wish to enjoy again. The people of this province—" big finish "—deserve no less."

Pause for effect as a loud rustle goes through the room, everybody hauling themselves up and awake after my monologue, getting ready for the jousting match, the serve and volley, the exchange of blows.

"Now, I'll take some questions."

Forest of raised hands. The opening shot is the no-brainer. How can DN expect the citizenry to believe it stands for non-violence when one of the alleged violent offenders last night held a DN membership card? No problem: over 15,000 British Columbians have a DN membership card. Within those numbers are bound to be some misguided individuals, we're checking our rolls to be sure he actually is a member, blah blah.

Emily Langford, CBC-TV's Ms. More-Righteous-Than-You'll-Ever-Be, wishes to push it. "As usual, Mr. Packard, I hear a lot of sanctimonious and self-serving crocodile tears from you about government-sponsored violence in Indonesia. What I don't hear from you is some expression of outrage that a member of your organization—I won't call it a political party since you have yet to elect even a single member to the provincial legislature in Victoria—would take part in such despicable and cowardly acts as we saw last night."

Who couldn't love such a sweetheart? "In the first place, Ms. Langford, under the Canadian justice system the men charged with these offenses are not guilty until a court of law has found them to be so. In the second place—" fending off the sudden resurgence of waving hands "—there are two aspects to what occurred last night. One aspect is criminal acts against defenceless people. Such behaviour is intolerable, and exactly what my government will put a rapid end to by increasing funding for every dimension of public safety.

"The other aspect, though, is the targeting of a certain establishment, a nightclub that caters primarily to wealthy economic immigrants of a specific ethnic origin. Hard-working *Canadians* of the same ethnic extraction are unlikely to be found there." Or so the briefing notes claim. Who among the reporters here would know whether this information was true or not?

"Such targetings, as with incidents of tasselling and beatering, are the inevitable consequence of this province's social crisis. No other *political party*—" lots of emphasis on the latter two words "—has been willing to provide any alternative but lip service to our drift toward disaster."

I attempt to recognize another waving hand but Sweet Emily won't leave it alone.

"I still don't hear a repudiation of violence, Mr. Packard."

"The whole existence of Democracy Now is an attempt to offer British Columbians an alternative to violence, to taking matters into their own hands in dealing with the present situation. We are the only party that offers a non-violent solution to the current slide toward a made-in-BC Djakarta."

"So you mean to tell me—"

I cut her off. I remember another approach The Crip suggested at the office one day when we were kicking around ideas on how to better handle these meet-the-press sessions.

"No, no. You tell me, Ms. Langford: do you vote?"

"What?"

"Do you vote?"

"Why?"

"On election day, your editorial duties permitting, do you do your duty as a citizen and go to your assigned polling booth and cast your vote for one of this province's political parties?"

Her voice suspicious: "Yes, I do. Why?"

"So you support one of BC's political parties?"

"I don't know what you're getting at, but it won't—"

"From the tone of your questions, Ms. Langford, I can guess that the political party you favour isn't Democracy Now."

An appreciative chuckle from here and there in the assembly. Ms. Shrill-Mouth isn't the most popular gal among her colleagues. I also sense a little extra electricity in the hall, the faces pointed at me in-trigued to hear where I'm headed with this.

"Ordinarily when you cover a crime," I resume, "I don't see you mentioning whether the suspect is a member of the Liberal Party, or the New Democratic Party, or the Conservatives. Let me guess why you don't include this information in your news report. It isn't because you're a supporter of one of those parties. Oh no. You're too profes-sional a reporter to let your personal political inclinations interfere with your news judgment. In fact, because you are a professional reporter, you understand that it is not relevant that a burglar is an NDP member, or that a bunch of white-collar criminals are card-carrying supporters of the Liberal Party or the Conservative Party."

The lady in question starts to splutter. I ride right over.

"I think if you covered politics in this province fairly, you'd find that every party has its share of members who break the law." Pause for effect. To my surprise I hear applause from scattered places around the room.

"Thank you," I acknowledge the approval. "No party condones illegal behaviour. Democracy Now doesn't either. I'd like to see a news climate where we're not treated any differently than anybody else."

The Right-on Sister's demeanor resembles an apoplectic volcano. "What you're implying, Mr. Packard, is that ... is that I—"

"I'm going to answer someone else's question now, out of fairness," I interrupt. I survey the hall. "Yes. You, there."

Some gentleman with a rather red nose wants to know about the Djakarta Now connection. How is it possible that the suspects in this case could be Democracy Now members and yet simultaneously possess Djakarta Now material? Especially given my assurances that Democracy Now is peace-loving, non-violent, etc., etc.

This is such old ground that I wonder if Red Nose is one of The Crip's plants. But in honour of "repeat, repeat, repeat" and The Big Truth, I steer my tractor across this well-plowed stretch of soil.

"Democracy Now and Djakarta Now have no connection with each other." This has been our iron-clad principle since the beginning: an airtight firewall erected and maintained to separate the two DNs. Let people surmise what they will. Yet let there be no shred of evidence of collusion. So far the barrier has held, although with the Samuel Billy defection—which is sure to be raised by somebody in the room the instant I reiterate our standard denial—a few good dents have been placed in the Great Firewall. Nothing we can't handle, however:

"People desire solutions to our present crisis. My guess is that anyone who harbours belief in both organizations is simply hedging their bets. I surmise, and I stress that this is only my idea, that their attitude is: 'Not necessarily violence, but violence if necessary.' I take this attitude as a spur to us in Democracy Now to succeed. For if we fail, if we do not successfully convince the electorate to vote us in as the next government of this province, all British Columbians face the spectre of many more of our fellow citizens adopting violence as a solution to redress their grievances."

Next up is a minor local celebrity, who a couple of months back had

been demoted from writing a popular sports column to general assignment duties. He had been discovered accepting perks from the loser
management of the loser NHL team all Vancouverites root for and love.
"You're making these goons sound like political scientists."

Shrug. And the next question is? In the fourth row centre a half-
dozen young people are perched, looking out of place in scruffy jeans
and face hardware among the suited, sport-jacketed, dress-skirted, or
casually-but-fashionably-attired journos surrounding them. I surmise
these young folks are from the universities' student newspapers or radio stations—not big supporters of DN, to put it mildly. But, hey, hands
across the generations. I point to an earnest-looking bespectacled girl
with stringy hair and multiple nose rings.

"If you have no connection with Djakarta Now," she squeaks breath-
lessly, exhibiting a stud through her tongue, "why is there a Djakarta
Now bumper sticker on the back of your van?"

Damn good question. A rising buzz of voices in the hall. Out of
the mouths of children. I sweep around to direct a meaningful glance
at The Crip, but he's angled down speaking into a small lavaliere mic
clipped to his lapel. Heads undoubtedly are going to roll: the Muscle
are supposed to keep watch over party property, as well as their other
duties. After a moment he glances up at me. His expression is blank.
No help here. I turn back to my questioner.

"I wasn't aware of any such sign," I stall. Could these kids have
attached it themselves, to cause trouble? Or do we have an agent pro-
vocateur in our own ranks? Perhaps some misguided zealot lurking
among the Muscle? Or maybe the kid is just faking, to throw me off my
stride. "I can't imagine how it got there. Probably somebody intended
to discredit us."

"You'll tear the bumper sticker off, now you know it's there?"
Squeaky again. "To show you distance yourself from Djakarta Now?"

Talk about a leading question. This is sounding more like a set-up;
I figure to stay proactive. "I might. But then again, I might just leave it
on as yet another reminder to myself and others of the consequences if
Democracy Now does not expend every effort to persuade the voters
to elect us into office."

Back to a question from an adult. "Mr. Packard, you insist as always
there is no collusion between Democracy Now and Djakarta Now. But

you're well aware that a former member of your Executive Council was pretty vocal last September in claiming that these organizations are actually two sides of the same coin. Do you think—"

In order to deflect a jab like this, at one time I would have adopted a testy, exasperated voice. Our image consultant ixnayed using that tone. My reply is strictly Mr. Sincere.

"I'd be very pleased to review *once again*—" heavy emphasis on the last two words "—our relations with Mr. Samuel Billy, and his, shall we say, addictive difficulties which led him to make some statements he has since recanted." I glance around the room, as though for support. "I think this is old news. But if you want me to run through the events yet again.... "

"Spin," somebody calls from a middle row. "You mean, spin the events again."

I shrug. "These are the facts. Mr. Billy was a First Peoples activist from Haida Gwaii. He saw parallels between the devastation his tribe suffered from the occupation of their homelands by the influx of whites in the 1800s, and the consequences for all British Columbians of today's immigration policies. DN welcomed his participation in our party, and he subsequently became a member of our Executive Council. We were not aware at the time that he had, as he himself has freely admitted, a serious drinking problem. Once we became aware of the extent of his regrettable addiction, and its effect on his political work, he was asked to resign. Mr. Billy subsequently has sought treatment for his problem."

Red Nose resurfaces. "Mr. Billy claimed he witnessed co-ordination at the highest levels of your party between Democracy Now and Djakarta Now."

I released the Long-Suffering Sigh. Image consultant be damned. "Yes, I recall those accusations. They were not backed by any tangible evidence. Mr. Billy later withdrew his statements, when challenged to produce proof in a court of law. As he said at the time, his statements were made under the influence of his problem. He said he was hurt and angry about being asked to leave the Executive Council, and had intemperately lashed out. We accepted his apology."

"Very noble of you, I'm sure." This from Vauxhall Smith, the recently transplanted Brit who is the afternoon paper's newest political columnist. His previous exposure to Canadian issues consists of eleven months in total on the Toronto *Globe and Mail*. But he radiates a sort of languorous self-confidence that convinces himself and presumably his editors, if not his readers, that he already comprehends everything worth knowing about the backwater politics of his newly adopted country.

"Whether or not evidential links exist between your organization and any other," the pudgy columnist drawls, "the pertinent question is—"

"What about the bumper sticker on his van?" Squeaky suddenly interjects.

"Please, please. It's veddy bad manners to interrupt," Pudgy scolds. "I believe I have the floor."

"You certainly do, Mr. Smith," I assure him, obligingly.

"You must be aware, Mr. Packard, that at a gathering of delegates from the BC Federation of Labour on the weekend at Kamloops—an anti-racism convention or some such—your organization and Djakarta Now were equally condemned."

Shrug.

"Those in attendance proclaimed they find equally repugnant such measures as your 'Don't Spit on Canada' campaign and the offenses commonly known as tasselling and beatering promoted by Djakarta Now."

"What's your point, Mr. Smith?"

"Wouldn't you agree that there exists a widespread impression that there is no difference between the viewpoints of your party and of Djakarta Now?"

"No, I most certainly wouldn't agree. Our party has proposed policies we feel will remedy a crisis caused by government decisions that have proven extremely harmful to British Columbians' quality of life. We are placing our proposals before the electorate, via the normal, democratic, parliamentary process. On the other hand, Djakarta Now seems to me a spontaneous reaction of our citizens, a form of protest that arises understandably and naturally because people feel the old-line parties have ignored their concerns. We are in fact the antithesis of Djakarta Now."

"Strange how this difference seems to have eluded some of your

supporters," Pudgy muses. "But let that go. You're aware I'm no unthinking advocate of the trade union movement in this province. Their
leadership, however, does consist of socially aware men and women,
however wrong-headed I must regard their methods and approaches.
Can you account for why a group of such knowledgeable and informed
individuals as assembled in Kamloops this past weekend were unable
to distinguish between your organization's activities and those of
Djakarta Now?"

"I have observed publicly many times, Mr. Smith—" this guy, like
Langford, is easy meat, given his unpopularity among his colleagues
"—that the officials of the BC Federation of Labour have a remarkably
poor track record at endorsing causes that benefit their members. For
years they have pumped money and support into the New Democratic
Party. That party, when in office, has consistently legislated strikers
back to work, brought in wage controls in the public sector, altered
proposed labour legislation whenever the business sector has complained, and engaged in similar behaviour that is very far from ben-
eficial to ordinary working people of this province. It's not clear to
me exactly what advantage the NDP *does* offer the trade unions, other
than providing high-paying government and NDP party jobs to scores of
former union leaders.

"All that aside, I'm pleased that the BC Federation of Labour has
taken a strong anti-racist stance, just as Democracy Now has."

Groans and hoots, as expected. I keep my demeanor grave, and continue. "Yet the BC Fed's stance is not enough. The trade union leadership have proposed not a single concrete suggestion that could resolve
our present difficulties, other than blind support for the NDP. And that
is a stance which union members, in droves, reject each and every election day.

"The unions' only other attempts to combat racism involve the
same measures they apply to every issue they oppose. They trot out
the tired and ineffective five Ps of the Left: posters, pamphlets, pickets,
placards, and parades. British Columbians of every viewpoint understand these are toothless gestures, although they evidently make par-
ticipants in these undertakings feel good about themselves. I suppose
that's something."

A patter of appreciative mirth and applause sounds again from various quarters of the hall. Pudgy, however, has his teeth sunk in this bone.

"Yes, to be sure, but what about the unions' observation that there is no essential difference between actions endorsed by your party and by Djakarta Now?"

"I can't account for that position. Our 'Don't Spit on Canada' campaign was enthusiastically received by the general public." This is accurate. Our billboards and TV spots captured all kinds of people gobbing on sidewalks and in public parks and even at beaches. We showed men, women, young, old. Most were Ching-chongs, of course, but we were careful to include a couple of popular baseball and basketball heroes, one black and one white.

Once the spots began to run and the billboards went up, our polling revealed that an astonishing cross-section of the population supported the campaign. Every age group and political persuasion. Our popularity surged in the campaign's wake: that's when we first nearly broke through the ever-elusive 10 per cent approval rating which the Suits and The Crip insist is the threshold for significant rapid growth.

Hard to believe, in retrospect, that the campaign was so hotly debated in Council. Was it too wuss? Would it alienate young people, who constantly watch their favourite sports stars hawking greenies out on the field or the ice, or sidelined on the bench? Should our slogan be 'Don't Spit on BC'? Or do we capitalize on national patriotism? I have to admit, I wasn't particularly in favour of the campaign, since it seemed to me irrelevant. I didn't feel as strongly opposed as some members did, though. Adam and a few other old-timers believed the Gob Job, as they tagged the campaign, would confuse or annoy our core support, and signal that we were drifting from the ideas that attracted people to DN in the first place. The Suits and others who waxed positive about the Gob Job were convinced it would add a more respectable image to the party's message. And the campaign would simultaneously imply that cultures from afar were infecting even our noble multi-millionaire hockey and ball stars.

People are everlastingly unfathomable, which is why they're so fascinating. You never know what will stir them up. Consider a one-legged fund-raiser for cancer, stumping awkwardly down the Trans-Canada Highway. Why would that image so touch people, when official campaigns orchestrated by the best and brightest minds of the country's finest advertising agencies never came close to inspiring people to part with their dough in such large amounts? In our case, donations and praise literally showered in. Tons of letters to the editor of the "I don't agree with Democracy Now but I support that wonderful campaign" variety. Players' associations passed resolutions saying that their members henceforth would discreetly use handkerchiefs if they felt the need to publicly expectorate. Little old ladies arrived at our storefront offices, trying to give us their pension money. Adam and a few of the Muscle took up ostentatiously gobbing about this time, in protest against all this nicey-nicey, until The Crip read them the riot act. But there's no question the campaign moved us forward.

"Our 'Don't Spit on Canada' initiative," I continue, "was an important contribution, according to every media report I've encountered, toward curing a bothersome social ill. In contrast, tasselling and beatering are both acts of vandalism against private property. Far from solving anything, these activities are no more and no less than a regrettable, but understandable, expression of British Columbians' opposition to the consequences of the current immigration laws."

Both the latter forms of amusement sprang up without encouragement from anybody. All that Djakarta Now had to do was publicize and organize them. Tasselling takes its name from the red-tasselled doodads that Hongers like to suspend from their inside rear-view mirrors. Good luck charms, I think. The idea in tasselling is to key, break windows, slash tires, kick dents in and otherwise trash any car in a parkade or at the curb sporting a tassel. Preferred targets are BMWs, Porsches, and anything else high-end. The biggest spasm of tasselling was Djakarta Now's famous Tassel Night last October, which was remarkably well promoted via word of mouth to high school and street kids. For some reason, the announced evening also caught the imagination of some Paki and other towelhead gangs. General mayhem ensued, and the cops claimed to have been caught unawares. The papers went on and on about "Kristallnacht" and such. But the damage was exclusively directed at Chinky-owned vehicles, except for a few manicured lawns that had gasoline poured on them to create an additional garden feature: a flaming D. Tassels almost disappeared from sight thereafter. The boys then began tasselling any cars that have collections of cutesy stuffed animals on the dashboard or rear window shelf. Pooh Bears and whatever are favourite decorations of Hongers, too, especially young females. Since Christmas, tasselling incidents have been pretty sporadic, although the media can be relied on to puff up each occurrence out of all proportion.

Beatering has never enjoyed the same popularity, which makes sense since it involves more risk. This sport consists of employing an old beater to intentionally bash into some Ching-chong's expensive new SUV or Infiniti or shitty little Prelude or Precidia. Preferably while the driver is making some big important deal on a cell phone. You can imagine how Mr. or Ms. High-and-Mighty Honger must feel the instant they realize that the smoke-belching wreck driven by a couple of scuzzy dudes they were sneering at just a few seconds ago is actually going to touch their precious new Range Rover. And not just touch, but smash the living crap out of. That's when they discover that the tubular rhino guards they had installed as a pricey extra option—to protect them from all the rhinos that wander the streets of Vancouver—aren't worth diddly. But by then Mr. and Mrs. Slant are in a game of bumper cars that they really, really never wanted to play.

Since technically this is hit-and-run, our people adopt various strategies. The most common is to steal the beater to begin with, or, if the vehicle is cheap enough, get a friend to buy it and report it stolen. The wreck can then be abandoned not far from the scene of the crime, and everybody walks. Or phony ID is used to register the beater. When the fun first started, the cops traced several suspect vehicles to one Kingsway car lot operated by a couple of guys who were not overly fond of their Boat neighbors and customers. So the business wasn't perhaps as rigorous in their paperwork as they might be. That lot had a high rate of reported thefts of vehicles from the property, too, until the City shut them down.

Overall, beatering involves much more preparation than just a stroll through a parking structure obliterating a few windshields or inserting the blade of your Leatherman into some Gook's radials. To engage in road work, as the boys call it, you have to be more dedicated to raising a little hell. I've been effectively banned from road work since Ernie and I last fall smacked a Honger at the wheel of a shitbox Honda—complete with a spoiler, as if the riceburner needed one. I've known

Ernie since he was one of the Muscle in the early days, and he's pretty cool under pressure. Which trait was useful, because we came within an inch of getting popped. We knocked the worthless Gookmobile up onto the curb on Cambie in broad daylight, when he least expected it. Then we turned up Forty-first, intending to deke into a side street a block or two along, ditch our wheels, and grab a bus home. But the City was tearing up the road just in from the corner on Forty-first. Probably to facilitate new sewer lines for some Ching-chong's monster house under construction. Not only was traffic crawling, but a cop was parked to ensure everybody was obeying the construction zone speed limit. Mr. Stove-in-Honda no doubt had already been whining into his cell. We were going to brazen out inching through the jam past the cop, until we saw his rack lights suddenly come on. I had to do a one-eighty across traffic, over a corner of somebody's lawn, then peel through the neighbourhoods down toward Forty-ninth. Once we shook the cop, we left the beater in a back lane and Ernie and I split in different directions.

The Action Faction gave me a hard time when they found out. Ernie must have bragged to somebody about our close call. I was treated to the full lecture about too big a risk to what we had already achieved, etc., etc. Probably I could have asserted myself as Leader, except I had to agree with the point about consequences to the movement if I was nailed. I joked that my popularity would soar. Yet I understood their worry. I also can imagine Marcie wouldn't think too highly of me being caught. Since then it's been strictly parking lots, and on the QT. Nothing to compare to road work, but like Marcie says, suits and ties aren't really who I am. It's not like there isn't some rush available in the big parkades, either: the smell of concrete and oil, noises of traffic in the street outside echoing off the cement floor and roof. Ears alert for the elevator doors opening on this level, voices, footsteps. Eyes scanning the vehicles to make sure no inadvertent witnesses are sitting in their cars for some reason. Mostly I go by myself, although sometimes Lard-butt Adam is up for it. He may not be good for much, but at least he can keep his mouth shut. There's an edge to Adam, too. Once when we came across a Honger Lexus, he unlocked it through the kicked-in window and shit in the driver's seat. Fuck the Suits.

Pudgy Vauxhall Smith isn't through with me. "Even if you dispute the findings of the Kamloops conference, I presume you do condemn such acts of vandalism as tasselling."

"As I said last October, Mr. Smith, I condemn the situation that leads otherwise law-abiding citizens to go to extremes like this to express their discontent with the government's immigration policies."

"What if you knew a member of Democracy Now had participated in such acts? Would you condemn such people? Would DN expel them?"

"This is getting hypothetical. I already said we do not condone illegal behaviour. But I have never witnessed members or supporters of Democracy Now engaged in tasselling or beatering. Have you, Mr. Smith?"

As much fun as fielding these questions is, I start to hope the media will run out of juice. I feel I'm on top of everything they've thrown at me so far. But you never know what curve balls can get pitched, even when you're ahead in the game. Then, too, my ribs are clammy from sweating under the damn TV lights.

A dozen more hands are hoisted aloft, though. Time to select a visible minority; keep this an equal opportunity press conference. An Oriental face. "Yes?"

"Mr. Packard, Chinese Business Improvement Association is stating—"

A commotion in the fourth row. The group of young people are on their feet, raising a white cloth bundle, no, a banner they unfurl. TV cameras swing toward them, seated reporters complaining as other camera and sound guys shove along the rows of chairs in the direction of the kids for a better shot, better sound. The banner proclaims, in badly hand-painted letters, "Democracy Now: Racist and Anti-Immigrant." How original.

A squad of Muscle form around me at the podium—protection, I guess. Others have left their posts along the walls and in the seats and lumber purposefully toward the kids and their banner, which sags as a picket fence of microphones is inserted into the protesters' faces. I get a better idea than the Muscle, however. I scan about for The Crip; he's already positioned himself just to my left, no doubt primed with suggestions for damage control. We have procedures for handling hecklers and disrupters at rallies. This is the first time a press conference has been interrupted, yet I'm certain The Crip's brain has already generated a scheme how to turn this to our advantage.

I beat him to the punch. "Call 'em off."

"What? I want to—"

"Call off the Muscle. I have another way to handle this."

"Like what?"

"Trust me. Call 'em off."

The Crip offers me a cautionary, you-better-be-right look, and talks into his lapel. I lean into my mic.

"Mr. Stenson. Is Mr. Stenson here? Could Mr. Stenson come forward, please?"

Stenson writes a think-piece column for the morning tabloid. He is sort of their resident intellectual, which on that paper means somebody who doesn't move their lips when they read. He's also vice-president of the press corps' union, and has been on our case about the presence of the Muscle at these little firefights. The Crip and I have met with him over the issue of "intimidation" of reporters. Our boys routinely check press credentials before admitting anybody: basic security. Stenson has been threatening a boycott. I know we're too newsworthy for his threat to be serious, yet it seemed best to negotiate a truce. The Crip's tactic is never to get sidetracked from the main issues; a beef with the media would consume no end of time and effort better spent on more productive ventures. I have no quarrel with that approach. The Crip's bon mot on this brushfire was: "Never get in a wrestling match with a pig. Win or lose, you end up covered with mud and smelling bad."

Stenson is usually at our press conferences, though I haven't noticed him today. "Mr. Stenson, please? Is Mr. Stenson here?" Lots of uproar in the hall: besides the scrum around the students, the seated reporters are busily chattering to each other. Sort of like a class at school when there's a fire drill. Everybody finds themselves outside, released from the tedium, excited by the escape from the familiar routine. The Muscle have returned to their posts as ordered, yet I can see their hands twitch in and out of fists as they shift their weight from foot to foot. They're ready for action. Who knows what The Crip told them.

Stenson bobs up in front of the dais. Grey hair, and tweed jacket and tie.

"Mr. Stenson, I'm going to let you handle this disruption."

"Say again?"

"At our last meeting, you insisted that the presence of members of our Security Service is unnecessary because only authorized, responsible members of the working press ever attend these events. Now this has happened."

"What do you want me to do, Mr. Packard?"

"This isn't a political forum. It's supposed to be a news conference. Either you bring this disruption to a halt your way, or we'll take steps to end it how we see fit."

Stenson heaves himself onto the dais. Standing beside me at the mic, he broadcasts a number of appeals for order. The hubbub eventually subsides.

"There's a time and a place for everything," Stenson chides, wagging his finger at the student journalist-wannabes, threatening them and their cohorts with permanent banishment from professional activities, from future employment, the works. The kids' banner is duly rolled up in the hot glare of the TV lights, and a couple of Stenson's henchmen, who he calls forward, confiscate the bundle of cloth.

He covers the mic. "You want them chucked out?"

"No. I have something to say to them."

He stares at me. "I'll bet you have."

I rotate toward The Crip, who is seated again, while Stenson clambers off the dais and is absorbed into the now-calmer rows of the hall. I give Bruce a wink, and mouth: "Watch this." I swing back to the mic.

"The slogans on your banner—" I point toward the students "—are all accusations DN has heard before. We've shown repeatedly these claims are false. Yet either you young people haven't been listening, or haven't thought these matters through. Let's take your first accusation, that Democracy Now is racist."

As I speak, I deliberately make eye contact with each face down the line of subdued-looking youngsters. "What I say constitutes Racism 101: people aren't racist because they are evil, or stupid, or misinformed. That's why exhortations that racism is bad have absolutely no effect. People adopt racist views because they feel powerless. When people feel powerless, they look around for somebody to blame. As a rule, those who are blamed are, if anything, in a more powerless position than the blamers.

"The citizens of this province have a lot to feel powerless about. They have seen their quality of life eroded badly in the past several years, and are threatened with even more of the same. That brings me to your second charge, that Democracy Now is anti-immigrant. I'll deal with that in a sec. Before I do, I want to stress that the cure for feeling powerless is to exercise power."

Pregnant pause to glance around; most of the reporters in the room are listening, although God knows they're familiar with this rap from me. A number are reviewing their notes, thinking about what they are going to write concerning the student's whoop-de-do. I sail ahead. "If people are convinced that nothing in the existing political structure provides them with power over their lives, over what is happening to them, they are going to exercise power another way. That's the crisis British Columbia is in: the threat of another Djakarta, here, where it should never happen. I can't say this too often: Democracy Now is about preventing this Armageddon from occurring. *Democracy*, because that is the socially responsible way the powerless can right wrongs that affect them. And Democracy *Now*, because in a crisis people won't wait forever for a resolution of their problems.

"We live in a social climate, though, where to even raise questions about immigration is to be branded 'racist' or 'anti-immigrant.' Democracy Now isn't anti-immigrant. In this province we are all immigrants, except for the original inhabitants who were swamped by our arrival here.

"The questions remain, however. What should the rate of immigration be into this country, into this province? Who gets to decide? How large a population is optimum for British Columbia? Who gets to decide? Why is it *racist* or *anti-immigrant* to talk about these questions?"

Pause to let all this float in the air. I'm into the rhythm of my little speech: I'm cooking, I'm cooking. Most of the clump of students are gawking up at me, feeling a bit guilty, I figure, at having caused such a ruckus. Yet more media types along the rows are beginning to fidget or whisper to each other—shop talk or gossip, probably. I can hear the ambient noise level increase. Screw 'em: I'm going to keep on to the end. Repeat, repeat.

"Democracy Now is not against immigration. We *are* against

*occupation.* When I can drive mile after mile through a commercial district in a suburb like Richmond and see hardly a single sign in English, it's clear BC is suffering from *occupation*, not immigration. When a bus pulls by me on the freeway covered in Chinese lettering, where the only words in English are on the licence plate, I know that whoever owns that bus and whoever that bus is hauling are *occupiers*, not immigrants. I can go into certain suburban malls, and 100 per cent of the sales staff are Chinese. If you ask them something in English, nobody behind the counter can understand a word. Every shopper around you is gibbering in Mandarin or Cantonese and the salespeople are jabbering right back. That mall might be physically located in Greater Vancouver, but at that moment you know you are in occupied territory."

I recap the federal immigration policies that have allowed the wealthy from offshore to buy Canadian citizenship for themselves and their families with money the federal government terms *investment.* But such funds are not investment in productive enterprises that actually employ people; most of the investment has been in real estate. The result of this mad arrangement has been skyrocketing house prices that have driven the cost of housing beyond the means of ordinary British Columbians.

"Hundreds of thousands of good citizens, hard-working people who were born and raised in this city, have been forced to leave their native place, the city where their jobs are, if they want to fulfill the dream most of us have of owning their own homes. Our citizens have been displaced by a merciless occupying force, by the wielders of obscene amounts of offshore cash. This dirty money, like as not, was squeezed from the occupiers' own countrymen forced to work in factories under horrible conditions and paid a disgusting pittance compared to what any of us in this room would consider a fair wage. *If* this wealth was amassed legally at all."

A raspy tickle starts at the back of my throat. This often happens when I launch into a rant. I could stop to take a sip of water, but I've found that once I commence swallowing water, I have to keep slurping it. Also, if I'm cranked enough—like today—my hand will quiver, and that to me is bad optics: shakily hoisting a glass to my lips, like some wheezy old geezer. Far better not to have water anywhere near me at the podium: too much temptation. Instead, I attempt to just suck saliva, make like a camel and do without.

Hardly anyone in the room is still digging me. Even the students' eyes have glazed over. But the red lights glow on the TV cameras, and I know the recording tapes are turning in the cassettes. "Think of it as broadcasting," was The Crip's advice once when I mentioned that at a certain point during my "repeat, repeat, repeat" presentations at these events the media people tune out. "You never know what snippet of our message will be picked up by some reporter and used. We've got to send a lot of words into the ozone, and we've got to send those words out a lot of times, for even a few bits of our message to get through to Mr. and Mrs. Average Voter."

A couple of weeks ago, when I was whining about how futile these moments at the podium can seem, somebody on The Crip's staff showed me a statistic that amazed me. The Communications team keeps records of the amount of airtime and print exposure the media allow us. When you chart the total column-inches and seconds of sound bites we receive, the line is headed steeply upwards. The wall between ourselves and the audience is increasingly porous.

So I swallow a couple more times, and soldier on. "Faced with a federally sanctioned—no, federally encouraged occupation, what recourse is available to a citizen of this province? We of Democracy Now believe the democratic process must not be allowed to fail. That is why we are putting before the electorate what we know to be the best alternative to the current slide into chaos."

I scan the room. "To date, I daresay a majority of you gentlemen and ladies have spoken out against our proposals, either by omission or commission." I watch more eyes in the rows lift toward me as I set forth on this tack. Nothing like a threat of media-bashing to get the attention of the media. Either that, or they could tell from having heard the gist of my lecture before that I'm drawing to a close.

"As important as a free press is to a democratic system, even reporters need to be reminded from time to time that they are not the voters. The voters of BC are the ones who will determine whether what Democracy Now proposes is preferable to the inaction of the other political parties.

"Democracy Now believes that the most recent wave of Asian

arrivals are not immigrants in the old meaning of the word. These are wealthy men and women. They do not seek, as most immigrants to Canada did in the past, a place to begin a new life for themselves in a land of opportunity. Instead, these greedy people simply desire a safe hideout for themselves, and their money, and their extended families—very extended, I might add—in order to escape for a time from the storms of economic uncertainty in their homeland.

"Far from severing themselves from their old lives, they want it both ways. They have seized the opportunity Canada provides that lets them keep grinding their fellow citizens back home, while enjoying every possible Canadian benefit for themselves, their swollen bank accounts, and their host of relatives.

"Rather than adapting to Canadian beliefs and traditions, these people have tried as hard as they can to recreate the economic and social conditions here that they left behind. Make no mistake. Theirs is a world characterized by merciless exploitation of anybody they believe weaker than or inferior to themselves, a world of government violence, corporate violence, gang violence. And of conspicuous consumption of luxury goods by a few in the midst of widespread poverty."

I have to clear my throat a couple of times: the itchy tickle is becoming worse.

"Now that the difficulties in their own country that precipitated their removal here have passed, it is high time for them to go home. The moment has come for them to end their occupation of portions of our province. My government, once elected, will offer them a simple choice: repatriation or expropriation."

Pause to let whoever is listening get the message loud and clear. Then tick off the scenario previously announced: "For six months after we take office, we will supply every assistance to help these people return to their own country. Once six months have elapsed, we will initiate expropriation proceedings against their economic holdings in BC.

"We anticipate a period of economic readjustment will follow from these expropriations. We are prepared to fully and fairly compensate all genuine British Columbians negatively impacted by these measures required to end the occupation peacefully. For example, my staff predicts a sag in the real estate market due to the sudden sell-off of many, many properties in the Greater Vancouver region. We will be monitoring this closely. If an authentic British Columbian family has to move and sells their home at a loss during this period, we will see they are compensated for the difference.

"We will be insisting that the full costs of the repatriation and expropriation period be borne by the federal government. Ottawa's policies precipitated this crisis. The perpetrator of the mess must pay for the cleanup."

Summarize the statistics to demonstrate how for decades British Columbians have contributed far more in taxes to the federal government than the province has received back in transfer payments. "The time has come to call in that marker. These cleanup costs represent compensation rightfully owed the citizens of BC. Such compensation is no different from how the federal government paid redress to British Columbians of Japanese descent, who were forcibly interned and otherwise treated in such a racist manner during and immediately after the Second World War. The federal government also has rightfully compensated British Columbians of aboriginal descent who were forcibly confined in the network of residential schools, where they were subject to the horrors of institutionalized racism, physical and sexual abuse, and other crimes.

"Ottawa's financial obligation in the present situation totals far, far less than paying the costs of a Djakarta. Should another Djakarta erupt here, consider just the financial implications. An expensive mobilization of the Canadian Forces to aid the civil power to restore order. Millions, if not billions, in property damage. Untold loss of productive capacity and hence tax revenue. The financial burden of providing ongoing protection of the homes and businesses of those occupiers who survive. Plus years of court costs and time in sorting out responsibility for the rioting and destruction. All this will add up to an enormously greater expenditure than the sum required to ensure an orderly departure of those who sought in such a cynical way to take advantage of Canadians' justly famous generosity, our good nature."

I swivel from the mic to cough three or four times, trying to shake the scratchies from my windpipe. The Crip approaches the podium.

"You sure you don't want some water, Bryan?" he whispers.

I shake my head. "How am I doing?"

"Fine. But let's wrap it. I think they've got more than their money's worth. Take a couple more questions. Then shut it down and we'll go for some lunch."

I consider his point. Maybe I have been overdoing the "repeat, repeat" stuff. I try to lighten the mood by announcing to the assembly that I've just been advised our rental of the auditorium is about to expire, which means there's time for only a few more questions. Nobody laughs, but I see some interest reappearing in the upturned faces.

Somebody ventures the hoary query about how do our expropriation plans differ from the expropriation of Japanese-Canadians' property in the 1940s. Back at him with the list: the Japanese posed no threat to social stability, were true immigrants contributing to the wealth and welfare of the communities in which they lived and to which they were assimilated. The Nips were fishermen, loggers, artisans, not real estate speculators and sweatshop owners, blah-blah-de-blah.

A radio guy wonders how we plan to proceed if the feds flatly refuse to help pay for the cleanup. This eventuality was well covered last summer when we unveiled the expropriation program. Yet if he's anxious to hear it again, I am, as ever, willing.

Before I can start, Ms. Righteous Emily Langford reinserts her CBC-TV beak into the proceedings. "Excuse me. I believe just before the students began their protest you had a question from Mr. Chu of the Chinese-language press pool."

"You're right, Ms. Langford. My apologies. Before I take that question, though: with regard to the feds, we stated in August that our legal team has prepared a number of options that will allow us to put effective pressure on Ottawa, if needed. First, we believe that our election will serve as a wake-up call to the federal government to recognize the severity of the problem it has created and work with us to resolve the crisis. Second, they are aware BC's ports are the door through which a significant percentage of this country's trade flows. Shut that door to all but BC exports and imports, and Ottawa might well see the wisdom of helping solve the crisis they precipitated. Thirdly, the federal government now has legislation in place that describes the procedure by which a province can legally withdraw from Confederation. Such legislation was adopted in response to Quebec's threat to separate, of course. Yet nothing would prevent British Columbians, too, reaching the conclusion, under a certain set of circumstances, that Ottawa's

attitude toward us warrants a referendum on BC's continued participation in Confederation.

"That's old news, however. As to the gentleman's question earlier:
that question was?" I look around to locate him.

Before I can pick out His Orientalness, Ms. Langford is frothing at
me.

"Your little scenarios are pure fantasy, Mr. Packard, and you know
it. The federal government would *never* let you carry out your vicious
little plans, even if by some miracle you and your thugs managed to get
yourselves elected. Which also will never happen."

"Then you have nothing to worry about, do you, Ms. Langford?"
Mr. Smooth. As long as I stay even-tempered, which one of us looks
like the raving loon?

"Let me remind you again," I continue, all reason and light, "it is
the *voters* who will determine whether Democracy Now has the privilege of serving them. But if your comment really means to ask, 'How
speedily and successfully does your government, once elected, intend
to put your programs into effect?', I have a two-word answer for you:
'Don't blink.'"

My throat is suddenly fluid again—a positive outcome of Ms.
Righteous' hissy-fit. "Now where's the gentleman who previously
wanted to ask me something?"

He pops up. "Um, yes, Mr. Packard. I ask if you are aware Mr.
Len Chang, who is head of Chinese Business Improvement Association,
state last Saturday at community meeting in Richmond that his association see you and Djakarta Now as two heads on a same body. He
mean that—"

Obviously, more than just we are capable of adopting The Crip's
"repeat, repeat" tactic. I intervene to block this quick. "I read the news
accounts of that meeting. But I think we've already dealt fully this
morning with that slander. Do you have a real question? Otherwise,
what I have to say to your Mr. Chang is: how long has he lived in this
country? I've read his bio, and it's my understanding that he's been in
Canada less than four years. Can you imagine the reaction if I moved
to China and immediately started criticizing the Chinese people for
their political system, started trying to tell the Chinese people that this
organization is good and that one is bad? I'd get deported at best.

Probably I'd be executed. Maybe when your Mr. Chang has lived in BC longer, he—"

Ms. Langford is on her feet, pointing a red-lacquered fingernail in my direction, and actually shrieking. "If that attitude isn't racism, I don't know what is!"

Nothing like these outbursts to reveal the professionally detached, unbiased reporting style of our just-the-facts media. I decide to switch on a bit of the old indignation myself. "Ms. Langford! I resent the constant trotting out of this shopworn accusation. Democracy Now has never been, is not now, and never will be racist. *You* may consider us such, but our polling indicates we have considerable support even in the Downtown Eastside, a riding that as you know includes Chinatown."

Some muted groans and jeers from the assembled media. Maybe I've exaggerated our popularity in the district a tad, but I know how to get under her skin.

"The story you folks are either afraid to cover, or have missed entirely, is the resentment toward the recent influx of wealthy so-called immigrants on the part of longtime Canadians of Chinese origin, such as those in the Chinatown area. For lots of reasons, our fellow British Columbians of Chinese descent have been reluctant to speak out publicly. But remember, these good folks did not fly over here first class, buying up expensive property right and left. On the contrary, these were poor, hard-working men imported as indentured labour to build the railroads, and to work in our fish camps and sawmills. Shoulder to shoulder with the rest of this province, they contributed something considerably more tangible to our communities than just opening wallets stuffed with ill-gotten gains. They suffered horrific discrimination, including disenfranchisement, anti-Oriental riots, blacklisting by labour unions, as well as the breakup of families.

"Today, because of the widespread antagonism directed toward the recent occupiers of our province, real Canadians of Chinese descent again are threatened. The forces of justifiable anger paint with a wide brush. The risk to the well-being of our genuine citizens of Chinese heritage is considerable. It's no surprise that the do-nothing stance of the other political parties has resulted in the endorsement of Democracy Now steadily increasing among citizens of Chinese descent. So far this support for DN has been anonymous, out of the limelight. But it is no less real for all that."

Keep 'em wondering. Maybe what I'm saying is true? "All of us in DN look forward to that day, which I promise you will come soon, when Democracy Now will have among the members of its Executive Council representatives of this growing source of support for our party." I silently raise the fervent prayer that whoever it is on Council not turn out to be another Samuel Billy.

The Crip is at my elbow. I cover the mic with a hand.

"Let's wrap it, Bryan. Take one more—the guy in the brown suit, about the middle row, off to your right."

"Two in from the aisle?"

"That's him." The Crip withdraws.

"Ladies and gentleman, our timekeeper insists we really have to bring these proceedings to a close. I can take only one additional question. I'm afraid I'll have to be firm on that."

Show of sweeping around the room, scanning the upraised hands. "You, sir. In brown. Yes, you."

The Crip's man tosses me the chestnut about how-can-you-ever-expect-to-be-elected-if-you're-a-one-issue-party. I rattle back the catechism: the effects of irresponsible immigration polices negatively impact *every* aspect of life in BC—housing, transportation, employment, education, health care, resource use. How although the primary effect is on Greater Vancouver, the spillover reaches all corners of the province. The occupiers will not be content to squat forever where they have established their beachhead. Hence our surging approval rate upcountry, where people are anxious to preserve their standard of living. Mr. Billy notwithstanding, our approval numbers are headed upwards among First Peoples, too, since they have already endured massive unwanted immigration. They have no desire to repeat their miserable experiences of having their own language and customs superseded, of being forced to live in places not of their own choosing under substandard conditions, of being strangers in their own land.

"For these reasons," I conclude, over the rustle of about half the room starting to pack their gear, "DN will run candidates in nearly every riding in the province in the next provincial election. The only exceptions will be those portions of Greater Vancouver, such as segments of Richmond and Surrey, that we have identified as Occupied Ridings. Outside of these, we are confident that the voters of BC will place their trust in us to form the next government."

I step away from the podium. Instantly, I'm in my post-speech fog, shoulders registering a release of tension I wasn't previously aware of, brain bumbling along in neutral or worse. My people are all around me, murmuring praise and administering slaps on the back. I follow where I'm guided: down a rear corridor to the sidewalk, along which a lineup of our vans waits, engines idling. The air outside, even here in downtown, is moist and cool after the heat of the TV lights. Somebody in front of me fumbles with a van door. A couple of seagulls call and answer repeatedly above the din of traffic, their cries reverberating off the glass towers looming over the street where we stand. Through a gap between a couple of the office buildings, I glimpse the blue North Shore mountains. The summits of the peaks glisten with a late spring snow.

The Crip rides with me this time, and keeps babbling in my ear, enthusiastic over something. I don't have the energy to process what he's nattering about. Then we aren't driving any more and I'm being escorted into the upscale beer-and-burger place we frequent at Cambie and Broadway. Several tables have been put together for us toward the windows, and Muscle are everywhere.

A beer is in front of me, and a menu. I order, drink deep, and sit back. My brain starts to clear somewhat.

The Council members who had been on the platform are here, talking among themselves. Also some Suits I hadn't seen at the press conference. Among those joining us for lunch is Roger Kees, the Suit I probably have the best relationship with. Roger is a tall, grey-haired lawyer who chairs the Funding group. He doesn't say much in Council, yet when he contributes something in his soft-spoken voice, it's worth listening to. Cell phones are ringing and being answered by the Suits and also by various of our staffers who are present—the work never stops. At three of the tables nearby, groups of Muscle are chowing down. Others are on their feet, having established a sort of perimeter around our encampment.

The woman from The Crip's staff who introduced me at the podium this morning leads up an older couple who insist on shaking my hand. Smiles on all sides. The male is wearing a neatly ironed plaid shirt and pipeline corporation windbreaker; he probably has in a trouser pocket the gold watch awarded him for decades of faithful service. Thin white hair combed slickly back. She is dressed in a sturdy skirt and cardigan.

"Ye're a right guid 'un, Bryan," I'm informed in a Scots twang, as the male holds onto my fingers a little too long.

"We love Canada; it's been a verra guid life for us here," the wife adds.

He enunciates their worry. "We hate to see this country ruint. They've ruint Great Britain, withoot a doot." Then, hurriedly. "I'm nae racist; don't take me wrong. A pairson is happiest wi' his aine, that's awl." The wife vigorously nods agreement. Our staffer guides the couple away, content. People never fail to be interesting.

The duo's retreat takes them past where Adam stands beside one of the tables of Muscle, yukking it up. At last a procession of waiters and waitresses materializes by our table, and my burger is in front of me. With each bite, I regain a little more energy. A couple of people from the office crouch at my elbow to brief me on the balance of the day's schedule, including a TV interview that has just been arranged for four P.M. Most of my attention is on my fries. But I know I have a quick bounce-back time.

The tapping of cutlery on glass begins where Priscilla, our lemon-mouthed lawyer, is on her feet. The Crip is alongside her.

"First off, I want to congratulate Bryan for a first-rate job under difficult circumstances this morning," Priscilla announces, pointing her chin at me. Applause rolls around the tables. She purses her lips, which I've learned to identify as an indication of her being friendly. "Bryan, with your ability to banter with some distinctly unpleasant individuals, it's not hard to see why you'll make such an excellent premier." To accompany her clumsy attempt at dispensing light-hearted approval, she produces her version of laughter: some breathy hyperventilation. A hard person to warm up to.

Jollity disposed of, she continues. "As some of you know, and others don't, our Communications Director has just informed us of the best news. Our polling last Thursday and Friday, the numbers from which were analyzed this morning, shows that for the first time ever we have exceeded the 10 per cent approval rating."

Another, louder round of clapping, mixed with "Yee-haw"s from the Muscle tables. I dimly recall this had been the substance of what Bruce had been trying to pound in my ear during the ride to the restaurant. He's talking now, explaining that once this crucial point is reached, support can be expected to rise from its own momentum to plateau at 15 to 20 per cent. Beyond that, he warns, we still have plenty of work to do. A staffer gives the breakdown of the poll results riding by riding. We scored as high as 13 per cent in some places, and as low as 4 per cent in others. But everywhere the numbers are better than ever.

A great cacophony of cheerful noise erupts as Priscilla and The Crip resume their seats. The waitresses are offering coffee, and a couple of our guys are fiddling with the restaurant's TV monitors. The sets have been pumping out country music videos. We are approaching the top-of-the-hour, though, and everybody leans forward to learn what the media has made of the morning's festivities.

Right after the prime minister's trip to Brazil, there I am in all my glory arriving at the hotel and at the dais. A voice-over provides an update on police investigation into the crime, with some tape of cops in the nightclub and the suspects' house. Then the announcer sums up the press conference. "In keeping with his usual style, Democracy Now leader Bryan Packard lectured, harangued and berated the media as he offered his party's reaction to last evening's events." The students' little protest is featured, as well as Stenson appearing positively googly as he begs for order. A brief bit of the back-and-forth between Emily Langford and myself. Then a goodly chunk of my riff on Racism 101, which is unexpected. Must be a slow news day. I have to admit I look pretty solid, pretty impressive at the podium, calmly and majestically laying down the law. I sneak a peek around our tables to see what other people's reaction is—no man being a hero to his valet, as the maxim goes. Every face is aimed worshipfully up at my flickering image, like flowers turned to the sun. What never fails to amaze me is that The Crip's shit works. Not all of it, of course, but enough. Hell, if I even impress myself, something weird definitely must be happening.

Marcie grilled me once on how much of what I say is Bruce's, how much mine, and how much of it I really believe. We were snuggling side-by-side on her couch watching some TV flick; I had my arm around her. A commercial was on, so she had her incredibly intense eyes aimed toward me.

I told her the truth—it's about 50 per cent Bruce, 50 per cent me. The extra factor I bring to the mix is my ability to think fast on my feet. I've always had the gift of the gab. Mrs. Myers, my grade ten Socials teacher at John Oliver High, told me about six times I had the smarts and quick mind to be a big success at whatever I wanted if I'd only apply myself. Marcie asked where I get my ideas for my snappy comebacks, when they *are* mine. I struggled to respond to that one, since I'm not entirely sure.

"The process is sort of connect-the-dots," was my eventual explanation. "When I know I'm right about something, I concentrate on that conviction. The words to express it either surface or they don't. Most times, they do—they're right on my tongue. A lot of it is being willing to vocalize what people secretly feel, but most are reluctant to admit out loud. Speaking the unspeakable has been fun ever since I was a kid. That's why people seem to appreciate my blather, I guess."

The movie commenced again, so I couldn't answer her about how much of my palaver I actually stand behind. I weighed her question while the film was rolling. Sometimes I'll stretch things in the heat of argument—like today, when I mentioned our support among Canadian-born Ching-chongs. If I sense a comment of mine is going to engage people—startle them, make them chuckle, make them think—I'm not too worried about whether I completely endorse it. I'm convinced I'm actually *more* effective as a public speaker because I'm not 100 per cent behind every word I utter. That gap gives me room to move, dance around, enjoy myself—people pick up on that energy, that flash. The Crip told me once it's important never to believe your own propaganda. I think he's dead right. Propaganda is for the rubes; you have to reserve for yourself the initiative to move, to not get trapped into protecting too narrow a vision. The idea is to stay on the offensive.

That time at Marcie's, I passed all this on to her during the next commercial break, but she didn't particularly react. She just gave me that "Hmmmm" she does when she wants to chew something over.

In the restaurant, four of The Crip's team at the far end of our cluster of tables are clicking stopwatches and scribbling on clipboards like crazy. In addition to monitoring our overall coverage, Communications has divided and subdivided every *plank* of our platform for analysis. That lets them keep on top of the airtime and column-inches devoted to each individual point we're trying to put across. Adam and some others mock this pencilneck activity. But on a day like today, there's no doubt in my mind that this obsessive attention to detail is the route to success.

The talking torso on the tube shifts to a fatal house fire in Burnaby, and the tables around me erupt in cheers, yips, whistles, and even some high-fives among the Muscle. Glasses are lifted in my direction, more blows to my back and shoulders, so I haul myself to my feet, invent some hee-haw caution about us getting turfed from the restaurant if we can't restrain ourselves. Then, as Mr. Sincere, I thank them all, couldn't be done without the marvellous work by each and every one of you, a privilege to be part of such a crew, important milestone reached, the road to victory ahead, let's celebrate. And sit down. More wild yells and clapping, and a happy clamour of talk swells. Suddenly I want to tell Marcie.

I push through well-wishers ("Thanks for your support, thank you") to the payphones outside the can. I'm old-fashioned enough to dislike cell phones. They may have their use in business, but I think people look stupid walking down the street or standing in the aisles at Safeway talking to themselves. On top of that, cell phoners to me seem pathetic. They imagine they're flaunting some hip image, when they really reveal a desperate need to appear in demand, connected, important. Also, I consider what I have to say on the phone a private matter. That's why I prefer even hunching into the semi-seclusion of the payphone mini-booths like in this burger joint to yakking where any yobo can over-hear half my conversation and speculate on the rest.

I reach Marcie at her work on the third ring.

"Marcie Rothwell. How may I help you."

"Uh, yes, this is the leader of a noted British Columbia political party calling, a party now ranked as the choice of just over 10 per cent of the eligible voters."

Marcie never misses a beat. "I'm sorry. If you're phoning to solicit funds, I gave at the office."

I keep the repartee going. "Actually, that wasn't the purpose of my call, although all donations are fully tax deductible. Perhaps you'd consider an extra donation?"

"No, I don't think so."

"In that case, how about you and I going for dinner tonight?"

"Let ... me ... see," Marcie drawls. "Would that mean I'd have to pay for 10 per cent of the meal? Or that you'd only pay for 10 per cent of the meal?"

"You're 100 per cent in my books. I'll pay the whole shot."

"Then let me check my calendar." She pauses. This is how she has me hooked: I can never predict what she'll say next. Was this check-my-calendar routine a little jab at me for having to cancel a number of dates lately due to party emergencies? She's back on the line. "Yes, I seem to have an opening. What did you say your name was?"

"Hey, I did good this morning," I burst out. Our teasing was fun, but I want her to know.

"Dad just phoned. He saw you on the telly. He was singing your praises, although I'm sworn to secrecy on that."

"He liked what I said?"

"Of course not. But he likes you. Admires you, even. 'If only Bry wasn't a fascist,' are his exact words. Followed by a big sigh."

"Yeah, we get along, me and your dad. In a sort of argumentative way."

"It's worse than that, I'm afraid. Mum told me he was defending you down at the Legion."

"What? I didn't know there were any Legion members who don't support us."

"Not Daddy's friends. Apparently Bertie started in—you remember Bertie? You've met him over at my parents'?"

I've been introduced to four or five of her dad's pals, but can't keep them straight. Mostly Limey machinists like him, and diehard socialists to a man.

"Anyhow—"Marcie reads my silence correctly "—it doesn't matter if you don't remember. Bertie launched in with 'How's your Nazi son-in-law?' and Mum says Dad got quite hot on your behalf. Not your ideas, naturally, but you as a person and your willingness to stand for something."

When I don't respond immediately, she again interprets my thoughts.

"Now don't go and panic over the phrase 'son-in-law.'" She speaks more quickly, which I know means she has shifted momentarily into defensive mode. "I assure you I don't expect you to ever make an honest woman of me. Probably my parents don't either. Especially given your line of work. It's just some of Daddy's friends ribbing him."

I realize I better say something. "Actually, I was more concerned about the phrase 'Nazi,'" I joke.

"Ahh," Marcie says, opaquely.

"I'm glad your dad stood up for me, though. I like your dad."

"You can't marry *him*. He's taken."

Is that an edge to her voice? Does all this kidding around hide a more serious subject? To my astonishment, I don't feel threatened by the idea of taking my relationship with The Divine Ms. M up a notch or two. I find the unexpected turns of her mind exhilarating. "Marcie, seems like you and I should talk."

"Don't let my dad and his pals stampede you into any rash decisions. Matters with you and me are fine as they are. I didn't do well as a minister's wife, and I don't suppose I'd be any better linked up with a *prime* minister, or whatever it is you're attempting to become."

Marcie had been married for six years to a United Church reverend, who I'd gathered hadn't been too popular with her father. On the other hand, she had made it clear to hubby that she was decidedly not going to adopt the traditional duties of a minister's wife—chairing the Ladies' Auxiliary, teaching Sunday School or whatever. She was raised in a pretty secular household, and, for all I could tell, marrying the Rev had been an act of delayed teenage rebellion.

He had accepted her terms—who wouldn't?—and tried to function while respecting them. But his employers, the good parishioners of the Saint Building-Fund Church or wherever he got hired, expected to acquire a team of two for one salary. The church movers and shakers became miffed when they learned about Marcie's deal, and this put some strain on the holy matrimony. With Marcie pursuing her own career as a corporate librarian—which now involved an impressive knowledge of computers—the marriage had withered away.

Some of this information I received from the horse's mouth, and some in a more rough-and-ready form from her dad. He thoroughly relishes an argument; when we first met, he was prepared to bark and bluster me into submission just like he had cowed the Rev. But I seem to have a natural talent for verbal confrontation. Mrs. Myers wasn't the only teacher to tell me I have a flair for rapidly absorbing facts and utilizing them. The teachers invariably complained, though, that my talents at gathering information would be better employed to complete my assignments, rather than trying to apply what I'd learned to talk my way out of whatever I was supposed to be doing.

Marcie's dad honed his debating skills in the union hall, and I perfected mine in the street—neither place having room for rhetorical niceties. Plus we were both graduates of countless beer parlour seminars, though I'd mostly given that up when party work became so consuming. But he and I are a match at lobbing ideas and insults at each other.

Her dad was born in Nottingham just before the last big one, and emigrated to Canada when he finished his National Service in 1956. His background was horny-handed Brit trade unionism. He served as a table officer with the union virtually every place he worked. Over the years, he has picked up his ticket as both a pipe fitter and a machinist, which is kind of rare. I met him when he was working as a half-assed millwright at the sawmill. Usually one trade is enough for anybody. Since Marcie's so unique, she has to have inherited it from somewhere.

Limeys like him, who inhaled an us-or-them unionism with their childhood gruel or cold porridge or whatever story of deprivation-during-the-Blitz they tell you, have for a long time dominated the unions here. They did so even though the organizations nominally are branches of—that is, officially subservient to—US unions. Hence the general Lefty tinge to the Canadian union movement which our Yankee brothers and sisters never understand. And hence the unthinking, unwavering, institutionalized union support for the New Democrats.

To Marcie's dad, somebody like me doesn't add up—someone descended from similar roots, who has worked blue collar, but with entirely different ambitions than the achievement of a trade union paradise. My father's father was a Cockney from London, who arrived on this continent after the turn of the century—a glover, my mom told me. He was employed first in factory towns in upper New York State, and then drifted north to Hamilton, Ontario. My dad worked at about anything he could, zigging and zagging westward. Finally Dad was pretty badly mangled on a logging show near Cultus Lake in the Fraser Valley. He died when I was five, so I have only vague memories of a bedroom my sister and I were supposed to stay out of, and be quiet when we were nearby, and of an old man propped in a chair in a shaft of sunlight in our front room. My mom is Polish or Lithuanian, depending on which of my uncles is bending your ear. When my dad died she took us back to the prairies where most of her family had settled. So I partly grew up in Abbotsford, mainly rural in those days, and partly out in Regina. Like my dad, I left home first chance I could, and knew my goal was to get back to BC I did a stint on the tugs, shipping out of the CBRT hall in Vancouver during the days when you could get work sooner or later by hanging around the dispatcher and waiting for a call no member wanted to take. Then I was more interested in spending time in town, and hired on at the mill. This worky-worky stuff earns me points in Marcie's dad's eyes. But he can't comprehend why I didn't adopt the same set of pinko blinders he wears.

So we hassle back and forth, which keeps me sharp for the media scrums. We'll never agree. Yet I know he's told Marcie that he prefers somebody who'll stand firm behind even a wrong-headed view, compared to some "mealy-mouthed sack of shit," as he quaintly puts it, "who twists and turns dispensing stink depending how the prevailing wind blows."

That attitude of her dad's might even be the reason I appeal to Marcie. She once told me that the Rev in private could be quite passionate in his beliefs, too, despite not being able to measure up to her dad's baiting and goading—turn the other cheek, and all that. Growing up in that household, Marcie of course couldn't get a word in straight ahead, so both she and her mom became experts in a kind of guerrilla war: sly little digs that, if you don't look sharp, will kill you with the death of the ten thousand pinpricks. Between them, they've cunningly boxed the old man into a few situations he still talks about, like how they got him to take Marcie as a little girl to Disneyland—a place he loathes. Last summer the old man was manoeuvred into taking her mom to Reno to gamble, which she'd always wanted to do: another victory for her and Marcie's relentless, underhanded method of warfare as opposed to the heavy artillery barrages and big noisy frontal assaults he favours.

So I never underestimate Marcie, and after nailing down the details about when I'll pick her up after work, I stroll back through the restaurant thinking about what to say on the issue of where our relationship might go from here. I recognize any talk about marriage will be quite a challenge, except that probably between her and her mom my fate was sealed months ago. Yet I'm looking forward to discovering how Marcie and I will bat the subject around.

In fact, I'm feeling damn fine about how the day has unfolded. Hard not to conclude I aced the press conference. We've had exceptional coverage at least from one TV newscast, and generally all the media take the same tack: "They drink each other's bathwater," as The Crip put it one day. We've crested the much-fretted-about 10 per cent approval rating. That number never meant much to me but, hey, if it keeps the troops enthusiastic. And from the hints The Big M is dropping—or at least, they're hints as far as I can tell—she and I might be en route to a closer tangle, which is great by me. I'm decidedly bouncing as I return past the eatery's other patrons toward our tables.

As I draw closer, however, I can see our bunch has thinned; several of them have probably headed back to work. The tables have been rearranged, too. One cluster is now ringed by a group that I realize consists solely of Council members. They're deep in animated conversation, but fall quiet as I approach. Adam reaches across and peels an empty chair from a nearby table, then shifts over to make a place for me beside him.

All heads rotate in my direction. I've never seen members of the Council regroup in this manner after an employee-attended lunch. Priscilla's lips are contorted into what I decide is for her a smile brimming with delight. "We've got more good news for you, Bryan," she sing-songs. The Crip, seated next to her, has replaced his customary stony face with an off-kilter grin. The world must have turned upside down if these two look this pleased. "Tell him, Roger," Priscilla beams.

The Funding chair gravely regards me. "Elliot Anderton has asked to see you and me in his office at nine AM tomorrow."

The Crip barely waits for Roger to finish. "We've cancelled the balance of your schedule for today, Bryan." His voice uncharacteristically chirps. "We all have lots of prep work to do. This potentially could be the biggest break DN ever had."

He's right about that. Elliot Anderton is a huge BC success story, unmatched except by the owners of the giant forest companies that flourished in the fifties and sixties. Anderton started on Vancouver Island selling logging equipment, and three decades later has a finger, if not an entire hand, in dozens of commercial ventures. His core holdings are a chain of construction equipment dealerships, but he owns or controls breweries, fish processing and marketing corporations, a string of discount electronics stores, a national cable television company, a couple of mines, a dozen community newspapers, and probably much more that nobody is aware of. He was the scandal of the day when a few years ago he paid the current prime minister an undisclosed sum to deliver a motivational talk to the annual convention of his company presidents and managers. Somehow, Anderton has become friends with the chair of the US Federal Reserve, and from time to time there are photos of the two of them with their heads together at some world financial conference. More recently, he tried to buy a number of mid-sized city airports across Canada. The federal transport ministry in the nineties had downloaded responsibility for these, which in practice meant the feds offloaded them to consortiums dominated by the civic governments of the municipalities the airfields served. The airports aren't exactly money-makers, and Anderton last month proposed to six or seven city councils across the country that he take these white elephants off their hands. The editorial writers had a field day of paranoia about the possibility of Anderton controlling the nation's air travel. Last I remember, a couple of cities are still mulling over his offer.

If Anderton is considering putting serious money behind Democracy Now, there is no telling what we might accomplish. I can understand why Priscilla and The Crip are so atypically overjoyed.

"How did this come about?" I ask.

"Roger has been working on him for months," Priscilla declares.

"He watched today's press conference," Roger says quietly. "Liked what he saw."

I feel my face flush; I *am* good. I can't wait to inform Marcie. "He saw the news clip?"

"He saw the whole thing," The Crip jumps in. "One of those cameras this morning was cable. He ordered a live feed direct to his office."

"Nobody told me," I point out. "How did he happen to order that particular arrangement?"

No response from anybody. "Roger?" Priscilla prompts.

"He's been interested in us for some while now," Roger offers slowly. "But we have to proceed with our eyes open. Mr. Anderton is not a man who gives you something for nothing. We may already possess whatever he wants. Or he may require something of us. Or both. We should determine what's on his mind, before we get carried away."

People's faces suddenly adopt a sombre look.

Except Adam's. "Are you people nuts?" Lard-butt demands. "Roger has to warn us not to get too excited. He's a lawyer and that's his job. Me, I'm only a dumb guy. But this is fucking fantastic."

Adam scopes the faces around the tables, then heaves himself to his feet to address us. Our people still present at the other tables must have heard the news while I was on the phone. "Elliott Anderton wouldn't bother contacting us if he wasn't convinced we're *worth* his time and money. We've got the guy right here—" Adam begins pounding me on the back "—who can sell totem poles to the Indians."

I watch eyes light up. Heads nod. A hum of happier chatter rises.

"Think of it: Elliott Anderton." Adam is stoked. "Elliott fucking Anderton. You think this isn't going to make a difference? A huge difference? Victoria is as good as ours, man. It's *ours*."

Murmurs of agreement sound, then coalesce into a steadily rising tone as people confirm Adam's sentiment with their neighbors. Someone starts to clap, and the sound becomes general. A voice yells: "Damn straight, Adam." He stops hammering my back. I observe Roger lean forward, frowning, probably about to interject a word. But he overrules himself and settles back. For an instant a faint smile flickers about his lips, then evaporates.

Adam is basking in widespread approbation, for once. He glances left along the tables, then right, then lifts both arms over his head, hands balled into fists, in a corny victory gesture. "What a team we are," he bellows. "What a bunch of winners." The racket around us crescendos. People are hollering, seconding Adam's declaration. I'm aware of a fervent glow in Adam's eyes I've never observed before. But then he seldom is the centre of anybody's approval. Above his head, he brandishes his fists in wild jubilation.

"Look at us," he hoots. "Look at us. Can *anybody* stand in our way?"

# The Rock Eaters

Glancing up from his struggle to knot his tie, he caught her grinning at him in the mirror. "What's *your* problem?" he mock-growled.

She stepped forward to lean against his back, and wrapped her arms around him. "You're so handsome." Her tone was light, jokey, and she kissed the base of his neck, where she knew he was ticklish.

His shoulders involuntarily hunched his shirt collar vertically to protect the exposed skin. "Quit it," he snapped. "I've got to finish."

"Want me to tie it?"

Their eyes met in the mirror. He noticed she was wearing more makeup than he had seen her apply before.

"Thanks but no thanks." His voice was rueful. "A man's gotta do what a man's gotta do." He swivelled toward her. "You all set?"

She was wearing a sheath mini-dress he did not know she owned; he assumed it was for special occasions. He thought she looked extra appealing in it, with her long legs in pantyhose and high heels. Usually she was in jeans when not wearing her uniform for work.

She rotated in a circle, a little unsteady on her heels. "Is this a knock-'em-dead outfit, or what?"

He scrutinized her with pretend exaggerated care. Her hair had been swirled up and pinned; she seemed simultaneously more grown-up and more desirable. He sighed as if resigned. "It'll have to do, I guess."

"Alan!" Her voice sounded outraged, but her eyes were laughing.

He faced the mirror above the bedroom dresser to fumble with the tie again. "You look better than me, anyhow. Plus a damn sight more gorgeous than the Wisps, of which no doubt there'll be plenty on hand today."

She bent in to kiss his neck once more. He jumped. "You're such a hottie," she said.

"Leave me alone," he grumped. "We're running late."

"So hurry up." She moved toward the bedroom door. "And you better not call them 'Wisps' in public."

"'Slimers,' then. How's this?" She stopped. He had done a passable job with the knot, but the thinner part of the tie extended two inches below the strip of green cloth's wider end.

"Let's see you in your sports jacket."

He lifted the garment from the bed, shrugged into it, and buttoned it up.

Her thumb and first finger joined to form a circle of approval. "Perfect. I'll have a hard time keeping my hands off you."

"Yeah, right," he scoffed. He squinted at his clothes in the mirror. "Seriously, Janice,—" she heard an anxious note in his words "—do I look all right?"

The pickup was only four years old. He had had the vehicle retrofitted, however, with digital gauges from an earlier era when the factory-issue windshield cracked during the first winter he owned the truck. The original glass had incorporated Heads Up Display instrumentation.

"Whoever decided on HUD for pickups never lived in the country," Alan pronounced about once a month between December and March. "You pay through the nose for the fantasy Detroit wants you to have that you're piloting a jet fighter." Sand deposited by Oregon's highways maintenance crews for traction on snowy roads often included small stones. Tires propelled the bits of gravel aloft at high speed: a menace to passing vehicles, or ones following behind. By spring, nearly everybody local had a chipped windscreen. Some of the collisions with flying bits of stone produced cracks that soon extended across the width of the glass. The insurance deductible on a HUD windshield was four times that on an old-fashioned one.

"What a way to spend Saturday," Alan said as they traversed the shovelled path to the Dodge. "We could have been snowmobiling with Dougie and Ron."

"*You* could have gone snowmobiling," Janice corrected him. She was wearing boots along with her heavy coat. Clutched in her hands was a bag holding her good shoes to change back into when they arrived at the ceremony. "I work Saturdays now, remember? I only got today off in your honour."

"Hah."

They climbed into the cab by their respective doors. He let the truck idle.

"Scoff if you like," Janice resumed. "To lots of other people, what you did is a big deal. That's why—"

"Anybody on the crew would have done what I did. I just happened—"

"We've been through this, Alan. Several times. Yeah, anybody else *could* have. But you *did* it. That's why the spotlight is on *you*." She snuggled closer to him across the bench seat. "That's why you're the man of the hour."

"Ugh." He made a face. Yet he put his arm around her. "Hopefully we can sneak into town, get this over with, and be home again before anybody notices."

"I wouldn't count on it."

Alan inched the truck down the snow-blowered driveway; twin high whip-antennas oscillated as the pickup bumped toward the mailbox. The vehicle paused, swung onto the plowed and sanded road and accelerated. Branches of the pines along either side of the route were weighted with white. Snow completely covered the ridges that delimited the narrow valley; the sky above was a flawless blue. Here and there the wintry forest opened where a driveway led off to a house, over whose roof woodsmoke lifted from a metal or brick chimney.

They approached the freeway on-ramp and seconds later the truck was speeding south up the grade. Both lanes of Interstate Five were cleared to bare asphalt. Janice reached toward the dash, activated the on-board, and scrolled the built-in mouse to select Audio, then Lyle Lovett, then "Cowgirl Spurs" from his latest release.

Twenty-five kilometres further, as the highway descended toward the city of Grants Pass, they saw the sign. Janice shrieked with delight, pointing forward.

"Oh, my God," Alan said.

Two tapering steel poles hoisted the Denny's logo up from the valley bottom to above the bench the interstate followed here. As always, the huge sign displayed the revolving green light on top, and the accompanying OWT symbol under the restaurant's name. *Suit-free dining* and *E-Z lockage* were proclaimed first in English, and then in two of the five main Pelarean languages. The latter inscriptions resembled Chinese ideograms, but were popularly known as "hieroglyphics." Like the ancient Egyptian form of writing, the squiggles and semi-representational figures indicated sounds rather than concepts.

Two new additions to the sign were evident. A white banner attached between the poles below the familiar metal and plastic announced in red letters: *Restaurant Temporarily Closed. Next OWT hospitality available southbound at Mt. Shasta, California, 198 kms.* The message was repeated twice more in Pelarean calligraphy.

A second banner, in English only, advised the travelling public: *Honor our fire volunteers, honor our hero. Saturday, Dec. 16, 2 p.m. Grants Pass City Hall.*

They drove in silence for a few seconds. Then Janice began to laugh.

"What's so jeezly funny?"

She put her hands over her mouth to stifle her giggles. "Sorry."

"'Our hero', my ass. I hope nobody I know sees that."

"I was just laughing because you said you wanted to get this over with quietly."

"It's embarrassing. Not to mention an insult to the rest of the crew."

She darted her face in to kiss his cheek.

They slowed for the exit. The Rogue Valley Motel signboard there ordinarily soared ten metres upwards to advise travellers of room specials, or to offer some cheery seasonal message like *Let it snow* late in the fall. Now the board suggested potential clients should *Salute our hero. 2 p.m. City Hall.*

"If I didn't know better," she said, gesturing toward the motel with her hand, "I'd say you made quite an impression on the business community."

"This is dumb."

"And, Mr. Hero, just maybe you've impressed the community at large."

From the intersection at the bottom of the ramp, waiting for the long light, they could stare up a street of gas stations, fast food outlets, car dealerships, and several motels. Tucked under the freeway embankment was a wooden construction hoarding around Denny's. Rebuilding was definitely underway.

Unlike some other waitresses, Janice had not minded working The Swamp. The manager, Mary-Ellen, emphasized when Janice had been hired at Denny's three years previously that nobody on staff was forced to take shifts in the OWT Area, the official name for the portion of the building where the Pelareans were served. "Denny's gets a big subsidy from the government, from OWT, and from I don't know who else to provide meals to their kind," Mary-Ellen had said. "As far as I'm concerned, I'm running a restaurant for Oregonians and regular tourists. If none of our staff is willing to suit up and go in there, that's not my problem."

Janice was never certain, though, that her willingness to take shifts in The Swamp was not an important reason Mary-Ellen hired her. "I think you're right," Alan had confirmed when she drove back to Bond Creek with the good news she had landed the job and offered her explanation for her success. She had been applying for the past month every place she could think of, both in the valley and over the hill in Grants Pass, after she was laid off as a cashier at Brophy's Hardware. The discount big box store at the Rogue River Mall south of town had finally put the Grants Pass firm into bankruptcy, following two years of dwindling sales.

Janice had worked at Brophy's for five years, since her first marriage ended. Over dinner the day she received her notice, Alan had suggested they move in together. She thought about his offer for a week, then accepted. After dating for eight months, they were spending most nights at his place. Consolidating households probably was only a matter of time. Why not now?

"I'll bet catering to the Wisps was a condition for old man Jackson buying the Denny's franchise," Alan had said as they celebrated her hiring with the steak special and a bottle of red at the Bond Valley Grill. "Head office would likely be pissed if Jackson or Mary-Ellen couldn't find anybody to mop up the Rock Munchers' drool."

"Alan!" Janice had scolded.

"Anyway," Alan had advised, "once you've built up some hours, you can tell them to shove The Swamp. You know Bennett Wong, works with me? His sister was a waitress there for a while and he says it was pretty miserable."

The OWT Area reproduced an environment of high humidity, engineered to match a desirable location on the Pelarean home world. The effect was created by a ceiling sprinkler and floor drainage system whose constant operation kept the atmosphere misted, and walls and eating stations damp. The Area was also bathed in a reddish glow from lamps that simulated the spectrum of the Pelarean sun. Air was replaced by the mix of gases required by the off-worlders, pressurized to the correct level, so the wait staff rather than the customers wore sealed suits inside the Area. A docking airlock on the Area's outside wall permitted Pelareans to step directly from their OWT Winnebagos or Airstreams into the portion of the restaurant dedicated to their comfort, without having to don protective gear.

When she started at Denny's, Janice discovered about half of the waitresses and waiters declined to work The Swamp. They were adamant that the suits were too cumbersome, the physical conditions of The Swamp were oppressive and the visitors' eating habits were repulsive. Other employees, like herself, quickly became used to providing service in the Area, and tolerated or even enjoyed working at the interface between two self-conscious life forms.

The Swamp's environment was not so different from a Terran environment that the required serving suit had to be as rigid or bulky as an astronaut's. Rather, the restaurant's gear resembled a scuba diver's equipment, although with boots and gloves. The helmet, however, could have belonged to a 1950s movie spaceman. Instead of air being available to the server through a mouthpiece, life-support was pumped into a clear bubble helmet that allowed the customer to view a range of human facial expressions—particularly the smile that OWT and Denny's wanted bestowed on the Area's clientele.

The suits were equipped with ConVerse translating devices, speech-activated on both sides of the transaction. They handled English and the five Pelarean languages selected by OWT as most representative of the visitors' home planet. The ConVerse had a learning component. Once the translator sensed and registered a particular visitor's choice of language, the device could handle nearly any request or comment either party uttered. In addition, menus and phrase books at each eating station featured photos and sentences that a staff member or the Pelareans could point at if the ConVerse proved inadequate. That technique, plus the translator, plus smiles, plus gestures, got Janice through most shifts without any more hitches than occurred on the restaurant's Terran side. In either location, she decided, some customers were cranky or demanding or downright rude, but the majority were pleasant and a few awfully interesting.

Her eyes rapidly adjusted at the start of each shift to operating in a red-lit space. The food prep room for the Area was illuminated identically, as was the break room for staff working an OWT shift. What was harder to get used to was the off-world cuisine itself, and method of ingestion.

A staple of the Pelarean diet, roughly equivalent to protein for humans, was minerals. When Pelareans opened communications with Earth, and particularly when the ferry craft from their orbiting ships eventually touched down at LAX and humanity had its first 3-D look at the off-worlders, what was hardest to absorb was that these beings' closest Earth counterpart was a stalk of grain. No question that the Pelarean technologies were in advance of Terran. Yet humans seemed prepared, at least in science fiction books and movies, to accept a mental or physical challenge from Bug-Eyed Monsters, or from fearsome tentacle-equipped creatures, or from oversized bipedal versions of familiar animals, reptiles, insects or crustaceans. More taxing to the Terran ego was being bested scientifically by some enlarged cereal plants, even if they were wearing impressively tailored garments.

Terran exobiologists hypothesized that an analogy for the Pelareans' development—only an analogy, the scientists stressed repeatedly—was a scenario that had intelligent life on Earth evolving from grasses that became mobile, rather than from fish that migrated onto land. The scientists' best guess was that root structures of the proto-Pelareans transformed themselves into a means of propulsion: the visitors' four supple protuberances that extended from the bottom of the torso. Why individual rooted organisms desired so strongly to alter their location remained unknown. The consensus among biological theorists was that humans would need to comprehend more of Pelarean prehistory, and that to date stayed a blank.

The hypothesis regarding Pelarean development further speculated that other roots migrated to the upper-middle torso to form the four arms: two short, two long, the latter with four finger-ish subdivisions. The shorter arms functioned in ways similar to humans' opposable thumbs. At the top of the stalk, the ur-kernels began to specialize into organs of sight, of which four were arranged around the head-like upper extremity. Apparently the brain that took shape concurrently with these other changes processed visual stimuli from a 360-degree circumference. Other topside organs collected data on sound and scent, and scholars believed Pelareans could detect temperature signatures, that is, could distinguish if what they were observing was hot, cold, or some in-between place on the thermal spectrum. A mouth-like opening, ringed with secretion-producing orifices, was external evidence of the development of an inner digestive capacity that replaced the lower tendrils as the means to absorb nutrients required to sustain life.

Immediately following Contact, Pelareans imported all their comestible minerals. But Terran geologists, after analysis of such rocks, proposed that certain basalts might be a match. Hawaiian lavas were pronounced a delicacy by Pelarean gourmets, leading even to some export trade as well as the addition of these to OWT Area menus. Also at the suggestion of geologists, off-world tourists found granites palatable, with ones from the Cascade mountains of the Pacific Northwest particularly prized.

Preparation of minerals of whatever origin involved a sequence of heating, freezing and pulverizing the stone into edible dimensions and textures. Acidic sauces of distinctive types marked the differing Pelarean cuisines. Also on the menu were bowls of soil of various mineral compositions, which fulfilled approximately the same role in the off-worlders' diet as soups or salads for humans. Soil mixes continued to be imported by OWT, although attempts were initiated to manufacture Terran versions. A range of fluids were also imported and available to customers. Some liquids produced an effect resembling that of soft drinks or fruit juices on humans; other selections altered the visitors' body chemistry in pleasurable ways reminiscent of alcohol's impact on Earth-dwellers. A variety of imported, packaged treats comprised of unknown ingredients were sold to be eaten off-premises, presumably as snacks.

The food prep staff in Denny's OWT Area followed OWT manuals by rote, and the kitchen space was overseen by random inspections by OWT officials. Decanting sand-like dirt from a ten-kilogram bag into a bowl and then offering it for consumption, even to an off-worlder, was difficult for employees to become accustomed to, despite assurances from OWT inspectors and Denny's upper management that the concoctions were appreciated by the customers as delicious and hearty. A jargon terminology based mainly on pet foods sprang up among Area staffers. Some famed Pelarean regional dishes were briskly referred to as "Kibbles and Bits" or "Rabbit Pellets" or "Puppy Chow." Liquids offered on the menu became known variously as "Paint Thinner" or "Nail Polish Remover" or "Battery Acid."

Waitresses and waiters, unlike prep area employees, were protected by their suits from the harsh smells of some of the off-world comestibles. But wait staff had to become used to witnessing the eating habits of the visitors. Nutrients were extracted by Pelareans by flooding the cuisine, while it was held by the arms or utensils, with secretions that dissolved minerals useful to the organism and that subsequently assisted in bearing these tidbits into the body. Whereas humans coated their food with saliva inside their mouths, Pelareans secreted energetically over theirs *before* bringing it within their equivalent of lips. Also, a loud sucking noise was emitted when the off-worlders' mouths reabsorbed nourishment-laden secretions once the morsel had been sufficiently coated.

Forbearance toward the sights and sounds within the Area was acquired easily by some new wait staff, but others refused shifts in The Swamp after an initial tryout, or from the day they were hired.

Pelarean dining techniques and diet became a source of scorn and revulsion well beyond the hospitality industry. And a parallel origin for anti-off-worlder statements and jokes arose from the emergence of Pelareans onto the North American highway network.

Adapted Airstream trailers took to the roads initially, once the visitors' intense desire to view firsthand the Terran landscape and civilization became evident. These trailers were pulled by cars driven by OWT employees, and in the early months formed convoys of twenty or thirty units. But many Pelareans chafed at the restrictions implicit in these guided tours, and soon were at the wheel of large RVs rebuilt to ensure their occupants' biological well-being, with controls and instrumentation modified to enable them to navigate the bus-sized vehicles.

The towed trailers—still used by the more timid—and self-propelled motor homes were readily identified by the OWT flashing green lights mounted on the roof, front and rear. Installed for purposes of safety, the lights additionally drew attention to the Pelareans' presence. They thus became a focus for human resentment. Besides possessing other supposed negative attributes, off-worlders were regarded as bad drivers, although statistically an accident involving them was rare. "How do you make Rock Eaters go blind?" one joke asked. Answer: "Put a steering wheel in front of them."

A contributing factor to sentiment hostile to Pelareans and to OWT was no doubt fear of the visitors' advanced technologies. They had achieved interstellar travel at a time when humans had barely established a semi-permanent scientific outpost on Mars. No Pelareans had ever brandished or even referred to a weapon of any sort, yet the menace implied by their evident scientific sophistication was enhanced by their stature. The stockiest of the Pelareans tipped the scales at under fifty kilograms, and a majority of full-grown ones reached somewhat over two metres high. Because of their apparent physical weakness—hence the derogatory term, "Wisps"—their superiority in brain-power bothered insecure humans even more.

Besides oral disparaging references and humour, bumper stickers opposing the visitors appeared, frequently affixed to vehicles that also paraded pithy sayings denouncing gun control, environmental protection, and other liberal causes. "Pelarean = Anti-Terran" was one slogan, and another pilloried the OWT as "Organized World Traitors." For about a year, the stylized representation of a lawnmower—presumably advocating cutting down the grass-like Pelareans—was reproduced in a number of display media, the way Confederate flag decals, T-shirts and belt buckles were sold. A number of states adopted laws forbidding the public display of the lawnmower image, claiming it indicated an intent to commit a crime. After numerous lower-court cases, the federal Supreme Court upheld the ban, arguing Constitutionally guaranteed free speech did not include the right to threaten bodily harm. The image continued to be seen, however, usually in the form of graffiti. More often, oblique expressions of dislike of Pelareans were affixed to vehicles or reproduced on clothing: "Bag 'Em"—accompanied by the still-legal outline of a lawnmower's clippings bag—or "I <u>Smoke</u> Grass" or "Another American Against the Grain."

Very few overt acts of hostility were directed at the off-worlders, notwithstanding a persistent, small number of diehards suspicious of the Pelareans' presence on the planet. Yet despite a television and print campaign conducted by federal and state agencies intended to educate people why "Rock Eater" or "Wisp" were offensive, such derisive terms for the visitors passed into ordinary speech.

Janice had spoken to Alan soon after they started dating about his and his friends' casual use of the put-downs. "How would you feel if you were known as a 'Flesh Eater' or 'Lump'?"

"Wouldn't bother me."

"I'll bet."

Alan curbed his slang references to the off-worlders at first when he was around Janice, but the terms were common currency at the sawmill where he was one of the dayshift millwrights. Nobody on staff at Denny's referred to Pelareans by the offensive labels while at work. Off duty, the names might creep into their talk. And Janice realized from shifts she was assigned on the Terran side of the restaurant that some of the wait staff who never served in The Swamp harboured decidedly antagonistic feelings toward the visitors. "I'm not prejudiced. But we don't go traipsing around their planet," was a repeated objection.

Alan had been up in the steel when his pager sounded. One of the drying sheds was not maintaining temperature, and the other millwright was busy realigning the largest head saw. A diagnostic on the dryer's heat system using the building's computer revealed nothing amiss. But during a visual check of the facility, Alan noticed that one of the ceiling vents was open when at this stage of the cycle it should have been shut.

He located the lift by the tool crib and drove it into place. A few minutes later he had extended and set the jacks for stability and had hoisted himself in the bucket five metres over the floor among the steel roof trusses. The vent had seized, and the electric motor that powered it had fried out attempting to reconfigure the louvres to their proper position.

The lift returned Alan to the ground. He walked back to the millwrights' station and selected the tools he needed. Barry at Stores confirmed they had a vent motor in stock if Alan could not revive the burned-out one. Alan mused on his return route to the dryer that Barry's response was the first positive news of the morning. As Alan was being lofted toward the balky vent again, his pager shrilled.

He cursed at the interruption. Most often a summons concerned a minor problem somebody could fix themselves but chose not to, preferring instead to halt operations and yell for a millwright. Alan's intention was to ignore the page until he had the dryer back on line. But when he twisted to observe the readout, the message line advised him: FIRE.

The word puzzled him for a second. He was not part of the mill's fire team. His connection with fire suppression was his participation in the Bond Creek volunteer crew. Being a member of the Bond Creek Fire Department involved spending Tuesday nights with the boys—and a couple of women—familiarizing themselves with the equipment, running through procedural drills, being taught additional rescue and safety techniques. Then almost everybody drove over to Sherman's Highway Bar, or the lounge at the Bond Valley Grill, to knock back a few and relax. Most fire department callouts occurred in the spring, when people burned off their pasture grass. Inevitably somebody who had been drinking during this chore would be unable to stop the flames from spreading to his fences, barn, garage, or occasionally house. The volunteers also attended infrequent highway accidents on the back roads, or a little more often on the sixteen-kilometre stretch of I-5 designated by the

State Police as the Bond Creek department's responsibility for accident backup.

But the pager flashing the word FIRE belonged to Rogue River Wood Products. If there was a situation in Bond Creek, nobody would contact him here at work in Grants Pass. Enough of the guys were employed closer to the hall during the day, or were at home in the valley, to handle anything that might occur there. Alan hit the reply button.

The voice of the mill's dispatcher, Billy, rasped out of the device. "You've got OWT incident training, don't you?"

Alan was taken aback by the question. He couldn't think what this had to do with his job. "Yeah. So what?"

"GPFD wants you. At Denny's, up by the highway. Know where it is? I guess something's going on."

"They asked for me? I live in Bond Creek. They've got their own—"

"They said step on it. They're contacting everybody in the area who's had the training. Your name came up on the computer."

"You sure they asked for me? GPFD has an entire designated—"

"It's what they said. Must be something big. You going, or not? I have to let your supervisor know if you're away."

"I'm out of here. Tell Mike I've isolated the problem in Dryer Three to a defective top vent. Maybe he can get that useless bastard Gino to unstick it while I'm gone."

"Dryer Three, top vent. Roger on that, Alan."


Janice had lowered the novel she had been reading in bed when he had returned home from a Tuesday fire department evening last June and announced he had been selected to take a week of advanced OWT training in Portland. The powers-that-be wanted better prepared first responders if a volunteer crew reached the scene of a vehicular incident involving off-worlders before specialized state teams could arrive.

"Must be your payback for your attitude," Janice had needled Alan. "Now you'll be the local expert on saving the very ones you're always bad-mouthing. I think I detect some just deserts."

"I tried to get out of it," Alan complained. "Dougie said we're required to send somebody. His information is that a lot of the course is mechanical, about environmental systems. I'm the only millwright we have. Everybody at the firehall figured I was the obvious choice."

"Did they take into account how you talk about Pelareans?"

"I don't talk about them any different than anybody else."

"You don't?"

"Okay, *you're* more respectful."

"No kidding. But if you really don't like them, why on Earth—no pun intended—would you agree to do this Portland thing?"

"Smart ass. Because I get full pay, courtesy OWT. Dougie says they arrange my time off from the mill."

"You don't make any extra? No stipend?"

"We're volunteers, remember?" He started to remove his shirt. "Portland will mean a whole week doing something different than repairing hi-los, or steam pipes or log chain drives. I thought it would be kind of interesting. I'll get to see how they retrofit those Winnebagos."

"You're interested in that?"

He unclasped his watch and placed it on the dresser, then piled his wallet and change alongside. "Alan's the name, machinery's the game. Don't you forget it. I've never considered a chance to learn something new a waste. You never can tell when you might be able to apply what you've learned to some entirely different problem."

She shrugged, and was reabsorbed by her book until he crawled in beside her. She clicked off the bedside lamp.

Nearly 100 people attended the Portland course. Besides at least one rep from various rural outfits, firefighters from city departments participated—some taking the sessions as a refresher, and some, like Alan, encountering the material for the first time. He knew four volunteers from crews north and south of Bond Creek; they had all been at the same regional training intensives or department competitions occasionally held on Saturdays in Grants Pass or further south in Ashland. Two of the GPFD members in attendance he recognized as instructors at the Saturday events.

He phoned Janice every evening. She could tell from the excitement in his voice that he was enjoying the experience. About half the material was technical detail he was pleased to gain familiarity with: how the life-support systems in the RVs and trailers that conveyed Pelareans were constructed, and how to best preserve environmental integrity if the sub-systems became compromised. Equivalent systems used in hospitality structures—OWT portions of hotels and restaurants—were covered. First response medical training was part of the Portland course, too: what Terrans understood to date about Pelarean physiology, and the likely effects on biological functions of various degrees of life-support collapse. Use of OWT rescue suits, liaison with OWT medivac teams, and some basic exopsychology techniques for dealing with traumatized off-worlders during and after an incident were taught.

Part of each day, Alan reported to Janice, was spent on exploring emergency team members' attitudes toward Pelareans, and how this affected the quality of assistance provided. The standard operational reference to Pelareans was now "OW Personnel." And the Supreme Court had recently ruled that for law-enforcement purposes off-worlders were legally persons.

On Alan's return from Portland, though, Janice did not observe any change in his language regarding Pelareans. With his friends when she was present, or alone with her, he could still refer to off-worlders as "Wisps" or "Rock Gobblers" or even "Slimers." The latter was a label he had been delighted to hear used by some Denny's staffers at the employees' Christmas party. But she noted the frequency of his negative references to the visitors declined after Portland. He no longer had so much to say when a item on the nightly news involved Pelareans. And she sensed that part of his use of the offensive names around her originated from his idea that it was fun to provoke her automatic disapproval.

As the OWT briefers in Portland had reminded Alan and the other attendees, Terrans had learned a considerable amount about their visitors in the thirteen years since Contact. Yet more about the off-worlders remained mysterious. The Pelareans appeared to prefer it that way. As a species, or at least among those of their species that practiced spacefaring, they had quite a commercial streak. Certain information would be freely available. Beyond that, if you wanted to know, you had to pay.

Terrans had grasped the bare outlines of how the Pelareans could voyage so far so fast. Interstellar travel had been relegated by humans to science fiction because, even at the technologically unattainable speed of light, ships attempting to sail the vast distances between the stars would take dozens—even thousands—of years to complete a round trip. But the Pelareans crossed space within a timescale compatible with humans' experience of inter*planetary* travel. To accomplish this, the Pelareans built what they called The Road.

Physicists on Earth already had discovered that an anomaly of Einstein's Theory of Relativity was that inside a particle accelerator infinitesimal bits of matter could exceed the supposed universal speed limit: the velocity of light. The Pelareans had sufficient scientific and technological skills to transform the very route they wished to travel into an enormous particle accelerator, with their vessel as the particle. In some manner, the devices necessary to construct the accelerator, to propel a ship along The Road, were flung immense distances ahead of a Road-building vessel even while it was proceeding at unimaginable speeds. Thereafter, these components of the accelerator floated in space. Subsequent craft could ply The Road with different payloads than construction vessels had of necessity to bear.

Terrans had a million questions not only about the science involved in The Road, but also about the Pelareans' overall comprehension of the universe. What other technological marvels besides The Road were the off-worlders capable of? What different planetary civilizations had they identified? Was the science of any of these as advanced beyond the Pelareans' as they were beyond humans'? Curiosity about a myriad of aspects of the Pelareans themselves stayed unfulfilled— from reproductive organs and methods, to normal lifespan, to why an apparently nonaggressive species had so prospered, whereas on Earth, war—or more broadly, competition—continued to be the mother of invention.

The Pelareans behaved as though they had predetermined which questions they would be willing to answer in detail, which more vaguely, and which inquiries they would be completely silent about. Everything we have learned, they repeated, we are keen to impart. But you have to pay.

The visitors were unmoved by Terran scientists' protestations that knowledge on their planet was routinely shared without cost. The

Pelareans insisted that Earth's civilization was as commercial as their own. The basis for all interactions they had monitored on the planet, they declared, was an exchange of goods, or of tokens to which exchange value had been assigned. In vain were clerics of various faiths, and philosophy professors of contending schools, brought out to counter the visitors' perceptions regarding human values. To make matters worse, the situation was clearly a sellers' market.

In the end, the debate shrank to one focus: what did Terrans possess that the off-worlders desired; what might humans use as payment for what they wanted to know? The recognition that specific Terran substances could be ingested, even savoured, by the Pelareans raised a possibility. But the visitors were hardly starving. At last the solution was revealed by the Pelareans: the travellers to Earth were inveterate and eager tourists.

Thus the global Off-World Tourism agency was created, as a means to generate the planetary version of foreign exchange. OWT from the start suffered from internal dissension, since the countries that the Pelareans judged safest to visit—the most stable politically and which had the smallest possibility of natural disasters—were anxious to obtain the largest share of the money. But the Pelareans refused to deal except on a species-to-species basis. So a grudging international co-operation emerged, both in ensuring the best possible Terran experience for the visitors, and in establishing planetary priorities on what knowledge the newly earned money should buy. One consequence of this enforced perspective was the awarding of a Nobel Peace Prize jointly to OWT and its corresponding Pelarean Liaison Council two years after large-scale visitation of Earth began.

The Pelarean tourism councillors constantly reiterated to OWT that off-world visitors were engaged in a trip-of-a-lifetime, so their stay on Earth better be worth it for them. Despite the unthinkable velocities attained on The Road, the return voyage plus a few months' on-planet tourism meant for Pelareans the equivalent of a two-year investment of time. OWT was unable to ascertain what financial outlay was involved for each traveller, but speculated that the visitors were mainly affluent individuals. This assumed that the distribution of wealth among the Pelarean population followed lines similar to that in most cultures on Earth. Yet no credible basis for OWT's assumption was proposed, and when pressed on the subject, the off-worlders merely added Pelarean economics to the list of information Terrans wished to purchase.

The moment after Alan punched in his pickup's ignition code, he selected the fire department frequency on the audio. The GPFD base operator was asking Medford to dispatch an additional engine company. From the request and other chatter Alan heard as he gunned through town toward the restaurant, he deduced the fire was not yet contained. The dashboard clock read 10:50. Janice was working afternoons, so she would not even have left the house, he noted with relief. By now he had met a lot of the people she worked with. He wondered, since the blaze was serious enough to call in reinforcements, if everybody had made it out okay.

The stoplight at River Road delayed him; for the hundredth time, he wished volunteers were allowed flashing lights and sirens on their vehicles. By keeping the truck to the posted speed, he rolled without a hitch through all the intersections up Seventh. He could see a column of smoke ahead. Before he reached the fire, a cop had the street blocked and was rerouting traffic.

Alan explained who he was, drove past the barricade and parked near where a pumper was connected to a hydrant. He hurried forward; the OWT half of the building had flames visible in one of its windows. Hoses were sending streams of water against the structure. A ladder truck was deployed soaking the roof, where smoke was streaming from a skylight. More smoke appeared to be pulsing out of the Terran side of the restaurant as well.

An OWT Winnebago was being uncoupled from the building's vehicular airlock. The RV's revolving green lights added another colour to the fire department's reds and whites and the city cops' reds and blues. The motor home began to back away from the burning restaurant; one of the firefighters directed it through the maze of hoses, pumpers, engine company wagons and piles of snow left from the plowing of the restaurant's parking lot.

A ProtecTent temporary OWT shelter had been inflated on a snowy lawn between the parking area and Seventh. Two suit racks had been erected alongside the ProtecTent: green survival suits for the Pelareans, with their built-in thirty minutes of life-support, and bright orange rescue garments for Terrans, with the accompanying oxygen tanks. This was all standard procedure for an incident involving off-worlders; in Portland, they had practised this setup and Alan knew the GPFD periodically did drills involving this equipment.

He jogged over to the OWT site. Two guys in regular fire department running coats, helmets and boots flanked another wearing the orange Terran protective gear minus helmet and air tank. The man in the rescue suit, taller and stockier than the others, was speaking on a Com phone. Alan identified him from the Portland training sessions: Marty Something. Marty stood out in any group due to his height and bulk, and the self-confident way he carried his physique—like a professional wrestler, Alan had concluded. The three turned toward Alan as he approached.

"I'm Alan Bryland, with the Bond Creek bunch. I was paged. I think it's because I'm the OWT specialist for our department. What do we have?"

"I remember you," Marty said. "You were at Portland last summer, right?"

Alan nodded.

Marty extended a huge hand. "Marty Becker." They shook.

"We got both the OWT side and the other burning," one of the firefighters told Alan.

"Everybody out?"

"All *our* people," Marty said. "We ain't sure about OW Personnel. Two of them in the restaurant made it back to their RV. We couldn't get them to shift the damn Winnebago away from the lock. So Craig suited up and went to move it. They weren't going to let him inside."

"They're freaking?"

"They don't speak none of the languages in a ConVerse. Not besides basic tourist palaver: read a menu, rent a room. They didn't have clue one what Craig was asking them to do."

Alan shook his head. "Why isn't anything easy?"

"Ain't that the truth. We have to find out if there were more than two chowing down. I've been on the Com to some fool at OWT in San Francisco. He promised to locate somebody who speaks the lingo. But first I'm supposed to inform him where exactly the OW Personnel are from. If we could ask them that, for fuck's sake, we could ask them *ourselves* whether any others are still in the building."

"Like having a Hindu or something at a fire in Mexico," the other firefighter added. "Emergency response technician has Spanish, maybe a little English. How can he ask a Hindu if Grandma and Grandpa and the kids got out all right?"

"We'll have to go in, I guess," Alan said.

"No shit, Sherlock," Marty agreed. "We're just waiting to see if Craig wrings any info out of them. Moving the bus was the first priority."

Alan glanced around. Another engine company had pulled in, and was preparing to hose down the gas station south of the restaurant. The newly arrived crew began calmly but efficiently to connect and charge hose. "I'll suit up," he said.

"There's no need," Marty replied. "You can do backup."

Once Alan had made the offer, he was conscious of the adrenaline buzz that invariably started with the realization he was about to be front-line at an accident site or fire. "I was paged at work, so I don't have my turnout gear with me, anyhow. I've had the training; now's the chance to put it to use."

Marty studied him for a moment. "Okay. Your call."

By the time Alan had the suit and helmet on, and run through his life-support checks, the door airlock on the Winnebago had hissed and an orange-suited figure stepped out. Alan could see the figure extend a gloved hand with thumb down as he walked toward Marty.

"No speakee English," the man's voice fuzzed over the speaker. "No speakee any goddamn thing the useless ConVerse can make out at all. Big interspecies problem for communicating the most basic goddamn thing."

"You were probably talking to an idiot," Marty ventured.

"Or an idiot in shock. We got to go in," the voice said.

"Let's hit it," Marty replied. "Craig, this is Alan. Alan, Craig."

Craig raised a hand in greeting, as Marty hefted tank and helmet from the ground and began his checks. Alan, already sweating in his suit, asked Craig if the Denny's employees had been quizzed about how many ow Personnel were being served when the fire broke out.

"The staff didn't exit this side. This is the pressurized half; the other half is—"

"I know. My girlfriend is a waitress."

Marty's speaker-modified voice cut in. "She works here?"

"Yeah. Her shift doesn't start until one this afternoon. But I know some of the other waitresses, and they'll probably—"

"She works OWT?" Craig asked.

"Yes. I've seen the layout inside."

"Excellent," Craig said.

Marty was talking on the Com again. A firefighter gathered lamps, axes and a Halligan bar from a GPFD truck and brought them over to the orange-suited trio. Alan selected an axe and lamp and fitted the latter into the socket on top of his helmet.

Marty finished with the Com. "Ricardo, the officer in charge on the front side, says a waitress confirms another two OW Personnel were in there. We better hustle." He rigged his lamp, and grabbed the bar from the fireman.

"We'll need suits for them," Craig said. Marty nodded. Craig briskly crossed to the racks by the ProtecTent. He rummaged among a pile of gear on the ground nearby and extracted a canvas bag. Then he took down two of the green survival suits, carefully rolled them up and stowed them. After a second, he added a third.

The extra was to provide a margin of safety, Alan realized, like they had been taught in Portland. Craig slung the bag over his shoulder by its strap. Marty, trailed by Alan and Craig, started pacing toward the airlock that accessed the OWT Area from the sidewalk.

The calf of Alan's right leg began to throb, as usual at stressful moments. Though the rescue suits had a heat-resistant capability, as Alan approached the building he thought he could feel the temperature increase while he stepped over the tangle of hoses after Marty. Alan concentrated on recalling entry techniques they had rehearsed at the OWT course.

Marty lifted the cover to the Area status panel alongside the lock. He punched a couple of buttons. "Integrity is intact," the speaker on his suit announced. "These things are built like fucking bank vaults. But pressure is down from optimum. Might be a structural fault, nothing to do with the fire. Or could be a leak or—"

"Let's go," Craig urged. Alan could see Craig's fingers tighten and loosen repeatedly on the axe he was hefting.

The three entered the airlock. As the outer door sealed behind them, Alan fought a surge of panic. The emergency light in the elevator-sized compartment cast strange shadows. The sound of the commotion outside was muted.

In accordance with standard procedure, the three firemen crouched, as the compartment readjusted its environment to Pelarean specs. "Everybody okay?" Marty asked. The readout over the door into the restaurant raced through atmospheric percentages. Finally the sign indicated the space was inhabitable by unprotected Pelareans by flashing the message *Safe To Remove Suit*. The information was in English as well as the Pelarean languages, although an extra advisory in English warned: *Safe For Pelareans Only*. Marty stood and pushed the entry button. The inner door did not respond.

After jabbing the button several more times, Marty unlocked the control panel and keyed in an override. No reaction.

"It's designed to fail safe," Craig observed, from where he and Alan were hunkered. "Fire probably knocked out some circuits." The instructors in Portland, Alan was aware, had emphasized that OWT hospitality areas and vehicles were designed to convert to havens in the event of a risk to the internal environment.

"Locks aren't supposed to fail jammed tight," Marty said. "If they did, we couldn't get none of them out alive. We hack our way in through a wall or window, they'll die from lack of that crap they breathe." He worked his Halligan bar into the seam where the door parts intersected and applied pressure, cursing steadily.

"Your Rock Eater don't exactly breathe, Marty," Craig pointed out. "More like they suck in through their skin."

Marty stopped heaving on the bar and stared at Craig, who rose and added his weight to Marty's leverage, without effect. Alan stood, too, but the bar was too short for a third pair of hands. After a minute Craig stepped back.

"This ain't getting it," Marty noted the obvious.

"Let's try going in from the other side," Alan suggested.

"Huh?"

"If we can access the OWT food prep room from the regular restaurant, maybe the lock there is still operational."

"Make more sense to pry the Wisps out of their Winnebago and into the ProtecTent. Then we can connect the Winnebago to the vehicle lock and enter that way," Marty stated. Alan felt his face flush inside his helmet. *Of course*, he castigated himself. *What was I thinking?* Marty's idea was much simpler.

"Nice try, Marty," Craig said. "*You* want to tell them what you're intending to do? I couldn't get them to grasp even the concept of driving away from a building in flames. Now you want to explain that they have to put on this funky suit and go sit in a see-through structure, while we drive off in their only lifeline and reconnect it to a restaurant that's on fire? Good fucking luck."

Without a word, Marty started the cycle to readmit a Terran environment into the lock. Alarms jangled the instant he hit the *To Exit To Outside* button. Readouts flashed a warning for several seconds to suit up, along with information on how to cancel the exit procedure.

Marty was back on the Com as they waited. He spoke to his contact at OWT in San Francisco, but nobody had yet located a Pelarean linguist. "Incompetent assholes," Marty raged when the call ended. Then he was speaking to the front-side chief. Ricardo said he had three hoses into the building and he believed Marty could make it through to the OWT food prep station. He promised to relocate one of his crews to assist Marty's attack.

Just before the outer door of the lock irised open, Marty looked at Alan. "Good plan," Marty said.

He sprang clear of the building and trotted along the sidewalk with the others in tow. Alan was amazed at how fast Marty could cover ground in the awkward suit. As the three pounded around the last corner, a white helmet—which had to be Ricardo—stood near the regular entrance vestibule beckoning to them. "Go get 'em, boys," he urged as they passed. "But be careful."

They halted inside the smoky interior. A counter with its row of stools was dimly visible. Booths lined the north, west and south walls, below large windows. The suits' helmet lamps had automatically switched on as the available light lessened. "You lead," Marty directed Alan. He followed three hoses through the chocked-open kitchen doors.

The south and southeastern walls of the kitchen were a mass of charred studs. Flames flickered through the darkness from the ceiling at that end of the room; an officer and line man were aiming a hose at the blaze. A fluorescent light fixture dangled from one of its two chains. Beyond the kitchen, Alan knew, was a corridor with staff washrooms, break room, storerooms and the door to the Terran part of the OWT portion of the restaurant—the ordinarily red-lit food prep space, pantry, break room and washroom. The Swamp itself was beyond that.

Smoke was thicker in the corridor, but two of the hoses led through it. Another white helmet and line man were crouched a couple of metres into a storeroom, hitting the fire there with a stream of water. Alan found the third team kneeling at the entrance to the OWT section. They were too preoccupied with their hose to notice the newcomers' approach, but the line man shut down the nozzle at the officer's signal once Alan tapped him on the shoulder to announce their arrival.

Alan peered past them into the smoke-filled darkness. The space was illuminated by flames rippling along the south wall far to his right, and by the beams from the firefighters' lamps. The sound was the vibrato roar of a fire well established. Even in his suit, Alan could sense the blast of heat ahead. His right leg throbbed painfully.

The two men with the hose squeezed aside to let Alan and the others by. Alan hesitated at the threshold, staring in at the swirls of smoke fitfully lit by a gust of fire. *Why should I have to do this?* a part of his mind protested. *Why not just wait outside until those OWT morons in San Francisco find somebody to explain to the Rock Eaters how their stupid RV is needed for the rescue? If San Francisco fumbles the ball, the consequences won't be the fault of anyone here. OWT ought to be better prepared for a mess like this. Who would let creatures from another planet tool around our highways like tourists from Nebraska, when they don't have the slightest notion of the dangers they face?*

"What's up?" Marty's speaker crackled behind him. Without further thought, Alan squatted and began to duck-walk forward.

He mentally reviewed the floor plan. They had entered the OWT portion of the restaurant at the northwest corner of the large rectangular prep room, whose longest part opened out to his right. The servers' airlock was in the north*east* corner, directly across the room from the doorway now a metre behind him. Windows that looked into The Swamp covered the north wall to his left, and half the east wall to the right of the lock that was his destination. On the west wall were doors to the break room—off of which was the washroom —and to the pantry.

The blaze was now mainly entrenched on the southernmost expanse of the east wall, and the top half of the south wall. Alan swivelled to watch as a portion of the ceiling in the southwest corner burst into flame and spiralled down to land at the pantry door. The fire appeared to have earlier broken through the ceiling ahead: blackened, wet, and smouldering bits of material littered the route in front. A sizable chunk of wood and sheetrock had crashed down onto the nearest food prep table and spilled across the drenched floor tiles.

Visions of the fire blocking the rescue team's retreat froze Alan's progress a second time. He gazed desperately behind, intending to motion the men at the hose to tackle the threat represented by the blaze spreading along the west wall from the pantry toward the entrance portal. But the white helmet had followed immediately after them. He had assessed their predicament, and he and the line man were already pointing their nozzle toward the southwest quarter of the ceiling.

Alan heaved aside a piece of sopping, scorched wallboard and started to crawl on his hands and knees. He brought his axe forward each time he repositioned his right arm. A tangle of larger debris had to be circumnavigated; he shunted to his left, closer to the north wall. Unable to resist, he half-rose and peered through the windows into The Swamp. Whatever emergency lighting should have been operational had ceased, if in fact it had ever functioned. The window reflected back the beam from his helmet lamp. If he swung his head from side to side, he could discern through the glass a few eating stations. No sign of any living occupants. He lowered himself to the floor again and resumed his progress toward the servers' airlock.

Marty had halted behind him while he scanned The Swamp. But Craig had attempted to proceed to the right of a still-smoking heap of ceiling insulation, portions of blackened joists, shards of metal and shattered fluorescent tubes. "Shit," he suddenly bellowed, the eruption from his speaker audible above the pops and rumble of the flames, and the high-pressure jet of water.

Alan glanced back. Craig had snagged one leg of his suit on a nail protruding from a board in the rubble he was skirting. He sat to inspect the damage. A gash of several inches had been torn in the suit.

Marty's helmet lamp joined Craig's in examining the rip. "That's it for you, buddy," Marty said. "Your suit is toast."

"Shit," Craig repeated.

Seconds later, they reached the airlock. Marty uncovered the OWT Area status panel beside it. "Increased pressure loss," he reported. "Readings are in the yellow zone. Integrity ain't going to last much longer."

Craig unslung the pack containing the off-world survival suits and handed it to Alan. Then Alan and Marty were within the lock. This one was smaller than on the OWT side of the building, and without light other than that provided by their lamps. Panic swelled again in Alan as the outer door sealed.

As before, when the *Safe To Remove Suit* sign flashed, the inner door would not open. Nor did the override budge it. Marty and Alan yanked together on Marty's Halligan bar, without success. Marty uttered a non-stop string of obscenities while they waited for the lock to restore a Terran environment.

"No luck?" Craig greeted them. "I reckon that's it. Unless anybody has any other bright ideas, let's blow this Popsicle stand." All three rotated from where they were crouched to study the prep room's southwest corner, where the stream of water was battering the fire. As more of the ceiling in that area collapsed, the fire along the south wall flared. The water intermittently sprayed left to drench that area, before returning to its previous target.

A memory struck Alan. "There's … I think there's one other lock we could try."

Craig turned from observing the fire. "Say what?"

"The waitresses don't come in and out every time to pick up an order. There's a lock that the prep staff pass food through." Alan gestured along the east wall.

"How big?" Marty wanted to know.

"Same depth as the structural wall around The Swamp. About a metre."

"The Swamp?"

"What the waitresses call the OWT Area."

"I like that," Craig chuckled.

"How wide?"

"What?"

"How wide is the lock?"

"Sometimes a lot of orders are up at once, if the place is really busy. It has to be about two and a half metres lengthwise. Not very high, though."

"Could somebody squeeze through?"

"Lying down, they could. I think."

"Probably it's screwed, too," Craig offered.

"Probably," Marty agreed. "But let's make sure."

To approach the food airlock meant moving further south along the east wall, nearer the fire. They indicated their intent to the white helmet with gestures and as they advanced across the sodden floor the stream of water preceded them, directed always a short distance ahead of their route.

Alan carefully manoeuvred around heaps of burned and soaking litter. A counter two-thirds of a metre wide extended below the lock; they had to stand and lean over the projecting shelf to access the controls.

When the lock door opened, the space inside appeared to Alan like the interior of a coffin. "We should test it to see if it's going to fail, before somebody gets in," he suggested. The door dropped once more as Marty complied.

Two minutes later, the panel lit up green.

"The fucking thing works," Marty yelled. Craig, too, released a wordless hoot of joy. Despite himself, Alan's heart sank.

Then he was staring into the open casket again. "Take the controls, Craig," Marty said. "And for Christ's sake, while I'm in there, don't—"

"I'll go," Alan said.

"Huh?"

"You're too big, Marty," Alan pointed out. "I'll fit easier than you. Besides—" he tried to joke "—I've already got the suits here." He tugged on the pack strap.

"You don't have to," Marty said. "You're a volunteer. This is what they pay us for."

"Look at the size of the lock," Alan urged him.

"Let's not stand around and fucking argue," Craig interjected. "Let's get those goofs out of there before the roof caves, and who gets to go becomes irrelevant since we're fucking crisped."

"You sure?" Marty said to Alan.

"What I'm not sure about is what to say to the Wisps," Alan responded. The issue had repeatedly surfaced and vanished in his mind since they began the rescue attempt. "How do we convince them to put on these suits, if Craig couldn't get them to understand why they needed to disconnect from the building?"

Marty raised a massive hand in front of Alan's helmet. The hand contracted into a fist, which made a couple of short sideways thrusts in the air.

"My advice is to cold-cock 'em if they don't savvy," Marty said. "Act first, talk later. We didn't come all this way to take no for an answer. I agree with Craig: we got to get out of here."

The three glanced down the room at the inferno. The spurt of water now being directed in that direction seemed puny against an expanded sheet of fire. Alan doubted he would be as able as Marty to punch out the Rock Eaters. But he could improvise what to do once inside. *One step at a time*, an inner voice calmed him.

Putting down the axe, he climbed onto the counter and squeezed himself into the compartment. He concentrated on his breathing as the outer door shut. He tried to focus on what he might discover in The Swamp, rather than on how he was trapped in a burning building inside a tiny space lit only by his helmet lamp, wearing a suit with a finite amount of air, his life dependent now on two men he scarcely knew.


Alan found a parking place in the nearly full City Hall lot and nosed the pickup in. Most of his attention, though, was drawn to the three hulking TV news vans parked by the building's main doors, one of them having been driven up onto the snow-covered median between the street and the sidewalk. Satellite dishes atop the van roofs were aimed skyward, and cables snaked up the steps and through the entranceway. Four OWT motor homes, green lights flashing, were also lined up at the curb in the No Stopping zone.

He turned toward Janice, indicating with his hand the cluster of vehicles. "This better not be for me."

She touched his cheek. "Of course it's for you."

"This is ridiculous. I wasn't—"

"They want to celebrate what you did." She smoothed down a cow-lick on his head. "I *know* you didn't do it alone," she said, anticipating his frequent objection. "You've told them over and over. That's all you can do." She wondered if she should try to lighten the moment, or whether the impending media attention at the afternoon's ceremony had spooked him beyond humour. She decided to risk jocularity: "You shouldn't have ever told them your partner worked there. That it might have been *me* you were saving. That gave them too good an angle. You've got nobody to blame but yourself."

His sense of fun seemed to have evaporated. His hands gripped the steering wheel, and his expression was miserable. "You're right. I wasn't thinking. I didn't know what to say."

"I'm just kidding, Alan." She leaned to kiss his ear. "Really, you did fine. You'll do fine today, too."

"I wish this was over."

"Part of this has nothing to do with you, hon, if that's any conso-lation. When I talked to one of those guys from San Francisco who phoned, I got the distinct impression this is mainly about tourism. A lot of money is at stake. They want the Pelareans to feel safe. Publicizing what you fellows did on their behalf is meant to reassure them."

"*I* wouldn't be reassured if I was them. We about lost them."

"But you didn't. And that makes you a celebrity." She adopted a cheery tone. "A hero like you shouldn't be fussed by a few minutes of television exposure." Grasping the bag that contained her high-heeled shoes, she activated the door latch and stepped down from the truck.

He sat paralyzed for a moment before he also opened the door. The Swamp was a blur of impressions to him now. Despite his attempts to remain calm, the seconds he was crammed into the food lock, waiting for it to cycle, had filled him with almost unendurable anxiety.

The Wisps had been right there by the wall when he struggled out of the compartment. One was conscious and the other not; he assumed the environment in The Swamp had further degraded. He had laid out the suits, and the conscious one had correctly interpreted his gestures, despite Craig's experiences. The Pelarean had climbed into one suit, and had helped Alan bundle the limp off-worlder into another suit and into the lock. A few minutes later the lock reopened, and the second Wisp climbed in. Dreading the thought of clambering back into the box, Alan had edged over to fiddle with the controls of the servers' airlock. The door would not stir.

The food lock suddenly was ajar for him. Soaked in sweat, he had forced himself to enter. As he lay inside, he fought panic by thinking of Janice: of kissing her toes, her ankles, the backs of her legs, along her thighs. Then the lock was open, and Marty was assisting him into a room where three different teams were now pumping water at the walls and ceiling. No flames were showing, only smoke and steam. Craig and the rescued Pelareans were not in sight, but two men he did not know wearing orange suits were beside Marty. Next he recalled, he was sitting with his helmet off on a gurney in the front parking lot beside a mound of cleared snow, an ambulance guy checking him over as he debriefed to Marty and the other two orange suits. Alan felt simultaneously elated, and weary to the core. When the group of them walked around the building to return the suits to the rack and help take up the equipment, Alan saw that a huge helicopter with OWT markings had landed on Seventh close to the ProtecTent. Another OWT RV was alongside the aircraft—he guessed to tend the rescued OW Personnel.

Before he and Marty could strip off their suits, they were intercepted by a man in civilian clothes Marty recognized. The newcomer guided them onto Seventh toward where the cops had barricaded the street. A microphone stand had been erected, facing a clump of people standing on the pavement. Alan had balked when he realized four of the group they were approaching carried professional-looking TV cameras. Marty strode forward a few paces alone, then had halted and waved impatiently for Alan to catch up.


Alan's legs felt weighted with lead as he and Janice crossed the City Hall parking lot. As they neared the TV vehicles, he could feel the calf of his right leg begin to pulse. Janice slipped her arm through his and held on. Together they started up the stairs.

# Rage Together

# Land under the Snow

## I

I wouldn't believe what happened either, except I lived through it. I had driven up Silver Star Mountain one Wednesday morning in January to go cross-country skiing for a couple of hours before work. Silver Star is on the outskirts of Vernon, BC, a city of 32,000 where I have a practice. Optometry is a profession you can do just about anywhere, and after many years down on the Coast in Vancouver I wanted to live in a smaller centre. In Vernon, I had taken up cross-country as a way of enjoying the winters. The Okanagan Valley, where Vernon is situated, gets a goodly amount of snow, though the local boosters insist the area is Canada's version of Southern California. Every winter of the six I have lived here, a cold spell of twenty-below weather hits. You're forced to shovel a foot of snow out of your driveway each morning for a week. The highway south to Kelowna is closed due to icy conditions, or a blizzard. Yet somebody is sure to earnestly inform you: "This winter is very unusual for the Okanagan." I have yet to encounter what anyone is willing to call a typical winter.

Mondays and Wednesdays are slow days, so during the winter I don't book appointments until one P.M. That lets me head out after breakfast for an hour or two of skiing, and still have time to return home, shower, change, and be at the clinic by noon. Marie or Gail opens up, and there is ordinarily a pile of things for me to do before the first patient. But the ski is worth it. I arrive at the office cheerful, energized, glad to be living where I am and working at what I love.

Also, on weekday mornings hardly anybody is using the trails. Mostly retired folks are on the mountain: at the warming hut after my ski, having a coffee from my thermos before heading down to the city, I can glance around the room and note I'm the youngest guy there. That's not an experience you often have in public when you're in your mid-forties. Then, too, older folks generally stay on the beginner's routes: Woodland Bell, say. When I tackle an intermediate trail, or one of the advanced runs like Aberdeen or Black Prince, I can sometimes ski for an hour or more without meeting a soul. I'm immersed in the absolute stillness of the winter forest, and my thoughts.

That winter my girlfriend, Erin, could occasionally be convinced to accompany me. But she sold real estate, so inevitably she had some deal cooking she felt she had to tend to. Mornings are best for sales, she claims. I liked skiing with her: her skills are superior to mine, and she was always challenging me to take more risks. She showed me new techniques—the previous year I learned from her an easy procedure for lifting one ski out of the track to initiate a half-snowplow on a steep descent.

My ex, Beth, only liked downhill skiing. So I guess I had become used to sliding my skinny skis down a trail alone. As a result, I tend to be cautious. Every winter somebody on a cross-country trail in BC zips off the track, breaks a leg, and isn't found for a day or more. Since I'm most often by myself, I take a pack which holds a parka, my waxes, an extra ski tip, a whistle, matches, a couple of sandwiches and oranges and a granola bar or something sweet. Plus of course my thermos of coffee. I enjoy a pause alone in the winter woods, munching on a cookie or apple, swigging down a cup of steamy java, and listening to the crisp silence that rings in my ear so loud I'm deafened.

On this Wednesday, I had phoned Erin the night before to see if she wanted to go with me. We had been together Saturday night for a concert—the Edmonton Symphony was playing at Vernon's Rec Centre—and at that time she said she might be able to slip away mid-week. She and Pauline from her office were flogging these high-rise condos out by Okanagan Landing. They had some client who wanted a tour first thing Wednesday, and Pauline wasn't back from a jaunt to the Coast. Erin told me she couldn't make it after all.

I can't say I wasn't disappointed when Erin changed her mind like this. I know work is important to her. But, really, somebody else from their office could have shown a client an apartment. I believe Erin was letting me know, in a passive-aggressive way, that I was not the number one priority in her life.

I liked Erin a lot, probably loved her. But I'd never been sure why she was attracted to me. She is quite stylish and terribly successful at her business; when we were introduced at an art gallery opening three years ago, I was almost afraid to speak to her. I was aware she didn't think I was very tuned-in about fashion, although she helped me buy some clothes that I admit are a lot smarter-looking than what I used to wear. Nor did she consider me entrepreneurial enough. She definitely helped my practice grow with her suggestions on advertising and signage. Yet I believe I disappointed her by not adopting her ideas about franchising.

We enjoyed sex, when Erin's schedule permitted us to spend the night together. But an emotional distance remained between us that I had never been able to lessen. I felt I was tangled in a narrow outer sector of Erin's life, restricted to a surface layer of who she was, rather than fully meshed in a deepening relationship with her.

I wasn't happy with the status quo, and I'll bet if you could get her to be totally honest, she wasn't either. But she wouldn't take a step nearer, and I felt ridiculous when I tried. I'd explain about how much she meant to me, and how I really wished to spend more time with her. "That's nice, Ron," she'd say, and start telling me about some new property out by Swan Lake she had her eye on, or some scandal involving a city councillor and a proposed extension to the Village Green Mall.

We seemed to be drifting, skimming over top of a meaningful intimacy. I could imagine the possibility of a wonderful closeness with her.

But I was stuck when it came to improving our connection with each other. I'd puzzled for almost a year whether a satisfying relationship with her wasn't hopeless. Should I break up with her? How much time do you give to a relationship that, despite your best efforts, isn't changing for the better? Then we'd spend a weekend at a hotel together in Vancouver, and I'd remember how terrific she could be, how we truly communicated in those rare moments she appeared to want us to mesh emotionally. I'd start to anticipate a future for us as a couple. That bubble would quickly burst once we resumed daily life. I'd conclude again that the healthiest move for me was out of there. Yet when I was about to have that terminal talk with her, she'd make some loving and thoughtful gesture that left me more confused than before about the right thing to do. Especially when she subsequently reverted to her old behaviour toward me, toward us. Leave or stay? Hang in, or hit the silk? I'd obsessed over this decision until I was sick of it.

At the core, I was convinced from comments she made that in her heart of hearts she regarded optometrists like the popular image of accountants—rigid and stuffy and out-of-it, even if fiscally secure. Of course, we optometrists are people the same as anybody, with dreams and emotions. I managed to make huge changes in my life when I gave up my practice in Vancouver and reestablished it in Vernon. Beth and I had had to face our differences and decide to end the marriage—even if we didn't have kids, which made the transition simpler. Whatever Erin thought of me deep down, and despite her image of herself as worldly and hip and Ms. Okanagan Business incarnate, I'd actually been through more shifts in my life than she had. She grew up in the Okanagan Valley and, except for one trip to Australia immediately after high school, she's been here ever since. She has never married, and her longest relationship before me was a five-year affair with a married guy, a yacht broker in Kelowna. I might not have an ambition to be a multi-millionaire, even if I am financially comfortable. But all the money she'd accumulated hadn't resulted in her being a contented and well-adjusted person. She was awfully driven, no matter how many Realtor of the Year trophies she collected. I believed that a ski with me even once a week would do her more good than chalking up another condo sale.

Yet a ski by myself has its positive side, too. Working in a service profession as I do, time alone can be precious. I enjoy the peace of being away from cranky patients, the break from having to interact with too many people in one day. It's unbelievably restful to be surrounded by a depthless silence, broken only by the swish of my skis on snow, and the occasional calling of a overwintering bird. After a particularly strenuous uphill herringbone, the lack of sound can be so complete I can hear my heart hammering.

Also, for several weeks at a stretch between November and March, Vernon gets socked in under a low grey ceiling. Frequently, one reward for the drive up Silver Star—twenty minutes of steady climbing, including a couple of severe switchbacks—is a cloudless, bright blue sky that never fails to lift your spirits. Down on the Valley floor, smothered by the pervasive dark cover, everybody is gloomy. I certainly am aware of this bleak mood in my clinic. My staff becomes listless and grumpy. Even Marie, the young woman who handles the front counter and customarily sparkles, acts taciturn and withdrawn. In my work you're literally eyeball-to-eyeball with people; you'd have to be blind not to notice people's attitudes.

I'll be explaining applanation tonometry to a patient—the test for glaucoma, pressure in the eyeball, about which people often express fascination. But in the grey months, all I ever get is slack-jawed indifference: "Whatever you say, doctor. Can I go now?"

I purchased a few years ago some amazing retinal photography equipment. It's Polaroid, so in seconds I can present you with a picture of the back of your eyeball. I even have a little folder of especially intriguing photographs to show patients. Diabetes appears as a spray of black dots. Night-blindness manifests as blacked-out areas of the retina. I am able to place before you somebody who stared too long at a solar eclipse: looks like a splotch of ink dropped on blotting paper. That part of the patient's vision is history. Saddest of all, but pretty damn astounding, is a brain tumour revealed by a raised area on the retina—the neoplasm pressing on the rear of the eyeball. In one photo, this effect is a perfect doughnut formed around the optic nerve. Then on a September afternoon, we had a gentleman in off the street complaining that his eyes felt funny. I took one look at his retinal photo, recognized the diagnosis, and called for an ambulance to take him right up to the hospital. We'd caught him in the middle of a heart attack.

Usually my patients are as absorbed as I am by the tales these pictures tell. But in Vernon interest drops to nothing after a few weeks of living under the perpetual overcast. Because I spent most of my life in rainy old Vancouver, I'm not affected to the same extent. But that doesn't mean I don't feel exhilarated when, during my ascent of Silver Star Road, my station wagon bursts out of fog and cloud into glorious winter sunshine and that spectacular blue dome soaring above.

On that Wednesday, the weather on the mountain was perfect: a piercing dazzle of sun made the snow whiter than white. I checked the thermometer at the warming hut when I arrived; the temperature was nearly low enough for polar wax. A dump of fresh snow had fallen overnight but the track machine had already been out, at least along the routes closest to the parking lot.

I started on Woodland Bell, then swung onto Mystery, an intermediate trail. After an initial climb, I was about half an hour along Mystery when an opening appeared to my right that I didn't remember observing before.

A post, which looked new, supported a trail sign: *Freya*. The symbol was for intermediate, same as Mystery. No tracks had been set. But, despite the four or five inches of new snowfall, I could perceive indentations where tracks now covered by subsequent snows led away between the firs and pines. Since, as Erin frequently pointed out, I have a tendency to cling to habits and routines, I force myself at times to try things I never have before, in order not to let my life get stale. I lifted my skis out of the tracks on Mystery and proceeded along Freya. My pace was slower since I was breaking trail. But I was glad for the decrease in speed on a route I'd never skied previously. On Mystery I'm familiar with what comes next around each bend, with how precipitous the drop is down every hill, and whether there is a sharp turn at the bottom of a slope. Here, pushing through the new powder meant that even on a steep downhill I wouldn't be sliding faster than I was comfortable with. The rush of adrenaline I receive from swooping down a rapid descent can feel astonishingly rejuvenating. Yet I don't enjoy wiping out when I'm on skis by myself two or three kilometres into the back of beyond.

Freya angled mainly upwards for twenty-five minutes. I sensed the air grow ever colder as I struggled ahead and was glad for the exertion

that kept me sweaty and my heart pounding. The cardiovascular ben-
efits of cross-country are indisputable, and one of the real pluses of the
sport. But this day I was more pleased about how the effort required
was keeping me warm. When I picked up speed on occasional downward runs, an icy breeze raced through my sweater as if its thick wool
was tissue paper. A couple of times I thought about digging out my
parka from my pack and putting it on.

Still, I can't imagine a better definition of "pure" than the air striking my face as I swing my poles and shift my boards forward up a high
mountain track. Frozen crystals of unsullied oxygen are drawn into my
nasal passages and mouth with each breath. To inhale is to swallow
chilled sweet light. I sense a beneficent hoarfrost forming on the roof of
my mouth and at the entrance to my throat. Absorbing pristine cold air
on a sunlit day deep in the winter woods is like ingesting beauty itself.

I'd frequently tried to impress on Erin how she was missing the
chance to be surrounded by such austere delight when she didn't take
time to ski with me. That Wednesday, too, I thought how I would
have welcomed her presence amid the magic. I know she would have
savoured each moment in the forest. The branches of the alpine firs I
passed were coated with blobs of snow, so each small evergreen stood
in the blanket of white like an angel with multiple pinions folded
against its body, asleep or motionless. I tried to keep my attention on
the wonders I skied among, and not slip back into mulling over and
over Erin's absence and whether it wasn't additional confirmation of
the need to extricate myself from the relationship.

I encountered nobody. At one point Freya traversed what must have
been an old avalanche chute, and I could gaze out across the mountain-
ous white terrain. I stopped, panting, to marvel at valleys far below
delineated by the snakes of grey cloud that had settled into them. The
ridges above these clouds gleamed in the sunshine, slopes jagged with
snow-covered trees. Expanses of solid ivory revealed where the forest
had been clear-cut.

The woods closed around me again as I glided on. In the dimmer
illumination these trees allowed, I noticed when I paused for a breather
that my poles that morning were leaving blue shadows in the little
holes they made. Around the trunks of the firs and pines, snow-wells
had formed: circular concavities caused by the evergreen's branches

deflecting snowfall away from the base of the tree. The depths of the wells nearest the trail also emitted a bluish glow. This shadow is a phenomenon I have often observed under specific atmospheric conditions. After a few minutes, another gap occurred in the wall of the woods. When I halted to check out the view, I could peer down over a snowbank at the unending white forest that cloaked the mountainside I was on. I absently ran one ski back and forth in its track to prevent the wax sticking, as can happen in cold weather when the wax isn't precisely right. Even the edges of the ski produced a tiny blue shadow where they cut into the snow. Standing there, I idly pushed one of my poles as deep as I could into a trailside drift. When I withdrew the pole, I studied the bottom of the cylinder that resulted. The thought registered that the shadow evident is the identical tint of certain cloudless winter skies: not the vibrant blue above me that morning, but a mid-afternoon blue—a shade more sombre, though no less glowing.

Staring into the depression, I was struck suddenly by the notion that I was looking down at the top of a sky. Another world lay beneath the snow, revealed only when a breach in the white here uncovered that lower world's upper atmosphere. The snow I skied over was a thin coating that separated our biosphere from a different one below. The same instant the concept flickered through my consciousness, I felt the snow where I stood collapse and I plunged into space.

My first panicked explanation was that I had paused atop a cornice that had sheared off. Was Freya in development, unfinished, with the faint tracks I had followed left by somebody who had wandered from where the new trail was supposed to go? Why hadn't I stuck to Mystery, at least until the track machine had laid down a proper course along Freya?

These considerations surged through my mind in microseconds, swamped by a rising tide of terror. I was tensed for the sharp impact with the hillside below the trail, and an end-over-end tumble among the trees downslope until I smacked into something or lost momentum. Instead of such a landing, I continued to fall. Fall as through air.

My brain choked with fear. I hardly knew if I was upright or upside down. Occasionally in an airliner during turbulence, the craft will unexpectedly drop like a high-speed elevator while I grasp the seat arms in horror as the fall goes on much longer than I think the plane can safely withstand. This was such a descent, except unlike on board an aircraft, the drop did not cease.

I couldn't say if I was calm, or screamed. I fell. Time did not slow, but thickened to infinite density. At some point I became aware of a snowy field far underneath me. As in movies filmed from a parachutist's viewpoint, the field floated upwards in my direction, looming ever closer. Without warning, the ground struck the bottoms of my skis.

The blow propelled me sideways with shocking force; I rolled over repeatedly and ended with my face mashed into the snow's wet coldness, my pack shoved onto the back of my neck. My toque was lost, and my right ski had separated from my boot and vanished. The left ski had acted as a brake while I was spun several times head over heels. But the instant I stopped moving, I found the ski had become jammed at a severe angle in the snow, twisting my left ankle into a painful position.

I sat up, as best I could, terrified that my leg was broken. A gob of snow burned chillily down my neck. I frantically heaved my left ski around to free my leg and take the strain off my ankle. Nothing felt amiss, but I was breathless, trembling. One ski pole dangled from its loop around my right wrist. After properly positioning the pole, I levered myself vertical. Both knees were vibrating. I could see my other pole protruding from the snow three or four metres away, apparently intact. My missing ski had slid across the crusty snow to rest against a wooden post, part of a split-rail fence separating the field in which I stood from a nearby forest.

I brushed myself off, hunching my shoulders in discomfort as more icy wetness slipped down the neck of my shirt to be transformed into a clammy mass against my bare skin. I took a step toward my detached ski, and promptly sunk my ski-less leg into snow up to my thigh.

Using my pole, I managed to haul myself atop the crust again. In a series of lurches, and two face-plants caused by losing my balance as my boot went through, I closed the distance to my ski. A minute later I was properly mobile, and collected my other pole. I glanced around to determine where I was.

As near as I could fathom I had somehow tumbled entirely down the mountain, and so must be at the foot of Silver Star. Nothing around me looked familiar, so I assumed I had landed on an opposite side of the mountain from Vernon. Gnawing at my assessment of my situation was that no matter in which direction I scanned, no large peak was visible. Fields or woods stretched away to a line of rolling hills.

I was shivering uncontrollably. I knew I must be suffering from shock, and needed to warm myself. I unslung my pack and shrugged into my parka, which helped. I decided to ski in order to further raise my body temperature. No signs of human habitation were in view, although presumably the fence meant I was on somebody's farm. I resolved to ski the length of the field in the expectation of finding a gate or lane or other indication of how I might reach the road up Silver Star or the main highway, and thus gain some accurate sense of my location.

My cross-country technique at first resembled more of a trudge than an exemplary kick and glide. But I quickly warmed, and my shivering eased. I observed that the fence I was following eventually turned ninety degrees toward the closest woods. A tiny figure, also on skis, was moving along the intersecting fence line toward me.

As the space between us lessened, I could discern that the approaching skier was a large bearded man. He had shoulder-length hair, and a burly build wrapped in what appeared to be a fur jacket. Incongruous as it seemed, he resembled a biker on skis. While a considerable distance remained between us, he waved.

When we arrived face to face we stopped and regarded each other. He was costumed in leather and furs, as though he was practising to play the part of a Sasquatch in a pageant or other entertainment for Silver Star Resort. His face was weathered, lined, although I estimated he was about my age. His expression was melancholic, but that was no surprise given the weather we'd been having of late.

He began to speak to me in a sing-song language I didn't understand, although some words sounded like English cognates. German, I deduced. Erin often maintained that people don't realize how much BC Interior real estate already has been bought up by Germans. I know that occasionally when I'm driving in the back country I'll come across a Bed and Breakfast establishment that displays on its driveway gate a sign that announces *Zimmer Frei* or other German phrase. I've always taken such objects as quaint, a touch of Olde Bavaria employed by the hospitality industry to give visitors to the Valley a thrill. Here clearly was a German masquerading as his idea of a Bigfoot, just as I'd heard of adult Germans back in Europe dressing up and playacting as cowboys and Indians.

I lifted my hands, poles dangling, to show I didn't understand what he was saying. He switched to a heavily accented English, and touched one of his furry-mittened paws to his chest. "I am Hrolf. I saw you fall. You are all right, yes?"

"I'm fine," I replied. "A little shaken up, but otherwise okay."

He nodded. I had noticed while he was speaking that he had startlingly bad teeth. One of his front incisors was snapped off, another front tooth was blackened and the rest were yellowish. Some Europeans raised in the post-war years of the late forties and fifties had poor nutrition. But I reasoned that any German prosperous enough to own land in Canada would possess the funds for restorative orthodontics. This was a puzzling detail about the man. Perhaps he was a wealthy eccentric, which might also account for his bizarre cross-country attire.

"You know," I continued, aware I was babbling but not able to stop myself, "I'm not sure where I am. I was skiing—" I gestured upwards at the non-existent mountain "—and something caved in. Next moment, I'm down here. Is this your field? How far are we from Vernon?"

Hrolf's face remained brooding, solemn. "Your name?"

"I'm Ron Kerr," I said. Automatically, I pulled off a glove, fished my wallet out of the back pocket of my ski pants, and handed him my card. "Optometry. My clinic is on 32nd Avenue, in the 3300-block."

Hrolf squeezed the little white rectangle between the thumb and fingers of his hairy mitt. He brought the card awkwardly toward his face and examined it as though he'd never seen one before. He thrust it back toward me.

I waved it away. "Keep it. I've got lots."

He brought the card toward his face again, then looked around as though he didn't quite know what to do with it. He suddenly stuck his mitt up under his coat and when his hand returned the card was gone.

"I hope you don't mind me being here," I rattled on, "if this is your property. I don't quite understand how I got here. I know that sounds weird, but—"

"You fall, Ronkur," Hrolf interrupted.

"Yes, yes, I did. But—"

"You are not first. This is how we—" his mitt indicated me, then himself "—speak."

Here was a jump in logic I couldn't fathom. What was the connection between tumbles down the mountain and our opportunity to converse? Or could he mean that chance encounters with errant members of the North Okanagan Cross-Country Ski Club were how he learned English? How much English could anyone master offering assistance to lost skiers?

I decided he *was* referring to acquiring English, even though I was confused by the context for his comment. "You speak English well," I praised him. "Am I far from Silver Star Road? Or the highway? It sounds strange, but I'm all disoriented. Which direction is south?"

Hrolf gestured toward himself again with his mitted hand. "You come, Ronkur. We ski to village, home."

"Thanks, thank you," I blurted. "I really don't want to trouble you. If I can just use your phone when we get to your place, I can call my clinic and get somebody out here to pick me up. You'll probably have to give her directions, since I'm not sure ..."

Hrolf was regarding me with an intensity that caused my voice to trail off. "You are not where you were, Ronkur," he said, emphasizing his words as if to impart some momentous truth, although his comment seemed obvious.

Before I could respond, he lifted his skis and reversed his stance in his tracks. He gazed over his shoulder. "Come." Immediately he launched into a series of powerful strides along the route he had taken to meet me. After a brief hesitation, I followed him; I didn't know what else to do. As I watched the tails of his skis rise with each stroke, I realized his were wooden skis. Real antiques. But he was much more accomplished at cross-country than I, for all my high-end gear. Despite my best attempts, trying to recall everything my instructor—and Erin— ever told me about proper form, Hrolf pulled further away from me each minute.

The field we were crossing soon ended at the forest edge. We swung into the woods along a snow-covered trail about the width of a skate- skiing route. Passing through a treed area is always a little warmer than being out in an open space, and I became heated attempting to match Hrolf's speed. I finally stopped and took off my parka, and stuffed it into my pack. Hrolf had vanished ahead, although his tracks were visible. Our path wound amid a mixed evergreen and birch forest, the latter leafless in this season. Twice I glided by open meadows or perhaps frozen lakes covered by snow. I smelled smoke, faintly. A few minutes later as I rounded a bend, I found Hrolf had halted to wait for me. Beyond him several streams of smoke lifted from behind a ridge covered with firs, hemlock, and some cedar. He nodded as I approached, then kicked away to resume his relentless pace. I struggled up the rise and abruptly we were sliding down toward a replica of a primitive encampment.

*These Germans really take make-believe seriously*, I thought. *I can remember when we were kids camping out pretending to be Indians for a couple of days. These folks are into this reenactment big-time.*

The scene was straight out of Breughel's painting, *Hunters in the Snow*. Eight or nine large wooden barn-like structures were arranged in a semicircle, with smoke pouring from a fieldstone chimney at one end of each steeply gabled roof. Pens attached to or alongside each building contained small herds of cows, pigs, sheep or goats, sometimes a mix. The common central space in front of the barns consisted of dirty, compacted snow, worn flat by people crossing the area. Chickens were wandering about. Ski tracks led between the buildings and off into the countryside in most directions. About forty men and women of all ages were busy in the yard or walking purposefully from one of the wooden buildings to another. A small group was skinning an animal suspended from a tripod—a deer, I ascertained from its severed head resting on the snow nearby. A fire was burning, with something being heated or cooked in a metal pot hanging from a horizontal metal pole lashed between two posts. Three people on skis had just towed in a sledge heaped with small logs. Others had begun unloading the conveyance, and a man a short distance away was wielding an axe to chop the logs into what I presumed was firewood. Everyone was dressed in versions of the clothes my guide was wearing—furs and leathers. A murmur of conversation rose over the settlement, punctuated by outbursts of frantic barking from dogs tied up at the doorways of many of the larger buildings. As we approached the village, a young girl emerged from one of the barns and threw something to the dogs there. The dogs hungrily devoured whatever she had offered them.

I could observe no power lines or phone lines leading into the encampment. But I reassured myself that if these people were wealthy enough to act out their fantasies of who-knows-what, dozens of cell phones probably were around. Folks like these need to stay in touch with their businesses, if not their relatives back home. I felt a pang of guilt about being late to work myself. My watch read eleven-fifteen already and, wherever I was, I doubted I was going to be able to return to my house, shower, and get to the clinic in time to meet my one P.M. appointment. Gail or Marie could reschedule patients, but I needed to give my staff some idea of when I would be in.

I had the sense that almost everyone in the area in front of the buildings was staring at me as I trailed Hrolf toward one of the structures. I smiled and nodded in various directions. People's faces were grave or expressionless; most turned back immediately to their tasks. Hrolf was disconnecting from his skis. I perceived that his bindings consisted of some straps; his boots resembled Inuit mukluks.

I stuck my skis and poles beside his in a mound of snow. The dogs tethered near the door were yapping furiously at us. "Sestu! Sestu!" Hrolf said sharply. The snarls and barks faded. He opened the heavy door and motioned me to enter.

I shifted aside a thick cloth blanket or curtain just beyond the doorframe, and stepped into a sort of vestibule. The small room was much warmer than outside, filled with an odour of drying wool and leather. Pegs supporting garments lined the walls, and I hung my pack on one of them. Another hefty blanket marked a further doorway, and after Hrolf stripped off his coat and mitts I followed him through.

We stood in a sizable rectangular hall, dimly illuminated like a sombre church. At the opposite end of the room, a huge fireplace contained a roaring blaze, apparently the only heat source. The fire also provided most of the light in the interior, enhanced by two small windows cut into the rear wall, high up on either side of the chimney. Wooden shutters hung on hinges above these, propped open with sticks. A metal tripod had been placed at the left-hand side of the fireplace, from which a pot similar to the one I had seen outside dangled over flames. Other cookware rested on the hearth. Rafter beams were evident above me, and higher yet the angled roof. The floor was rough-cut planks, strewn here and there with swirls of cedar boughs. The centre of the hall was occupied by a large table, with benches on either side. Facing the fire, additional benches were situated, some with cushions. To the left of the fireplace was a smaller table, supporting an assortment of wooden boxes.

More benches were placed down each of the long walls of the room. These walls were lined with a series of large cupboards, the doors to which began about a metre from the floor and extended upwards another metre and a half. Though the room itself was warm, the odour was oppressive: musty, mildewy, smoky, and with a faint tinge of rotten meat, like when you sniff a cooked roast that has been in your fridge for a while, and detect a gamy scent. Also part of the olfactory mix was an off-putting sweeter smell, reminiscent of rancid butter.

To the right of the fire, a motherly-looking woman sat operating an antique spinning wheel. A elderly man on a stool nearby was amusing a five- or six-year-old boy, who was playing with wooden blocks. The three were dressed, as Hrolf was once he took off his coat, in a kind of pullover: short for the males, to form a loose shirt, and floor-length for the woman. The elderly man's pants were, like Hrolf's, of leather. Everything appeared homemade.

The three at the other end of the room glanced up as we entered, and the adults stood and walked toward us. Hrolf began to speak in that sing-song German of his, and the woman veered off to tend the fire. After Hrolf motioned me to sit at the table, and lowered himself onto the bench opposite me, the elderly man placed a wooden bowl in front of each of us, together with a wooden utensil shaped as a small ladle. The woman carried a pot from the fire and spooned out a thick stew. "Kjotsupa," she said to me, pointing at my steaming bowl and smiling.

"This is my wife, Edi," Hrolf said. "Her father, Carl. Ronkur," he added, indicating me.

"Hello," I nodded to both of them. The woman asked Hrolf a question, to which he did not reply.

"Thank you very much for the food," I said. "It looks delicious. I actually am quite hungry, after skiing. But you know, I'd feel more comfortable if I could just phone my clinic and advise them where I am and when I'll be back. I'm an optometrist," I explained. "And today's a work day. I go skiing in the mornings sometimes when I know we aren't busy at the office. Could I use a phone?"

Silence greeted my request. Then a flurry of conversation erupted between the woman and the elderly man. Each stood now to one side of the table: the elderly man behind me to my left, Edi behind her husband's left. In this proximity to them, I could note that, like Hrolf's, their teeth were poor. The mouth of the father-in-law, Carl, displayed mostly stumps of teeth. Edi's were better, but one of her lower incisors was missing, and one projected forward alarmingly. All were as yellowed as Hrolf's. He, meanwhile, contributed nothing to the dialogue that was occurring but bent to begin slurping his meal. After a couple of spoonfuls he glanced up and said: "Eat, Ronkur."

Obviously, my wish to use a phone wasn't about to be fulfilled immediately. I gingerly brought a spoonful of the stew to my lips. The concoction was quite hot, and savoury: I detected basil and sage and, I thought, garlic. Lumps of meat, possibly lamb or pork, plus carrots and turnips. I polished off the bowlful without pausing, and Edi bustled around and refilled it. I told her how tasty I found it, and then consumed that serving almost as speedily as the first. I attributed my tremendous appetite to the stress of my fall down the mountain, and the strangeness of my surroundings. Wait until Erin hears about this place, I mused. If she's bothered about Germans buying up the landscape, this medieval reenactment or whatever it is will send her completely around the bend.

Hrolf finished a second bowlful and started on a third. He uttered some suggestion to Edi, and she walked toward the fireplace and then out of my sight to the left. She emerged a few minutes later with a pitcher and two stoneware mugs. She poured one for each of us: clear water, which I gladly drank.

Meantime the little boy had become bored with his blocks, and approached the table. He scrambled onto the bench beside me, and gazed up at my face. I smiled at him, but his grave expression did not change. The woman spoke to him in a coaxing tone, but the boy ignored her.

"Thank you again for the marvellous lunch," I announced. "Great stew." I put every ounce of enthusiasm I had into my voice. In fact, I *did* like the meal; food always tastes better after exercise in the cold. "But," I continued, "could I use your phone now? I want to let my people know where I am, and when I'll be in to work."

"This is Usk," Hrolf said, indicating the boy. "Grandson."

"Hello, Usk," I responded, facing toward the child. "I'm Ron." The boy said nothing, lowering his head to inspect the planks of the table.

"He's shy," I proclaimed. Then, urgency creeping into my voice in spite of myself: "I really would like to use your phone now, please."

Hrolf fixed his eyes on me. His upper body seemed to swell. "Ronkur, you are not in that place."

I waited.

"You fall. You are in *this* place." He paused, as if searching for words.

"I don't understand," I said. "If *you* don't have a phone, can you tell me where the closest phone is?"

For a long spell I heard only the rustle and crackle of the fire, and the little boy humming tunelessly as he dug out a handful of shiny pebbles from his pocket and arranged and rearranged them on the bench.

"You are not first here, Ronkur," Hrolf stated after a while. "You fall. Every few winters, someone falls. I don't ... understand. But you are not in your place. Now you will live here, with us." The last was uttered in a tone of finality.

My brain was reeling. "I'm sorry," I said testily. "I'm *not* going to stay with you, much as I appreciate the offer. I have patients waiting. If you won't point me in the direction of the highway, I'll find it myself. Silver Star isn't exactly in the middle of the boonies. People live all around, and—"

Hrolf suddenly slapped his hand down on the table.

I jumped.

"We did not ask," he declared. "But you are here. Three years ago: Abejackson. Before him, a woman: Lindabbot."

"Others like me?" I asked. "Can I talk to them?"

"Gone."

A chill ascended my back. "Gone?"

"One day, gone. We never see again. Perhaps they rose." Hrolf's glowering intensity lent a sinister import to his words.

"Vernon's not that big a town," I started to argue. "If somebody went missing it would be all over the papers." My rational approach calmed me a little. "Frankly, I don't believe it. I'm not sure what game you're playing. If the bunch of you want to pretend to be pioneers, or peasants, or whatever you're supposed to be, that's fine. You probably even own this land fair and square. But I don't want to play. I've got responsibilities. I don't need to run off and be a Boy Scout or buffalo hunter or whichever fantasy you're acting out. If you won't tell me how to find a phone, or the road to Vernon, I'll be on my way."

Hrolf leaned toward me. "Three levels in the world. Three." He raised stubby fingers to indicate each division. "Asgard: gods' home. Midgard: this earth." He swept his hand around to encompass the hall. "Niflheim: roots of the world-ash, home of the dead." His hand returned to rest on the table top for a second, then lifted to display two fingers. "Midgard has levels, also, though we did not know before. Above: your place; under your place: here." His hand again pointed around the room.

He paused, then began again. "We do not fall. But some of you fall. Why? Ask the gods." He mused, briefly. "I understand 'phone.' Abejackson explain. No 'phone' here. This is our village, Urda. Five, six days from here: Verdandi. Then a sea: Skuld. Beyond Skuld...." He strove to find the words.

If he was acting, he was doing a good job. He seemed entirely sincere. But then, nuts I've seen interviewed on TV who believe they were abducted by flying saucers also project sincerity. I leaned across the table to match his posture. "Sounds to me like you're playing Vikings. Okay, I'm not going to spoil your fun. I *have* to get back to work, though. You may be rich enough to take time out from real life; I'm not. I need to get to a phone."

I stood. I thanked all of them again for the meal, and in the midst of a burst of agitated conversation between them strode out through the curtains, slipped on my pack, and opened the outer door. I put on my skis, pulled the loops of my poles over my gloves, and slid off.

At the lip of the bowl the encampment was in, I looked back. Hrolf was discernible at the door of the building, watching me. I waved once, but he didn't respond. I glided away down the tracks we had made earlier that morning.

I spent the rest of the short afternoon exploring the area. Retracing our route to the field where I landed, I skied hard in the opposite direction Hrolf had led me. Twenty minutes later the forest closed in again, so I skirted that region for a while. I was unaccustomed to this amount of skiing in one day, and eventually could feel my thigh muscles tighten and then ache whenever I halted for a breather.

As the afternoon waned, the cold increased. I discovered there was maybe 100 acres of open field, ringed on all sides by forest. Occasionally I came across a split-rail fence, and once a stone holding pen of a crude design. I scoured most carefully the southern part of the cleared region, guessing the compass heading based on where the descending sun sets in January in the Okanagan. My reasoning was that a south-bearing trail or road should lead down the valley toward Vernon. Yet I met only wooded hills. I struggled through the bush up a slope, to learn if I could glimpse the terrain further southward. I even detached from my skis to climb the tallest of a stand of cedar at the highest point of the rise. Aside from snow down my neck, I regained the ground no wiser. The view from between the branches showed unbroken forest undulating into the distance. A far-off mountain range was hazily visible to the west.

The unmarked condition of the forest bothered me as much as anything. There's no place in the BC Interior these days where you aren't aware of large clear-cuts in every viewscape. Also, no power lines crossed the landscape, and I noticed no contrails in the sky. In the Okanagan, which is on the main flight path between Vancouver and Eastern Canada, white lines left by jets flying overhead are always above you in a cloudless sky. Here was only unsullied blue, darkening as the sun dropped lower.

At dusk I arrived back where the trail led to Urda. I had long since finished the coffee I had packed in what seemed another lifetime, and was once more wearing my parka against the chill air. In a brief moment of panic as the light grew dimmer, I lost confidence I could find the route to the encampment. But to my relief, I located my original outbound tracks. Although I'd had a lot of opportunity to think while skiing, my mind kept angling off from any reasoned processing of where I might be. Eventually, my goal was simply to get in out of the cold. "Any port in a storm," I told myself, echoing a saying of my father's I first heard as a child one July, when he beached our little outboard runabout on an island in a lake to seek shelter from thunder and lightning. I was five or six. *About Usk's age*, I thought.

The return through the woods to Urda took longer than I anticipated, yet I knew I was worn down from the events of the day, not least my afternoon of somewhat desperate physical effort. Urda's dwellings were largely windowless, so the only signs of life when at last I skied over the edge of the bowl into the village were the embers of the various fires in the central area and the crescendo of barking my arrival generated. A man emerged from one structure, stared in my direction, and crossed to enter another building. I drew up in front of what I recalled was Hrolf's dwelling. I felt a little woozy. Uncertain of the etiquette for entry, I released my boots from my bindings and pondered my next move. Should I just walk in? Knock on the door? I realized I had seen no weapons, except a domestic-looking axe being employed to split wood. On the other hand, hunting must occur, since I had witnessed a deer being skinned. And people kept dogs tied up at the doorways, guards whose uproar currently was verging on the hysterical. What had Hrolf said to calm them? The dogs were unresponsive to my admonitions in English.

As I hesitated in front of the building, I caught a motion in the dusk behind me. I swung round. A man on skis glided to a stop a few feet from me. He said something that sounded courteous in that sing-song German, so I nodded back to him. He removed his skis, stuck them and his poles in the snow beside mine, and quieted the dogs with a command. He slapped the door hard with his mitt several times.

After some moments I heard a brief inquiry from within. My companion shouted some words, and the response was the sound of a bar being withdrawn. The door opened. My companion gestured me through, and I gratefully stepped into the odorous warmth of the vestibule.

When I pushed aside the second curtain, the hall was decidedly more crowded than at noon. Hrolf had risen from his seat at the table to greet us, and the benches were full. About two dozen adults were in the midst of the evening meal. No sign of the child, Usk. Hrolf offered introductions all around, but the names mostly entered and left my brain the same moment. I managed to retain that the man I had encountered outside was called Magnus. He was in his early twenties, and I subsequently deduced he had been sent after me by Hrolf at some point in the afternoon. Magnus seemed unaffected by having covered the distance I did, but perhaps he had known which route I was likely to travel, and had employed some shortcuts. To the extent I could determine, he was a relative of somebody at the table.

Hrolf introduced a strikingly attractive young woman as Signy. He was blunt about informing me she was a widow: "Signy, my daughter. Usk's mother. Husband is dead." Magnus clearly had his eye on her. He insisted on situating himself opposite her when we were waved to join the meal. He continually tried to engage her in conversation, although her responses were perfunctory, to my ears.

The hall was lit with small oil lamps, placed on the table and also on ledges around the walls. The large blaze in the fireplace sent wavering lights and shadows into the structure's interior. My head felt hot, although when I sat at the table I perceived a considerable temperature difference between my upper body and my feet, which were much cooler.

A few minutes after we were seated, my legs had stiffened to the point that I could barely move them. A wooden plate was passed to me by a middle-aged woman seated on my right. I confess I was too weary to pay much attention to the social dynamics of the meal's preparation or consumption. On the plate was a mound of aromatic meat and steamed or boiled carrots. I quickly shovelled it into my mouth with the spoon I had been handed. A cup was sent down the table for me: a syrupy drink of some liquid I couldn't identify. I didn't much care for its cloying taste, but it helped wash down the two platefuls of supper I finished. The drink was fermented, I discovered. As I was on a second cupful, an impression that I was extremely well cared for possessed me. My body relaxed, and around the table conversation had become boisterous. For the first time, I heard laughter mixed with the sing-song being spoken.

Hrolf asked me a few questions concerning my life previous to my arrival in his village. Despite my best intentions, my answers were interrupted with yawns. The opportunity to sit, the meal and the alcohol, in addition to the day's occurrences, had rendered me rather drowsy. A couple had left the table already, heading down the room toward the fireplace and then out of my sight to the left. When they reappeared, they opened one of the cupboards that lined the wall. I could see it contained a sleeping platform. Clothes hung on pegs all around the interior of the cubbyhole, with other items placed on shelving above. When the couple had removed some of their outer garments, they climbed into the space with the help of one of the benches that lined the perimeter of the hall. They called something back to the table. People still seated drinking responded in what sounded to me like a formulaic manner. The doors to the cupboard were then closed from the inside.

Hrolf said something to Magnus, who rose and beckoned me. I staggered as I stood up a little too rapidly, and on either side hands shot out to catch me, amid general merriment. I also stumbled trying to manoeuvre my aching legs over the bench. Magnus led me down the hall toward the fire, then through a passageway to the left by what appeared to be a pantry and kitchen area, and out a barred door.

We emerged into brutally cold air. A half-moon had risen, along with about a million stars, and I noted we were in a compound surrounded by high walls that extended from the dwelling. There were three small structures; from two of them came animal noises—obviously these were where livestock was confined for the night. A big dog materialized in the doorway of one of them and started to bark ferociously, but Magnus shouted something equally fierce at him and the beast wagged his tail and sat down. Magnus moved sure-footedly across the yard toward the third structure, which as we approached I could ascertain from the stink was a latrine. There were three cubicles, one larger than the other two. The place was icy, and lit only by moonlight through an opening high on the back wall. This was no place to linger. A semi-collapsed wooden box attached to a wall contained a mound of shards of moss, which I presumed served as toilet paper. When I emerged I tried to clean my hands in a pile of relatively white snow, although most of the yard was trampled and soiled, as could be expected of a barnyard. My hands were like two blocks of ice by the time we reentered the hall.

I thawed out briefly at the fire, and Magnus guided me to one of the sleeping-cupboards. Signy was standing on a bench, leaning in to arrange bedding. I lowered myself onto the seat, and with great difficulty unhooked and untied my gaiters and boots. Groggily I hoisted myself into the cupboard and swung the doors shut by two handles attached inside. I peeled off my sweater, shucked out of my ski pants, and pulled a sort of woollen quilt over me. Through the closed doors of the cupboard I could dimly hear conversation and laughter from the table. I shifted position a few times to try to find a comfortable arrangement for the aching muscles of my legs. Then I was suddenly asleep.

# II

I awoke to the sounds of talking, and peeked out to see a few members of the household already dressed and at breakfast. The fire at the end of the hall was relit and blazing away, if in fact the flames had been allowed to die out during the night. None of the people whose names I could recall was visible at the table, however.

I lay back to review the previous twenty-four hours, trying to grasp the dimensions of my predicament. If indeed I had been transported to a different world, dislocated both spatially and temporally from the one in which I had wakened the morning before, my situation made no scientific sense. I knew about a theory of parallel universes. But this ostensibly Nordic encampment was surely not what cosmologists or whoever posited such theories imagined. Hrolf's brief account at lunch of a three-layered universe matched ancient Norse beliefs, as I remembered reading about them. Yet to have the same ontological belief system appear in two different universes, not to mention a thousand years later in one than the other, was stretching theories too far. Nor could I recollect anything in Scandinavian myth about travel between parallel existences, although my familiarity with the subject was limited. Then I remembered the moon last evening. If I had fallen from my world to this, how could the moon be aloft in a sky *below* the planet that the moon orbited? I kicked myself for not having more closely observed the stars. Were the constellations the same? I must have been drunk not to pick up on such a potentially important clue to my whereabouts offered by the night sky. If the arrangements of the stars here were significantly altered from the upper world's, I'd have to conclude I was situated now in another part of the galaxy, or a different galaxy, or indeed, a different universe. Could the cross-country trails of Silver Star Mountain conceal a wormhole through space-time? The idea seemed absurd.

Yet when I tallied the evidence from yesterday, the balance of probability tilted alarmingly toward my having been thrust into an existence other than that in which I had begun the day. I focussed on Hrolf's casual mention that visitors like me who subsequently disappeared from Urda might have risen again. If a cosmic wormhole linked the worlds, did it function as a two-way portal? Or was "risen" a euphemism for "die," as in a person having risen to heaven or Valhalla? I pushed the latter speculation from me. Hrolf didn't seem menacing, just stern, solemn. Nor did people in Urda, or at least those in this dwelling, act very warlike. Except for the presence of the fierce dogs. Also, I read the Vernon paper every day; as I had told Hrolf, if somebody had vanished on Silver Star during the past few years I would have been aware of it. Certainly I would have seen a mention on the news if somebody reappeared after a mysterious absence. I resolved to question Hrolf further about his knowledge of transit between the two worlds. I wasn't sure he had much to add, but yesterday I had been thoroughly blitzed trying to comprehend what was occurring. Maybe Hrolf needed to be drawn out. Yet how adequate really was his English, especially for articulating abstract or difficult concepts?

By the time I had wriggled into my clothes and emerged from my cupboard, I was pleased to see Hrolf and Edi had joined the others at table. As soon as my feet touched the floor, I was struck again by the difference in temperature in the hall between the warmth of the room at chest height and the frigid air around my boots. No wonder the bed-cupboards were elevated. I glanced up at the rafters, and thought how this place could use a ceiling fan to circulate heat. Overall, I felt unshaved and dishevelled, with a sticky taste in my mouth. I aimed a general greeting toward the breakfasters, who now included the child, Usk, together with three other kids not encountered yesterday, and a couple of young teenagers. Everyone responded to me with some variety of "good morning" words. I headed toward the latrine.

Hrolf detached himself from the others and followed me to the outside door. Snow was madly eddying across the stockaded farmyard. The wind shrieked, and the flakes for a moment gusted nearly horizontal before resuming their tumultuous swirling. A blizzard was in progress; the notion struck me that I was fortunate I didn't fall into this kind of weather yesterday. Hrolf wouldn't have discovered me, and I'd have wandered blindly around and spent the night freezing in the fields or woods. Maybe the weather down here was always identical to that above? I had no way of verifying this hypothesis.

A dog lurched out of the white confusion of snow toward us, growling and barking. Hrolf taught me to shout, "Sestu!" repeatedly at the animal. The procedure seemed to work; the dog slunk away. I continued alone to the latrine and back, braced against the force of the wind.

Breakfast was a filling, though bland, type of hotcakes. I found myself wishing for an energizing cup of hot coffee. I knew I drank too much coffee at the office, and consoled myself that a period here in Urda without ingesting caffeine would probably be a tonic for my body. Yet a cup of clear water to wash down the meal just didn't provide the kick-start to the day I was accustomed to.

As I ate, men and women of the household emerged from their cupboards and joined the table. Others, finished their meal, carried their utensils toward what I had guessed the previous day was a pantry. I was considering emulating their example when Hrolf clambered to his feet, gathered his plate and spoon and cup, and motioned me to do the same.

In the adjoining space, a metal pot of hottish water was available for cleaning our breakfast things: a large shelf held already-drying plates and utensils. When we reentered the hall, Hrolf gestured that we should sit on a bench beside the fireplace.

"Bad storm," he announced. "We stay." He waved his arms, indicating the interior of the building. I didn't know whether his words were meant to be a command to me personally or a proclamation of a decision the people in the dwelling had reached. Before I could inquire further, his brow furrowed: "My sister, Munin, travels here with others."

"Today?" I asked. "She'll have been caught in the blizzard."

He nodded.

"When was she supposed to arrive?" I asked, as sympathetically as I could.

Hrolf shrugged. "Yesterday. Today. I was out to look when I saw you fall."

"I was going to ask you about this falling business," I began, seizing the opportunity. "What do you—"

Hrolf cut me off. "When storm is less, we ski to find them."

"Sounds like a good plan," I agreed. "What I want to know, though, involves—"

"This morning we work here," Hrolf decreed.

I gathered he didn't want to talk further about my preferred subject. I hoped again there wasn't some sinister reason behind his reluctance, but I tactfully switched topics. Using as simple a vocabulary as I could, I tried to elicit if he was the owner, or chief, or just a dominant character in the household. If I understood him correctly, he definitely was top dog. But he described himself as the "steward" of the dwelling, and of certain of the village's fields that were associated with the hall. "I do not own, like clothes, yes? Or skis. I *steward*. Abejackson, who fell like you, gave me that word." Hrolf seemed pleased with the term. He repeated, as if remembering some English lesson: "You *own* mitts? You *steward* field."

I liked the distinction. Erin and I argued about her devotion to the sacredness of property rights. She was convinced that when someone owns a piece of land they should be able to do absolutely anything they want with it. Land-use bylaws to her were an anathema. I had attempted numerous times to convince her that land is our link with the past and future. Land also is a link, in the present, to the community in which we are situated. I'd been a bit of a fire-breathing ecologist when I was younger, and continue to believe we need to see ourselves not as an isolated island but to acknowledge our debt to everyone around us.

I had become upset when the trees on the wooded lot across from my house near Kal Lake at the southern edge of Vernon were cut down by their new owner. At first, as the chain saws fired up, I thought, *Well, the guy doesn't like trees near his building site.* That's one excuse for clear-cutting you hear constantly in the BC Interior: "Damn trees were too close to the house." Then the owner adds either "Blocked the view" or "Shaded where we want the garden" or "Weed trees, anyway" or "Dangerous: might blow down onto the roof in a high wind." You might well ask why someone so opposed to trees would choose to build in a wooded area. In this case, as soon as the house across the road from me was completed, the *For Sale* sign went up. The dwelling was a spec house. But the tree-slaughter continued. On the weekends the guy would show up and, for lack of anything better to do, continued eradicating the forest. I'd be out gardening and hear that hideous whine and then the crump of a huge cottonwood or alder or spruce collapsing. If the tree was big enough, the earth on my place shook when it hit the ground. I felt so helpless, impotent. Angry, too.

Erin's attitude was that since the land was his, he could do whatever he wanted. I pointed out that he hadn't planted the trees. We jousted on this point, but the issue was hardly the main source of my frustration with our relationship.

I tried to explain to Hrolf how much I endorsed his notion of stewardship rather than ownership of his fields. I'm not sure he understood; I guess I launched into a bit of a rant. But I believe he did pick up a general sense of approval from me.

I probed further, and learned Hrolf had obtained his stewardship partly through family—he said his mother had been wealthy—and partly through his success at hunting and jewellery. Everything he said opened up dozens of questions, but to me his reference to "jewellery" seemed wildly incongruous. At first I thought I had misheard, or he had misspoken. Everyone I'd seen in the dwelling had been completely unadorned, except for a simple brooch-like pin securing their overshirt. This bear-like man appeared to be the last person I would imagine hunched over a table working on bracelets or rings.

When I voiced my doubts, Hrolf stood, ambled across to his and Edi's sleeping-cupboard, and returned carrying a small wooden box. He thrust it toward me.

Inside were intricately filigreed brooches, each wrapped in a square of cloth. Other packets held rings surmounted by amber, or blue-coloured and in one case jet-black stones. Armlets or bracelets, even a couple of necklaces cunningly formed of interwoven thick metal wires, all testified to considerable skill, at least to my eyes.

Hrolf watched me as I examined each of the box's contents. "Did you make these?" I asked. He nodded. "I'm impressed," I blurted, truthfully. I rambled on for a few moments about how accomplished his handiwork seemed to me. His face didn't change.

After a minute, he said: "This work honours Freyr." When I didn't respond, he added: "Freyr is god of the ground. From him are grass, trees, berries, apples, carrots, grains. For the animals and for us. Adornments thank him for these, and for beauty."

"Beauty" also wasn't a word I would have expected from this rough-looking individual. His tone of voice was nonchalant, however, as though he was reporting on the weather or asking at table if I wanted a refill of water. He held out his palms, and I repacked the box and passed it to him. He traversed the hall again to his sleeping-cupboard, and returned empty-handed.

I started to question him about how wealth was measured in Urda. Were there agreed-upon tokens—money—or were riches determined by mere possession or stewardship of objects like livestock or land? As nearly as I could comprehend his answers, a mixture of barter and of coins made from precious metals like silver or gold provided the medium of exchange. Hrolf was vague about where the coins were minted. "From Skuld," he said, gesturing toward one wall of the dwelling. I knew I'd heard the term before but went blank. "The sea, Skuld," he repeated.

"Coins are manufactured on the coast? Or the coins originate overseas?" I asked.

"From Skuld," he reiterated. For a moment I wondered if some technology existed at the seashore to refine metals from salt water, a process discussed and occasionally tried in my world. That degree of metallurgical know-how seemed beyond these people. Yet I had seen metal axe-blades in use the day before, and metal pots and knives in the kitchen. Somebody must understand smelting of ores.

I returned the conversation to what Hrolf had said about his mother having been wealthy. Curious about relations between men and women in Urda, I asked if certain kinds of work were done by men and other kinds by women? Our provincial professional organization, the Association of BC Optometrists, has been worried about how few women study for the doctorate. The ABCO claims that in 83 per cent of clinics in the province, the optometrist is a man and all the other staff are women. That's certainly true in my office. I've tried to encourage Gail and Marie to go back to school, and eventually become professionals themselves. Both have about 100 excuses.

Hrolf stared at me when I explained what I wanted to know about gender roles and status. I attempted to rephrase the question, and realized I better move from the abstract to the concrete. Obviously women could steward and own things, since he had said he inherited from his mother. I sketched our customs of marriage and divorce, using the settlement between my ex-wife Beth and me as an example. Similar arrangements were known to Hrolf, although they had no lawyers as such. He referred to a Formadur, which he translated as Speaker. I gathered that this individual combined the functions of conflict-resolution expert, judge and priest: an adjudicator between people, and between people and their gods. The Formadur was elected by the village, but also trained by the previous office-holder. Men and women above a certain age voted, but Hrolf was weak on English-language numbers, so I wasn't sure what the voting age was.

Household chores were assigned by rotation or by lot, I was a little unclear. Everyone had some task that was their responsibility, irrespective of gender. Assignments changed frequently. Hearing this, I asked that I be given some work. Hrolf expressed surprise when I stated my request. Part of the intent of my offer was to nudge him into revealing more of his knowledge, if any, about falling—and rising. I had the idea that if I obtained some information from him on the *duration* of my assignment, I might gain an opportunity to explore the matter of how long I was likely to be in Urda.

Instead of a direct reply, Hrolf launched into a series of questions about my occupation. I sketched out the practice of optometry. I realized as I spoke how little practical good I could be in this world, shorn of my diagnostic equipment, optical lab, and drugs. While I was capable of identifying problems and offering an approximate prognosis—in cases like cataracts, say—I was helpless to accomplish anything further. Hrolf declared himself familiar with glass, once I explained the substance to him. He appeared to regard it as a substitute for gems, although he had seen in another village a glass bottle. Glass for windows was unknown to him. With a bit of charcoal, I drew him a picture of eyeglasses, since apparently neither previous visitor from above had worn these. He listened politely, although I had no idea whether he grasped what I was saying, let alone believed me.

In the end, he arrived at the same conclusion about my potential contribution to the household as I had: that what I did for a living topside had no immediate application here below. I suggested kitchen detail, and he agreed. Yet he displayed no hurry to implement our plan. He and I continued to roost together by the hearth, talking. Around us the majority of residents had settled in for a morning's indoor activities, which appeared to principally involve mending. People stitched clothing, as well as leather constructions of one type or another: harnesses and snowshoe webbing and ski bindings and pack straps and some tangles of leather strips whose purpose wasn't apparent to me. Edi and another woman and man set up a portable loom, and the man seated himself and began to weave. Usk and the other children either assisted various adults, or at times grouped themselves to play a game involving small sticks of assorted lengths thrown on the floor. Another man brought in a three-metre-long sledge and used a drawknife to smooth the bottom of one of the runners.

Every so often, an explosion of dogs barking outside was audible. The person who subsequently entered the hall would be brushing snow off their leggings as they fumbled through the second set of curtains. The blizzard unquestionably was still howling, as I verified myself when I made another trip to the latrine. I deduced that some of the visitors who showed up at the door were gadding house-to-house on one excuse or another. The men and women who appeared through the curtains were greeted with much bantering talk. Herbal tea was kept steeping in a pot by the fireplace; the arrival of these visitors from other dwellings was the occasion for everyone at Hrolf's to pour themselves another cup as they worked and chatted. Intermittently, the discussion must have turned to me and my situation: heads suddenly would swivel in unison in my direction from a group seated at the dining table, or from an arrangement of benches elsewhere in the hall where men and women were attending to their projects by the light of a cluster of oil lamps. The storm made the interior space even gloomier than I had experienced yesterday. I marvelled that more of the inhabitants didn't exhibit signs of eye trouble. Of course, even if their vision gave them difficulties, my lack of understanding of their language would keep me ignorant of all but the most blatant symptoms.

About mid-morning, Hrolf conducted me into the pantry area, and introduced me to two people currently responsible for kitchen duties. I remained vague about the exact mechanism by which they had been selected, and still couldn't tell if their assignment was for a meal, a day, a week, a month. The two kitchen personnel were Olaf, a lanky teenager, and Gudrun, a stout woman in her late thirties. We all smiled and nodded to each other, and they directed a number of questions at Hrolf, likely concerning me. When he left, Gudrun beckoned me to follow her. She lifted a trap door in one corner of the room, collected and lit a couple of oil lamps, handed one to me and disappeared ahead down a rough plank ramp leading below.

The space we descended into had wood walls, but served as a cold cellar or larder. Smoked sides of meat hung in one area, and opened and unopened wooden barrels and boxes were piled on a dirt floor. Gudrun seized a metal bar hanging from a peg on one of the support beams. She pried off the lid of one box, revealing sawdust. A second box was selected, and once more the top was levered off. She restored the bar, and presented me with two wicker baskets, pantomiming that she wanted one filled from each barrel. Leaving her light on the ramp, she ascended into the pantry.

I discovered one of containers held carrots amid its sawdust, and the other, slightly wizened apples. While I was rummaging in the sawdust in search of the best-looking fruit, Olaf descended, nodded to me, and vanished into the darkness toward the back of the cellar. He returned seconds later, hoisted the lamp Gudrun had left, and again sought out something in a rear area. I could see him in a corner, bent over a number of wooden boxes. He extracted a sack from one, slung it across his shoulder, and picked his way amid the various shapes of containers to the ramp. When I finally rose from the depths myself—clutching baskets and lamps—I found him and Gudrun preparing a fish stew: the sack had contained smoked whitefish of some variety. At Gudrun's direction I pitched in, chopping carrots and onions, and later aiding her in devising an apple mash dessert. She and Olaf said little to each other; I had no sense of the relationship between them. But their silence did not seem sulky or hostile. Rather, the lack of conversation appeared either a matter of personality, or a wish not to exclude me from their normal job-related talk. So we three mainly worked in a companionable silence, under Gudrun's direction.

Then came the bustle of serving the meal, during which I helped ladle out the main course, and ensured water jugs were filled. The water was drawn from casks kept in a passageway accessible from the pantry. The passageway ended in a door to the outside; I presumed the casks could be removed for filling by means of this entrance. Ventilation slits in the door ensured that the chamber holding the row of casks was chilly. I had wondered how cold water could be produced at meals.

The ultimate source of the household's water was not discernible: a well nearby? A creek?

Those engaged in kitchen chores ate after the rest of the residents, although of course we had snacked and tasted throughout the preparation process. Then we did a general cleanup of the kitchen and pantry, and Gudrun shooed Olaf and me back into the hall.

Hrolf was sitting by the fireplace, speaking to a man I didn't know. Before I could relax from my domestic labours, he asked me if I wanted to ski out with them to try to locate his sister and her companions. He said the storm had calmed. I noticed fewer people were around the dwelling than had been present at lunch, and concluded that the weather had eased enough for the inhabitants to have resumed their ordinary outdoor tasks.

I was a bit weary from the strain of working for hours with people whose language I didn't speak. I said I would like to rest for a few minutes before we started. Hrolf agreed, and had just turned back to his companion when I heard the clamour of dogs outside. Almost immediately, there was much stamping of snow from feet in the vestibule and half a dozen people shouldered their way through the heavy curtains into the far end of the hall. Two I recognized, but the other four I hadn't seen previously.

Hrolf was striding down the length of the building; he boomed out some greeting. I speculated that the newcomers were the awaited visitors. When the commotion of welcoming the travellers began to subside, I was called forward to be introduced. Hrolf confirmed that indeed this was the overdue group for whom we were about to search. They had been on the fringes of the blizzard the whole distance from their farmstead of Leifsdahl, near the village of Verdandi. Two afternoons ago, they had been caught by the worst of the storm and had to construct a shelter and wait for daylight. He introduced me to his sister Munin, the only female in the party, and to Sigurd, a cousin of Signy's former husband. Two friends of Sigurd's had accompanied them. The latter would be staying in a different hall, I learned, since they had relatives who lived there. All four travellers were younger than me: Munin seemed the oldest, and one of the cousin's friends the youngest, about Olaf's age. All were chattering excitedly to whoever would listen, probably relating their adventures en route.

Gudrun bustled over with cups of hot tea. She launched into an intense conversation with Sigurd. Others contributed comments in a joking tone, which produced guffaws of laughter. I scarcely heard a word anyone uttered. I was transfixed by Munin.

She was the most beautiful woman I had ever encountered in my life. Her face glowed with energy and her pale blue eyes glittered with vigour and humour. A delightful network of tiny laugh-lines radiated out from the corners of her eyes when she smiled. She was short in stature, and had lustrous-looking hair, indisputably once brown but now streaked with silver. While her travelling clothes did not reveal much about the shape of her body, she moved with a swing and grace that suggested someone comfortable with themselves and their physical being.

I was dazzled. She appeared a few years younger than Hrolf, yet as sometimes happens in families, she possessed a radically different personality. Where he was a man of few words, she chattered away. He displayed a solemnity in response to everyday events that at times shaded into a dark brooding, as if on the conundrums and injustices of existence. She seemed not to allow her sensible nature to overpower her basically cheerful attitude toward life.

The sheer pleasure I felt in just gazing at her astounded and discomfited me. We were sitting at the table drinking tea; I was directly across from her. The language I did not know swirled around me, but I didn't care. My eyes couldn't get enough of watching Munin speak to her brother, his wife, her niece Signy, and to other members of Hrolf's household who approached to welcome her, including many who reentered the hall from outside. She evidently was a favourite of many who lived here. At various moments amid conversations, she gave a hug to Gudrun and some other women, including Edi and Signy. Munin was so unselfconscious in her bestowing of affection, I couldn't help but contrast her behaviuor with Erin's insincere greeting of her real estate colleagues at parties we attended, and the difficulty Erin had finding a good word to say about her mother, father or sister—her only sibling. Erin's complicated disapproval of her relatives could not have been less like Munin's wholehearted joy at reconnecting with family and friends. At one point, I became aware of Sigurd ushering the other two travellers toward the building's entrance. Mostly I was focussed only on Munin.

Then, during a lull in what I surmised was a catching-up on news, Munin rotated to face me. Her eyes twinkled with amusement. "And how are you liking your stay in Urda?" she asked in perfect English, although with a charming musical lilt to her pronunciation. "My brother tells me you are fitting in well with us here."

The speech was so unexpected I could only splutter. "What? You speak—? How—?"

She laughed merrily, relishing my surprise.

"Of course some of us speak English," she teased. "Did you think you had fallen among ignorant folk?"

"Your brother said— But, but you don't— Have you met other people who fell? I mean, where did you learn—?"

Her infectious laughter again. "No, no. I was in Urda for my winter visit when Abejackson came. He taught both Hrolf and me."

"You speak very well."

"Thank you. You haven't answered my question."

"Question?"

"How do you like being here?"

I managed to express my appreciation for Hrolf's hospitality, and a few other platitudes. Suddenly I was dying to explore innumerable subjects with Munin, first and foremost herself. Was she single, for example? Did she have children? How did she support herself, or was she part of a household like Hrolf's? If so, whose? Before I had the chance to commence, she was swept back into conversations in her own language. She did shoot me a bemused glance and a shrug, I believed as if to say: "Sorry. That's how it goes. We'll talk later." In any event, at that moment Gudrun tapped me on the shoulder and indicated good-naturedly that I was wanted in the pantry.

I performed my chores in a rather absent-minded fashion as Olaf, Gudrun, myself and another woman undertook supper preparation. A small table was arranged for the children and younger teens in one corner of the pantry area; they were tended by the woman who had joined the kitchen crew. The rest of us had to work around the lively pack of a half-dozen youngsters eating their evening meal.

In the hall, supper was marred by shouting: the first voices raised in anger I had heard since I had fallen. I was busy carrying around a platter of slices of an unidentifiable roast—goat? venison? I had perceived that Sigurd was seated beside Signy, while Magnus was across from her, as usual. All at once, Magnus began speaking loudly at Sigurd. Signy said something sharply to Magnus. Sigurd added a comment, and then Magnus was standing and yelling. The room became very still while he did so. Magnus extricated himself from the bench and stalked toward the vestibule. I heard the outer door open and shut. Sigurd stated something briefly but firmly, and the table laughed, nervously I thought. The hum of talk resumed. The children had assembled in the pantry doorway at the sounds of discord, staring wide-eyed at the scene of confrontation before Gudrun herded them from sight. I was eager to ask Munin what the argument was about, but understood that this question would just have to be added to my list.

As the kitchen staff eventually sat to eat, around us in the hall people were shifting benches toward the fireplace, bringing in arm-loads of wood, sweeping the hall floor with a cedar-bough broom, re-filling lamps. Fresh cedar boughs were placed in specific locations on the floor, although I could not understand why those particular spots were covered. In the midst of this activity, I felt I shouldn't dawdle over my meal. I noticed the rest of our KP detail were also eating more rapidly than I'd previously witnessed. We hurried through the last slices of some excellent cheese for dessert and returned to the pantry to tackle cleanup.

When Gudrun gave the signal that we were finished, I emerged into a hall transformed from how I had left it. The area had been reconfig-ured into a kind of auditorium: benches had been arranged in a series of semicircles facing the fireplace. Thronging the hall were perhaps 100 men, women and children, a majority of whom I had not seen before. I had been aware as I scrubbed pots and helped Olaf tidy away the chil-dren's table that the hubbub of voices from the hall was much louder than I had so far experienced it. But I was astounded to see so many individuals of all sizes and ages jammed into Hrolf's dwelling, standing together chatting or seated on the benches. And people were much bet-ter dressed than I had observed to date. The coarse clothing that up to now was standard attire had been replaced by gowns and loose-fitting shirts and pants for the men, and long dresses with a kind of cape or shawl over the shoulder for the women. The fabric of these costumes was of higher quality than everyday wear: some boasted fur trim for collars and cuffs. People's garments appeared tailored; certainly, the clothes were less clumsily cut and sewn than ordinary dress. The children wore miniature versions of their elders' outfits.

Also, people were ornamented for the first time with jewellery: glittering clasps and brooches were affixed to clothing, and necklaces and rings of varying degrees of complexity were also winking and flashing when gold or precious stones caught lamplight or firelight. The most spectacularly dressed in the crowd were a grey-haired couple attired in scarlet robes marked with horizontal black stripes. Broad golden collars were draped around their necks, much like a mayor's ceremonial chain of office. A circle of men and women were talking with the brilliantly dressed pair; among the group ranged around the couple were Hrolf and Edi—both elegant in cream-coloured gowns and multiple necklaces of what looked like amber and turquoise.

I gazed about at the clusters of intently conversing villagers, amidst whom kids darted from clump to clump in a state of high excitement. Suddenly someone grabbed hold of my hand. I jumped, and found Munin smiling at me. "Let's sit together," she said. "You must be wondering about dozens of things. My brother is not the most talkative of men."

She continued to grasp my hand as she navigated us safely through the mob, until she located space for us at the end of a bench. I was so pleased to be touched by her that the entire distance across the room I was sure I was blushing. She wore an emerald-green garment, much more shapely than her travelling clothes. A brown segmented necklace—constructed of painted bone, or a gemstone of some sort—supported a silver disk between her breasts. The disk had some of the filigreed designs I had seen in Hrolf's jewellery box; I guessed that he had given it to her.

Munin's eyes were animated as she swivelled toward me once we were settled. "So, is there anything about us you would like to know?" she began in that teasing tone I had experienced at lunch.

"I have only a billion questions," I responded, trying to equal her light-hearted approach. She was even more attractive seated next to me than she had been across the table earlier in the day. Her mouth displayed a few of the bad teeth characteristic of almost everyone I had met in Urda, but somehow hers merely made her more intriguing, delectable: a sign of a woman who had *lived*.

"Ask me just one," she laughed.

First and foremost I wanted to hear about her. She appeared so natural and open—about as different from Erin as anyone possibly could be. Erin considers herself always on duty: "In a small town, everybody is a potential client." Even when we were by ourselves, at her place or mine, she was ultracareful about how she dressed and acted. Her makeup had to be perfect, and I don't think she owned any item of clothing that didn't appear brand-new. Her living room, bathroom, kitchen resembled a store display or photo in a *House Beautiful* catalog. Nothing in her environment even hinted that an actual human being inhabited it. She said most people are slobs about the upkeep of their houses, so when she returned home from selling she liked a tasteful space to occupy. I could accept that. Except, trying to exist in her space, I felt like a bumbling intruder, a hapless despoiler of some prizewinning exhibit of interior decorating. When she was at my house I wasn't comfortable either, because I imagined her constantly judging my taste and my housekeeping against her pristine standard. I'm a bit of a neatnik, but I couldn't begin to be as fastidious as Erin in cooking or cleaning or laundry or personal hygiene, or just about any aspect of being alive.

I have to admit Erin never complained about me messing up her living room or bedroom by passing through them. She never offered a word of criticism about my place. But she didn't look too happy to watch me blundering around her condominium. Nor did she look that delighted hanging out at my house. She acted most relaxed when we were at some fancy restaurant or bar. Or shopping: she loved to browse through the more expensive clothing boutiques and high-end furniture or kitchen stores at Orchard Park Mall in Kelowna, or tonier establishment she patronized on trips we took to Vancouver or Seattle.

I always found Erin physically enticing. Our sex life was fine when it happened, although often she wasn't that interested. I've never understood how the chemistry of attraction works: some combination of her body build, gestures and facial expression seldom failed to generate in me a surge of lust. Yet she frequently declared she had a busy agenda tomorrow, or was too tired, or some such excuse. I've read that making love requires no more energy than walking up a flight of stairs two at a time. I'd asked her if I was doing something wrong, if she'd like me to perform differently. She said sex for her could bring up a lot of unpleasant memories. She claimed she wasn't abused by her father or anything, but had gone through a series of bad relationships when she was a teenager in high school. In addition to having low self-esteem, as can happen with any young person, she went steady with a boyfriend who smacked her around until her mother intervened and convinced her to break up with the guy.

As a consequence, a lot of the time when we slept together, we didn't make love. I tried to take my cues from her, because she was the one having difficulty with sex. I find it tough, however, to lie next to a person I feel drawn toward and have to be content with a hug. Some weekends I thought I'd go out of my mind with the sexual tension. Yet in the middle of the night she would reach over and hold my hand, or while I was cooking us breakfast she'd put her arms around me from behind and kiss me. I'd feel sorry for her, and sudden waves of love and tenderness for her were churned up in me and the cranky mood I'd been wallowing in would dissipate. For a while.

The worst times for feeling denied sexually occurred when we were travelling. Having escaped from everyday routines, just focussing on each other for hours in neutral environments like hotel rooms or a car turned me on. I felt we were indulging ourselves; why not sample the pleasures of the flesh, too? Occasionally she responded the same way, which was super. More often, she behaved as if she was even less interested in sex than usual. Maybe she was worried about what was happening back at the office.

I kept trying to talk to her about the whole phenomenon. A marriage counsellor Beth and I went to for about six months hammered into me the need to speak out about what's bugging me. "If you have a problem, Beth has a problem," the counsellor stressed repeatedly. "She needs to hear what you're bothered about." I never did learn to speak my mind fully with Beth; we had developed intricate ways of not discussing the open sores in our marriage. Those pathways of potential communication were blocked by insurmountable piles of stone by the time we acknowledged we both were in terminal despair of ever achieving a successful relationship. With Erin, I religiously tried to monitor what I was feeling and let her know before troubles became rooted. But Erin's typical reaction to me attempting to describe my feelings was to change the subject.

The contrast between how satisfying the very best times with Erin were, compared to the unsatisfactory quality of most of our interactions, verged on crazy-making for me. I'm sure our behaviour together wasn't emotionally healthy for her, either. The question consistently before me was: what should I do about the situation? Was our relationship salvageable? Or, as I frequently decided in the affirmative, was I stuck in a morass that I needed to extricate myself from if my life was ever going to become wholly enjoyable? If I felt unfulfilled and couldn't see a solution, why didn't I pull the plug? Was I fearful of being alone, of having to inaugurate the hunt for someone else? Was I paralyzed by a sense that Erin would be devastated at being forced to acknowledge that, despite her perfectionism in other areas of her life, our connection was flawed and we'd failed to craft a remedy? My internal debate about the right next step for me to take was circular, unrelenting, inconclusive. Any distraction from it during the day—squeezing in an emergency case at work, equipment breakdown in the lab, even landing in this impossible world—had its welcome aspect. Meeting Munin was the most effective counter I could imagine to my persistent weighing and evaluating of my alternatives with regard to Erin.

Seated by Munin, I absolutely savoured my delight at being around this effervescent and charming woman. Her beauty and, I'll admit, sexual attractiveness were a plus, of course. But in addition, I was extremely grateful to her for paying attention to me when, without doubt, she was the belle of the ball at Hrolf's. I told myself I wouldn't ever cheat on Erin. I had had two affairs during the years I was married to Beth. I never confessed to her, and I believe she never knew. But as soon as I obtained some perspective on these extracurricular activities, I recognized that I had managed to duplicate with the other women the same type of non-communication I hated in my life with Beth. Also, affairs are like working two jobs, as I did for a year between my BSC and grad school. Both moonlighting and affairs involve a gigantic expenditure of extra energy, constant schedule juggling, and some desperate transportation crises as you remember you have to be at an appointment across town immediately. Resentment at the increasing stress caused by these demands surfaces quickly, which hurts not only your relationship at home but also your performance at your jobs or your stolen hours with somebody else.

When Munin was nearby, warm and stunningly gorgeous, I can't claim the idea of greater physical intimacy between us didn't surface in my mind. But I knew I was the proverbial stranger in a strange land, and mostly I wanted to speak with her and to hear whatever she wished to tell me.

As we chatted, people increasingly selected places to sit, although the cocktail-party roar of conversation did not diminish. I observed a few rows ahead that Signy had established herself with Magnus to her left and Sigurd to her right. She bestowed her attention on first one and then the other. Magnus for a moment looked back over his shoulder to scan the crowd for some reason, and I could see his expression was distinctly unhappy.

Despite the racket around us, meanwhile, I learned from Munin that she was single, that she lived on a farm she jointly stewarded with another woman who *was* married. Munin had separated from a husband four years before, after a thirteen-year marriage. She and her ex had an eleven-year-old daughter, who currently lived with her father in a hamlet not far from the farm. Munin had one other sibling besides Hrolf, a younger brother who had been at sea for about three months. She and Hrolf didn't expect to hear news of him for another three or four months. Both parents were dead, although her mother had succumbed to an illness only the previous winter. The mother had lived in a hall at Skuld, with her youngest son. Munin then began to question me about my family and close relationships.

I had started telling her about Beth, when I became conscious that the ambient noise of people chattering had died away. I finished my sentence in a whisper. A procession involving the couple dressed in the scarlet robes paced through the hall on my right toward the fireplace. About ten men and women, including Hrolf and Edi, composed the processional party; all except the two in red carried lamps. The group ranged itself facing us, with the more spectacularly attired couple in the centre.

"Who are the two in the middle?" I whispered to Munin.

"The Formadur. The Speaker," she whispered back.

"Which? The man?"

She looked at me with surprise. "Both. No one person could presume to Speak. We say no one person or one god holds the world. Together they are Freyr and Freya."

"Freya?" I recalled that this was the name of the trail on Silver Star from which I had been catapulted into Urda.

"The goddess of the hearth: birth, death, love, marriage. Freyr and she are married."

"This is a religious ceremony?"

"All our gatherings celebrate the world. Since we are here in the world, we believe we should, as the prayer goes, 'praise, understand, enjoy, mourn.'"

During our exchange, the Formadurs had initiated a chant-and-response litany with the crowd. I gazed expectantly at Munin for a translation. But when I caught her eye, she shook her head impatiently, reciting along with the others. I understood why a minute or two later, when she and Sigurd and their two travelling companions stood up to utter a few ritualistic-sounding phrases. Then they remained standing while the audience, which now resembled more a congregation, chanted sentences toward them. I guessed this was some form of welcoming rite, and had my suspicion confirmed a second later when Munin yanked me to my feet. She alone gave the obviously expected answers to the chant aimed in my direction. A sinking sensation gripped me. Maybe the reason she had chosen to sit beside me was because such an arrangement was necessary for the ritual? I was astonished by how devastated I felt at the idea. But I was aware of her arm linking through mine, and when I glanced at her there was no mistaking the sincerity of her grin beaming in my direction. She announced something to the crowd which provoked a burst of laughter; I'm certain her statement wasn't part of the traditional litany. Then she pulled us down onto the bench, as the woman Formadur resumed reciting something.

"What did you say that was so funny?" I hissed.

Munin giggled.

"What?" I whispered, as sternly as I could.

Munin was blushing. She leaned toward me, and I inclined my head toward hers. "The Welcome invites the visitors to stay a long time," she whispered in my ear. "I added that I might hang on to this one forever."

"Oh," I said. I could feel my face burning. I was overjoyed and confused and a little frightened all at once. *Careful*, a voice inside me cautioned. *She does seem to like you a little. But don't read more into her actions than you should. She's everybody's friend. And you're very, very far from home.*

When I regained enough composure to glance again at Munin, she was smiling at me. In spite of the voice's warning, I grinned back.

The male Formadur was talking now. Edi, Hrolf and the others filed away from the front, leaving the scarlet-robed couple before the crowd. From the male Speaker's conversational tone of voice, and the suddenly more relaxed posture of people around me, I concluded we had finished the ceremonial part of the event. Since I couldn't fathom what the man was saying, I drifted off into some dreamy imaginary exchanges with Munin, where she and I were gabbing heart-to-heart for hours. I was abruptly returned to my actual surroundings when, in response to a certain sentence, the crowd loudly chanted some reply.

The scarlet-gowned male took a couple of steps to the rear and someone brought him a stool. The female watched him seat himself, then began to address the crowd in a different cadence, and with more arm and hand gestures than I had yet observed.

"What's going on?" I whispered to Munin.

"She is weaving a story," Munin replied, her voice very low. "This is a type we call a Mat, since it's not long."

"Weaving?" I asked.

"Yes. In our language, the grammar is more intricate for stories. More tenses."

"More than past, present and future?"

Munin nodded. "In weaving, we have also a never-was: sort of past and sort of now. Also a what-if tense, sort of now and sort of future."

My head was spinning at the possibilities. I had not done well at languages either in high school or college. At university I had elected to study Russian, where even personal pronouns are declined, an intricacy I found overwhelming. "What's her story about?"

Munin's face suddenly flushed. "A man travels a long way, and in a strange village he falls in love with a woman."

"What happens?"

"Shhh!"

After a moment I whispered to her: "Is this an old story? One you're familiar with?"

"Familiar?"

"Have you heard this story before?"

"Yes. But each weaving is different. Now you must be still."

The Formadur's voice continued to swell and fade for a few more minutes, interspersed with gesticulations for emphasis at several points. Then she was silent. The crowd stomped their feet on the floor in what was evidently applause. A stool was brought out for her, and she seated herself beside her male counterpart as three youngsters, Usk among them, walked hesitantly to the front. Each in turn spoke for a few minutes. The first was a little girl who appeared about seven years old; when she finished there was much "oohing" and "aahing" from the gathering, as well as enthusiastic foot-stomping.

"What did she say?" I inquired, feeling virtuous at not having directed any inquiries at Munin for some time.

"We encourage children to weave stories," Munin whispered. "They don't always make much sense. This was about flying rocks and a bird that became the moon."

When each of the kids had finished—I wanted to ask Munin if these short-short tales were called Handkerchiefs or Serviettes or some other fabric construct smaller than a Mat—I saw Sigurd rise and pick his way forward. He launched into a tale. I presume he was very good at weaving because I could see many of the women, including Munin and Signy, lean toward him raptly as he spoke. After one of his pauses in the narrative, there was audible sighing in the crowd. His hands, which had only made a few gestures at waist-level, all at once lifted dramatically in front of his face, punctuating some tense development in the plot. Then he was done. I saw two or three people wipe away tears as Sigurd threaded his way back to his seat through the wildly stomping audience. I wondered if Magnus would challenge him by trying to top the story we'd just heard, but Magnus displayed no inclination to compete.

A man and woman I did not know jointly wove a piece, followed by another man, and the entertainment or ceremony or whatever it was concluded when the Speakers stood and pronounced a few words. An energetic cacophony of voices immediately erupted from the crowd, as benches were scraped across the floor to the edges of the room or were repositioned elsewhere in the hall. The press of visitors thinned as children were collected and some adults disappeared. Hrolf and two other men brought out a barrel and tapped it; everyone still present seemed entitled to one drink of what proved to be a bitter ale. Several people had corralled Munin, and I wandered around slightly lost, sipping on my brew.

A man from another dwelling approached me. He had acquired a few English words, but after the initial "hello"s and "how are you?"s were over, we just smiled at each other. I tried to ask him the name of a number of objects, but I couldn't be sure if he comprehended what I was attempting to learn. I remembered, from my undergraduate years, a story related by a friend who was an Anthropology major. A field researcher studying a tribe elicited a list of their names for things and activities. Months later, when the anthropologist had gained a more complete knowledge of the native language, he became aware that his initially obtained names translated as "I-don't-understand" or "Why-do-you-want-to-know?" or "Could-you-repeat-the-question?" So I considered my interaction with this guy simply a friendly exchange, rather than a real learning opportunity.

When the barrel was empty—which did not take long—the remnant of the crowd took this as a signal to depart. The dwelling loomed larger and emptier than I'd known it, as the last of the guests vanished through the vestibule blankets. Munin was nowhere in sight. On my way to the latrine, I noticed the sky was clouded over so I was unable to determine whether the stars at Urda formed the same patterns as in the upper world. The night was too cold to linger, and I was glad to return to the hall. Only a few figures continued to move about, and I opened my sleeping-compartment and climbed in. I felt happy and excited, replaying the images of Munin talking to me and smiling, and the sensation of her soft hand holding mine. Somewhere in the course of my reverie, I slept.

# III

Munin wasn't at the breakfast table next morning, but hardly anyone was. I couldn't be certain if they all had woken before me and were occupied elsewhere with chores, or if the hall was indulging in a late sleep. After I had spooned down a bowl of thin, oatmeal-like cereal that I think had been sweetened with honey, Gudrun motioned me to the pantry. I felt somewhat guilty about not having participated in preparing breakfast. Yet no one had suggested to me I should be awake at a specified hour to help—I wasn't even sure how hours were measured in Urda. I had been too preoccupied with Munin the evening before to inquire what was expected of me, as a kitchen staffer, with regard to breakfast.

As it happened, this day's meals were much less regular than on the previous day, which reinforced my suspicion a holiday was occurring, or at least that the arrival of Munin and the others had precipitated a break from routine. Breakfast blended into lunch, as people kept showing up at the table wanting to eat. My tasks in the kitchen and the cellar kept me busy into the afternoon. I never minded fetching and carrying utensils or foodstuffs or preparing vegetables; these jobs were so different from my customary clinic and office duties that I enjoyed the kitchen milieu, as well as the sense I was being useful to the household.

Yet I was longing to see more of Munin. She wasn't in evidence at lunch, either. And though I tried to keep my attention on scraping a charred pot, or carrying in wood for the cook fire and oven from a woodpile in the yard, or chopping onions for rabbit stew—a young man named Snorri was skinning, cleaning and salting rabbits for part of the morning—I couldn't help wondering what Munin was up to and when we'd next have a chance to talk.

When I was released from the kitchen in mid-afternoon, the hall was empty. I was feeling a bit bored and decided I needed fresh air. I headed out for a ski. The light was already waning; I didn't venture far. After sliding across the central area of the village, I traversed the hill out of the bowl and picked up the route through the trees toward the fields where I had landed. The storm had wiped out any previous tracks, although at least one person had skied here since the new snow descended.

Dusk was gloomy in the evergreens as I poled back to Urda. But, as always, I felt rejuvenated by the exercise. Wherever I was, and whether or not I would ever get home, for the moment I perceived that my body and mind were toned up, competent, happy. The physical effort of the skiing, plus anticipation of more time spent with Munin, left me buzzed.

At supper, she was among those present. When, with the rest of the kitchen detail, I sat down at last to eat, she made room for me beside her. We spoke about the day's activities. Then she said Signy and Sigurd were going wooding the next day, and did I want to accompany them? Munin herself would be along.

I enthusiastically agreed, then pressed for details. Would her brother object to my leaving my kitchen assignment? What exactly was "wooding"? I presumed it had to do with collecting firewood. How far did we intend to travel? And, remembering the love-triangle that seemed to have formed with Sigurd's arrival, I asked if Magnus would go with us.

Munin's eyes sparkled at my flurry of questions. She assured me the trip was no problem as far as my obligations to the hall were concerned; another set of residents was due to assume mealtime chores. We would be gone two or three days: we would tow a large sledge to a camp some distance away, where wood had been cut and stockpiled against a time when transport over the snow was possible. Like summer or autumn wooding, winter wooding was also, in part, a ritual. Couples used the excursion as a formal betrothal announcement; the event thus was simultaneously a pre-nuptial honeymoon and work party. Wooding at this time of year was where, Munin blushed a little, the autumn children came from.

At the prospect of two or three days of Munin's companionship with fewer people around, I experienced a complicated flare of emotion. *Wow, this is great* mingled with *She seems so incredible, but, to be realistic, you scarcely know her.* I attempted to decide if she had engineered this opportunity for us to be together free of the continual social interactions with so many others at Hrolf's. After all, she had arrived only yesterday at Urda following a long trek, and might be expected to want a break from travel.

My head reeled as I sifted such considerations. Meanwhile she was explaining that, since Sigurd and her niece were undertaking the wooding to announce their intention to marry, Magnus definitely was to have no part in the expedition.

"Why don't the young couple go wooding by themselves?" I responded.

Munin appeared shocked. "This is a betrothal, not an elopement."

"Are we chaperones, then?" If children were expected as a result of the trip, I couldn't imagine what purpose guardians of propriety would serve.

Munin wasn't familiar with the concept of chaperones. Our presence, along with two more people, was partially to serve as witnesses. And to help fulfill the other reason for the journey—to bring back fire logs.

About half the village was out of doors next morning as we readied ourselves to leave. Dogs, for once released from their tethers, raced among us barking, and smoke and breath rose into a faultless blue sky. People clustered around Signy and Sigurd—there was backslapping and hugs and much laughter. Bundles of food and a couple of packs of extra clothing were placed on a wooden sledge, and, apparently by tradition, the first shift in harness pulling the sledge was taken by the betrothed couple.

I had talked late the previous evening with Munin, blissful in the presence of her liveliness, and at how from time to time our eyes met. Despite my ski that afternoon, I hadn't slept well. I had gone to bed still high from the joy I felt being around Munin, and lay awake wrestling with how I should respond to my feelings for her. Images of Erin kept interceding as I mentally replayed the aspects of Munin I especially cherished. To counter my guilt about Erin, I reminded myself I wasn't sure if I would ever see her again. I lacked the courage, though, to inquire from Munin what she knew about the return of visitors to the upper world. Or maybe I didn't want to investigate the possibility of *not* staying in Urda, while I was awash with pleasure at Munin's company. Her behaviour and words underscored that she was about as different from Erin in her overall personality as I could imagine.

Next morning I was groggy, until the crisp air and the community excitement around our departure prodded me fully awake. I noticed Magnus strapping on his skis, and speculated perhaps Munin had been wrong about his absence from our party. Had the three young people resolved their differences overnight? A glimpse of Magnus's shadowed face, though, made that hypothesis unlikely. Before we completed our preparations, Magnus shrugged into a pack and glided off by himself. He disappeared eastward down the trail I had taken the day before. Our party, when it finally heaved into motion, proceeded along a cut in the forest that tended generally southwest.

I asked Munin about Magnus as soon as we'd left Urda behind. She and I were skiing side by side, approximately in the tracks left by the sledge. Progress had been slow climbing out of the village, but our pace increased as the route snaked forward amid the firs and spruce, with only slight inclines up or down varying a generally level course.

"We call what Magnus is doing a 'love-ski,'" Munin told me, her face more desirable than ever as the exertion of skiing brought fresh red to her cheeks. "When somebody loses at love, they are prone to brood and be miserable, and thus to depress or anger others around them. So their parents or the people of their hall or the Formadur insist they take their broken heart away from the community for a time. If such events happen in winter, the removal from the village is by ski."

"How long will Magnus be gone?"

"A love-ski traditionally lasts as long as the winter wooding that prompts it; Magnus should be back at Urda about the same time as us. The love-ski, like an overland trip in another season, lets someone burn out all his jagged emotions, and adjust to the change in how he thought his life might unfold. Or she. Magnus will regain a sense of himself as an individual, with his own fate."

We skied in silence. I was recalling the pain of youthful relationships truncated through no wish of mine, and my own behaviour in response. Perhaps Munin was remembering similar incidents in her past.

"When you're in love," she resumed after a minute or two, "you start to think about 'we' and that's very pleasant. Magnus probably was planning in his head for Signy and himself, Signy and himself and their children. When such an important love is lost, you have to reacquaint yourself with your loneness. That's hurtful. But it's a part of love."

We paused at the brink of a gentle descent, waiting as Signy and Sigurd guided the sledge down the slope. "Did you go on a love-ski, or did your husband, when you separated?" I asked.

Munin knelt to adjust one of her bindings, then straightened. "No. That's for the young. I had my daughter to bring up." She hesitated. "My husband ... he went to sea for a time. At our age, we are expected to cope in a way Magnus can't yet."

We dropped down the hillside, and then between us was only the shushing sounds of our skis passing over the snow. Evergreens on either side of the route clutched white cloaks tightly to themselves.

When, an hour later, Munin and I took a turn hauling the sledge, I found the conveyance easier to pull than I had feared. Uphills required more of our strength, and I was curious how much effort would be needed when logs were piled on.

Our group halted for food around noon. Besides Munin and me, and the lovers, the other two in our party were Snorri, whom I had met in the kitchen, and a young man called Ymir. After lunch, these two fastened themselves into the sledge's harness. Underway again, we skied on through the slowly fading light.

Munin informed me, in answer to a general query of mine, that there were regions in most directions surrounding Urda known best for gathering wood or for hunting. Trails—narrow roads, really—were ancient means of access, although because of boggy expanses, travel was easier in the six months when the land was snow-covered. Two wide rivers north of Urda were troublesome to ford or ferry across—once frozen, they were no obstacle. We would not encounter the rivers on this trip, although Munin said I might enjoy a session of ice fishing on them, and on a couple of lakes the rivers fed.

Summer excursions were happy ones, Munin explained, despite the difficulties with crossing water. People appreciated the break from the cold, and a festive attitude enhanced these expeditions, without diminishing the seriousness of the tasks undertaken. Wooding or hunting outings in late summer and early fall were traditionally the source of spring children. Her own daughter was one such, she told me.

"You have no children," she stated, confirming information I had already shared with her.

"Not so far," I said. We glided side by side without talking for a bit. Perhaps she was waiting for me to elaborate on my attitudes to parenting. After an interval, she started to describe autumn travel.

This is the holiest time of year. Once the harvest is gathered and green things began to die, everyone can appreciate how all life is owed to Freyr and Freya. In this season, travellers occasionally encounter, standing motionless ahead of them on the trail or keeping pace alongside them in the woods, a boar surrounded by a golden light. Men and women to whom the boar reveals itself are accorded special powers—they often become Formadurs in their communities.

No such sighting by people from Urda had occurred for more than a decade, Munin said. But in her district last fall, a small group of woodcutters had chanced upon a boar with a vibrant golden glow emanating from it. The animal is regarded as a manifestation of Freyr, and hence of the Holy Couple. One of the logging party, a woman named Erna, announced she was called to attend the sacred boar. Against the advice of her companions, she trailed the boar as it trotted away into the forest. She hadn't been seen since.

Munin said that, similarly, the appearance of a solitary white swan deep in the woods is accounted a manifestation of Freya. I tried to probe whether Munin truly believed these creatures existed. She grinned at me, but I couldn't read from her expression whether she accepted these supposed verifications of her religion or whether she was skeptical about such revelations. Maybe she was agnostic in her views. Or perhaps she sensed she was explaining a set of ideas to someone who was entirely outside her belief system.

We arrived at a spot where another track led away to the right. The sledge unhesitatingly swung along it. I asked whether the route we had embarked on was how Munin had travelled from her home. She said no, that her party had intersected the main trail to Skuld, which from her description bore southeast from Urda. I asked if Hrolf ever visited her on her farm. Her reply was that he made an annual voyage each spring to the coast carrying furs to trade, and usually stopped off to see her on the return trip. I was surprised by her mention of a fur trade, because although a lot of people's clothing incorporated furs, I hadn't seen any evidence at Urda of trapping or drying pelts. Munin insisted the village was famous for the quality of its furs. I guessed that one of the outbuildings or even one of the main halls was designated for that work.

We reached the wooding camp late in the afternoon. At some identifiable bend in the trail, while Munin and I again were hauling the sledge, Snorri and Ymir had skied forward out of sight. Munin explained that they had gone to prepare for our arrival. When we glided at dusk into the small clearing that held a half-dozen huts, smoke was pouring out of the chimneys of two of them. Everybody jammed into one of these; the four of us who had just arrived crowded to the fireplace to warm ourselves. The hut had no windows, and was occasionally smoky if, because of wind or some other reason, the chimney failed to draw properly. The walls and floor were log; the floor had halfheartedly been smoothed by an adze.

Snorri and Ymir meantime unpacked the sledge; they also were responsible for kitchen duties, and began assembling a stew. Munin and her niece disappeared, and once they were gone there was a burst of joking between the young men. Sigurd opened a pack and quickly adorned himself with a necklace, bracelet, and multiple rings; by now I recognized the link for these people between jewellery and the divine, and thus speculated that this act by Sigurd was part of the marriage process. Sure enough, when Munin and Signy returned, the bride-to-be was similarly bedecked. The engaged couple looked remarkably solemn, I thought, but everybody else seemed in a jovial mood. We ate with a hearty appetite, and not long after supper Sigurd and Signy said what must have been goodnight, and slipped away to the other hut.

Rolls of blankets for us were unpacked by Ymir, and he made up four beds in a semicircle close to the fire. While this was occurring, Munin related what I presume was a series of short jokes; Snorri and Ymir released bellow after bellow of laughter. At least one of these humorous stories probably had me as the butt; the young men glanced over at me as they laughed. Munin may have gone too far with another attempt at comedy; a comment of hers provoked Ymir to chuckle but Snorri reacted as if he was offended. This in turn caused both Munin and Ymir to double over with merriment. Snorri continued to look dubious for several seconds, but eventually laughed himself.

I was in a cheerful frame of mind, in the presence of such high spirits, of young love in the next cabin, and of Munin. I went out into the dark to relieve myself before bed, and the snowy winter forest was pristine with cold and a spectacular sky. Myriads of stars arced above our tiny settlement, twinkling through the heavens. The constellations were exactly as I remembered them: Orion the Hunter soaring above, the Big Dipper indicating the Polestar, and the Milky Way sparkling its irregular ribbon across the night. Wherever this lower world was located, it existed under the identical arrangement of stars that my world's northern hemisphere offered. I experienced a twinge of both homesickness and exhilaration. I longed for my previous, familiar surroundings. Yet I knew with a rush of excitement that I was involved in a central adventure of my life.

Somebody emerged from our cabin and stepped through the snow toward the nearest trees. A few minutes later Munin approached me. She clutched my arm and stared upwards. My heart rate began to increase. We stood for a few minutes like this, and then she tugged me toward the hut. "Isn't it beautiful? But very cold. Let's go in." Her hand grasped mine as we returned through the snow and into the thick warmth of the cabin's interior. The young men were lying wrapped in their blankets beside the fire, apparently asleep.

I'm not certain how it happened, but Munin and I embraced and kissed for a long while just inside the door. I was acutely conscious of the sweet softness of her lips, as though I was an adolescent kissing a girl for the first time. Eventually we disentangled. Not only my heart, but my mind was racing. If I had any doubt about her affection for me, she had convincingly dispelled it. Yet I had no idea how to respond to this heady experience. Lack of privacy curtailed any immediate escalation of our physical attraction for one another. I knew now beyond question, though, that I was in love with Munin. However, in a different world, I was committed to Erin. If Munin and I became lovers, was I betraying Erin? Yet wasn't Erin literally in another universe, in a state of being as remote from this one as death is from life? On the other hand, wouldn't Erin be frantic with concern about my disappearance? I believed she was fond of me to that extent. How could I become physically involved with somebody else at the very moment Erin might be devastated with worry over my unexplained absence?

As I wrestled with such thoughts, Munin and I each arranged layers of blankets around ourselves to form, in effect, sleeping bags. She wriggled her blanket roll nearer mine until our faces were very close; we rubbed our icy noses together. Then we kissed through the chill air that lay along the floor. I reached one arm out of the warming cocoon of bedding and hugged her—to be more exact, hugged the mound of

blankets that covered her. She hummed a short "Mmmmm" of pleasure, and then turned over so her back was to me. "Goodnight," I heard
her say. I retracted my frozen arm into my bedroll. As if unable to end
the evening, she rotated in her wrap of blankets so we could kiss another time. After a while, she once more shifted her back toward me. I
watched the firelight play on the hut's rafters and the underside of the
steep roof.

When I woke, everyone was up but me. Munin was not in the hut,
but she entered a few minutes after I untangled myself from my bedding. She gave me a huge morning smile, but otherwise was no more or
less friendly than the day before. She did not comment about, nor react
in any other way to, our embraces the previous evening. I followed her
lead as to how to behave. Munin said she had carried the traditional
betrothal morning breakfast into the cabin next door: a certain kind of
cake that had been baked in Urda and included in our food sacks.

We didn't see Signy and Sigurd during the day. The rest of us loaded
the sledge from a stack of logs piled about a five-minute ski from the
huts. During the balance of the morning and short afternoon, we skied
around the area; Snorri was taking inventory of which woodpiles were
left in the vicinity. Everyone ate supper together, the bridal couple appearing somewhat subdued. After the meal, at our hut we rolled into
our blankets immediately once the cooking and eating utensils were
cleaned, in order to make an early start the next morning.

We set out in the tentativeness of first light, with three people at a
time pulling the loaded sledge, and everybody helping haul or push up
steeper inclines. I was pleased that I wasn't the tiredest on the return
trip; Ymir seemed more winded than I during the afternoon breaks.
We reached Urda just after dark. Hrolf and the others greeted us with
shouts, and quite a fuss was made over Sigurd and Signy. Magnus had
not returned but showed up about noon the next day. He indeed had a
calmer-looking demeanor; he embraced both of the betrothed pair and
that seemed to settle the matter.

In the days after the wooding expedition, there was increasing tension between Munin and me—an arousing kind of tension, as the issue
of how intimate we might become hung over us. I sensed she was waiting for me to declare myself. But since my own future felt suspended, I
couldn't decide whether I should take the extra step to add the physical

dimension to our caring for one another. My obligation toward Erin intruded on my love for Munin; I knew I did not want to feel that Munin and I were involved in an affair. Transported as I was to Urda, I obviously was unable to bring my relationship with Erin to any conclusion. I floated in a mood of excruciating frustration with my predicament.

Nevertheless, each waking hour I could, I arranged to spend with Munin. We never tired of discussing nearly every imaginable subject, except the parameters of our connection. I was aware I *should* bring this topic forward. But my thoughts about what best to do stayed chaotic, a swirl of "what-do-I-want?"s versus "what-is-right?"s. Most evenings, Munin and I sought out a darkened corner of the hall after people had gone to bed. We exchanged lengthy, delicious kisses. More than once, we proceeded rather farther, although technically we weren't lovers yet. Our activities were as if we had reverted to being a couple of kids necking: we explored each other's bodies to the fullest extent we dared. I remained tormented with an indecisiveness about whether to venture beyond this stage. Munin never uttered any reproach at my dithering, but always demonstrated an ardent physical response to me, as well as proving through our talks how much she and I revelled in a true meeting of minds.

A week passed. Then another. When I wasn't on kitchen detail, I frequently assisted either Munin, Hrolf or a different household inhabitant where I could: chopping firewood, or helping restock water barrels at a still-flowing stream, or acting as a weaver's assistant when Munin worked at the loom. On one errand or another, I visited each of the dwellings at Urda. The smallest of these was in fact devoted to trapping; I packed bales of furs for two days with Magnus, an old man named Bjorn, and a young woman called Tove who Magnus now displayed an interest in. I was slowly learning a few words in the language spoken at Urda—not enough for a conversation, but occasionally I understood the gist of dinner-table exchanges, or even kitchen gossip.

Munin continued to be a patient and unfailing source of information. In spite of my lack of resolution concerning her, I was at peace in Urda in a way that I recognized I had not been in the upper world. I skied almost every day, and that, plus the daily physical work, provided me with growing bodily strength and perfect health. I never even had a cold at Urda. As in my former life, however, skiing often caused my nose to run copiously after strenuous exertion in the icy air—having to herringbone up a sharp rise, for instance. But at night I would lie in my bed-cupboard and feel swathed in well-being, completely happy except for my nagging inability to resolve my moral dilemma around Erin and Munin. That aside, before sleep I savoured the promise of additional pleasing activities tomorrow—perhaps including a total surrender of myself to my love for Munin. The latter was like a wrapped present with my name on it. I felt elated simply knowing the package was there, even if so far I hadn't opened it.

The villagers at Urda possessed no calendars or clocks. Yet they displayed an ability to reckon time: they were capable of deriving, apparently from the light and the season, approximately how far from noon any given moment was. My digital watch provided me with a means of noting the days clicking by, though I often left the device in my sleeping-cupboard.

As I began my fourth week at Urda, I finally summoned the courage to ask Munin what she knew about rising back to the upper world. In mulling matters over, I had decided this information was vital if I was ever to resolve what to do about our relationship. She and I were by ourselves in the hall after lunch, lingering over tea before rejoining the others outdoors.

As soon as I introduced the subject, I could see she was uncomfortable. She lifted and lowered her cup several times before answering. Her features assumed an uncharacteristically sombre cast, and her posture became stiff. I was pretty nervous myself. In my mind I had formulated a sort of *Star Trek* ascent: "Beam me up, Scotty." I could visualize the atoms of my body dissolving, and then reassembling on the sidewalk of Barnard Avenue in the heart of downtown Vernon, to the shock and amazement of passersby. I was aware my fantasy of relocation to the upper world was ridiculous, but everything about my presence in Urda defied rationality.

"I ... I was friends with Abejackson," Munin began in a low tone, light from the fireplace illuminating half her face, and leaving half in shadow. "Not how I am friends with you. He was in a field when he left, with a man, Torvald, who is dead now. The day was windy, Torvald told me. Much snow was being carried into the air: like a blizzard, except it wasn't snowing."

"Powder snow?" I asked.

Munin shrugged. "Torvald said the snow seemed to circle around Abejackson. Then he rose."

"He rose," I repeated. "You mean...?" I held my hand out flat, fingers spread, and slowly lifted it to about the level of my eyes.

"That's what Torvald said."

I couldn't think what else to ask. The event seemed improbable.

"What about the woman visitor?" I inquired after a minute. "I forget her name."

"Lindabbot."

"Okay. Did she rise the same way?"

"No one knows," Munin stated. "She disappeared one afternoon when she was by herself."

"Nobody found a body?"

"There was never a sign of her. When she didn't return to the hall where she was being fostered—this was not at Urda, but another village—they set out to search for her next morning. It had snowed heavily, so no tracks. She was never seen again."

My mind tried to process the information. Finally I decided to reveal to Munin my original fear—that we upper-worlders perhaps were killed at some juncture, as too inconvenient or unsettling for people to tolerate.

Munin was appalled. "Why would we kill?" she blurted. "Life is hard enough without murder. Any killing here is through sickness—brain-sickness or love-sickness or sex-sickness. Everyone is taught to watch for signs of this illness in others, and to take steps or at least talk to the hall steward or Formadur about what they see." She paused. "Who would want to kill you?"

I had no answer.

"How can you even imagine we would do such a thing?" She broke into tears. My heart flipped over, and I stood, hurried around the table, and clumsily tried to embrace her, to comfort her. She pushed me away and sat looking at me, tears flowing down her face. I felt awful.

After a bit she reached her hand out and touched my arm. "I do not want you to leave. But what will happen *will* happen. None of us understand why people arrive from above. Or why they go away again. You do not understand it, either, as far as we can tell."

She wiped some tears from her face with her other hand. "But there is love between us, you and me. And our love is a fine thing. Isn't it?" She sniffled a little, then smiled at me, the water still on her cheeks. "Though neither of us knows what to do about it. What a pair," she concluded, her usual good humour returning to her voice. I felt simultaneously crushed by the uncertainties of my status in her life, and yet euphoric at the strength of her caring for me.

So matters remained for another week. I began to worry about when she might depart for her farm, her winter visit to her brother completed. I could no longer conceive of living at Urda without her.

She made no mention of leaving, and I was too fearful of the consequences of her return home to be able to explore the subject with her. My grasp of the language of the villagers continued to grow, but not to an extent to permit me to casually inquire of Hrolf or anyone else how long Munin's annual stay customarily lasted.

I finally achieved clarity about the future of our relationship during Sigurd's and Signy's wedding. A number of days after my discussion with Munin about rising, she informed me that the formal rite uniting Sigurd with her niece would occur a few nights later. On the evening of the nuptials, preparations for the event matched those of the welcoming ritual, when Munin and the other travellers arrived at Hrolf's. Again the hall was crammed with well-wishers, attired in their best.

I had been regretting that I had no other clothes but the ones I had fallen in, and these were long overdue for the laundry. I had succeeded in establishing a regime of *personal* cleanliness, at least: washing face and upper body in heated water daily, and arranging for a bath about every ten days—despite this activity being rare among Urda's residents. Utilizing a sharp, axe-blade-shaped device Hrolf had provided, I had begun to shave again. This activity was not unknown to the villagers, though all but four or five of the men I encountered were bearded.

Hours before the wedding, Munin drew me over to a bench and presented me with trousers, socks and a shirt of special-occasion quality that she had woven and sewed for me. I was staggered by this fresh proof of her love. By this point I was aware how much effort and how many hours were involved in producing clothes at Urda. And she had created this gift without me having a clue about her intent. My eyes teared as I stammered my thanks, and then we were locked in an embrace. She was teary as well.

"I have nothing for *you*," I said, feeling wretched.

She kissed my nose. "You are all I want from you."

"I want to give you something," I insisted miserably. Despite myself, despite the presence of others in the hall—who were looking determinedly in other directions—I started to cry. While I had been unable to resolve what to do about my passion for Munin, she had been toiling to present me with a loving, considerate gift.

Munin cradled my head against her breasts. She kissed and stroked my hair. "Go see if they fit," she said, when I had calmed a little. She gave me a push. "Try them on."

She eyed me critically when I emerged from the deserted pantry wearing my new outfit. "Not bad."

"They're terrific," I said. "Now nobody could tell I'm not *from* here."

She giggled. "They just might guess. But I have something else to show you."

She produced a cloth packet containing a filigreed gold brooch, and two gold rings displaying a bluish stone. "These are for you. From my brother."

Again, I didn't know what to say. "I … I thought I recognized Hrolf's handiwork," I stuttered. "He's an … an amazing craftsman."

She helped me attach the brooch, and then slipped one of the rings onto the middle finger of my left hand. She placed the other ring on my palm. "You give me a ring."

My hand shook with emotion as I threaded the ring onto her left hand's middle finger.

"Now we are joined by jewellery, besides our love," she said. I enfolded her in an embrace, overwhelmed by a renewed upwelling of tenderness toward her.

We held hands throughout the ceremony that formalized Signy's and Sigurd's union. Besides the nuptial couple, at the front were Signy's son Usk, the Formadur, Edi and Hrolf, and a couple from another hall who were stand-ins for Sigurd's parents. I was still dazed from Munin's gifts, and by how intense my feelings for her had become.

I heard the phrases of the ritual, but a steady roaring resounded inside my head. I trudged again through the wearisome maze of my dilemma regarding Erin. Then it was as if I stood at a familiar closed door—a door which, this time, I opened easily and stepped through. Why was I being true to Erin in this lower world, when if both women were present in either existence, I would without a moment's regret end things with Erin and commence a new life with Munin?

Whether or not I ever had the chance to tell Erin in person that I wanted to bring our relationship to a conclusion, my love for Munin was my choice hereafter. I felt an ache of sadness at my core at the idea that if I *was* returned to my own world, Munin would not be with me. Yet such a separation could not shake the rightness of finishing with Erin. If I was exiled from Munin, no one could replace her—even if I might someday find a person who shared a few of her qualities. But the sole means to acknowledge every dimension of the love Munin offered was to break up with Erin in both worlds, forever.

I recognized that I was as certain of this feeling now as I had been irresolute previously. I glanced at Munin's face, shining with gladness: at her niece's marriage? At holding hands with me? She felt my gaze on her and turned her head toward me, smiling. Our eyes met, and held. Did she sense I had reached some happy decision? Without thought, we bent toward each other and kissed. Abruptly, we were prodded in the back by the two women seated behind us. They grinned at us good-naturedly when we spun around to learn who had poked us. One of them leaned forward to whisper something to Munin, who blushed and laughed. She wouldn't tell me what had been said.

Indeed, we had little chance to talk alone once the ceremony was over. Munin was part of some additional women's ritual involving the bride, an event that took place in a different dwelling. I believe this occurred where the nuptial couple would spend the night. Certainly Sigurd did not linger at Hrolf's; I noticed when the hall emptied he was not among those residents who remained.

Nor had Munin returned by the time I carefully folded away my new garments and jewellery in my sleeping-cupboard. I wondered if I would next wear these at a rite officially linking Munin and me. I was burning to tell her about my resolution to begin a life together. But I consoled myself with the realization that, after so long a delay, another few hours would not matter.

She was not at breakfast, but others from the hall also were either sleeping in or had stayed elsewhere. Though I was impatient to speak privately to her, I knew I would have the chance after lunch, or at worst, supper.

Yet that morning, I ascended—a few days short of six weeks after I fell. I was out skiing with a man in his mid-thirties named Nels. He had been constructing a table in an outbuilding that served as a carpentry shop, and I had been helping him. Mostly I handed him items he pointed to, but he taught me how to sand smooth certain planks he needed, using an abrasive stone. I also held some boards while he fitted pegs to join these lengths of wood to other parts of the table. Naturally, my mind that day was full of lascivious and loving thoughts about Munin, anticipating what I hoped would happen that evening. But I managed to concentrate enough on the job to avoid major mistakes.

Late in the morning, Nels suggested a quick ski as a break. I was familiar by this time with most of the countryside close to Urda, and led us to a specific ridge trail I liked. The route up was strenuous, but the descent was fun and by now I was thoroughly acquainted with the only difficult patch—a double series of turns about three-quarters of the run back down the slope. Nels and I paused to regain our breath at the top. The trail ahead from here levelled out for quite a distance; I believe the route eventually led to a village much further south.

Nels launched himself downward first. I waited a few moments, and then started after him. I noted the time before I kicked into motion: I had secured my watch from my sleeping-compartment at Hrolf's before we left, because of a sort of study I had initiated for myself to determine which of the downhill runs nearest Urda was the longest. I know that time is frequently distorted in moments of intense concentration or excitement, and I thought it would be interesting to know conclusively which route provided the lengthiest descent. I had just gotten underway when I rose.

The ascent felt to me, paradoxically, like falling. I can't speculate what a witness on the ground would have seen, but the sensation to me was the bottom dropping out of the Earth—exactly as I experienced when I was first propelled to Urda. My initial thought was that a snow bridge across some hollow place on the hillside had collapsed under the combined weights of Nels and me.

As with my earlier freefall, time swelled to infinity while I endured the drop. Panic blocked my mind from comprehending anything but the sense of an endless downward plunge through air. At last I noticed between my skis a forested mountainside rising rapidly toward me. The tops of snowy evergreens surrounded me; branches whipped by, lashing at my body. Then I was hit hard by the snow.

I toppled forward, impelled face first across a drift. My left arm was wrenched underneath me, so in part I skidded on that, twisting my left shoulder. A jolt of pain seared my neck. I lay stunned for a minute. When my breathing eased, I observed that my poles and skis were still attached, unbroken. After couple of unsuccessful attempts, I levered myself upright. I was shaky, but alive.

I beat snow from my clothes, and cautiously took stock of my surroundings. A considerable depression in the snow that was my point of impact was evident, as was the gouged-out path that marked my precipitous slide from there to where I stood, legs vibrating.

Suddenly I believed I recognized this cluster of trees. The angle of the slope, the specific groves of pines and firs, resembled a stretch on Mystery, a downhill portion just before the route rejoins Woodland Bell.

Or was I mistaken? These woods *appeared* to be a place on Silver Star I had often skied, but was this wishful projection? I gazed about me at the wintry evergreens, trying to judge. A wind flowed through the trees' upper branches, then quieted.

I sidestepped up the thick snow of the embankment where I had landed, and discovered at the top a trail on which a cross-country ski track had been set. I resolved to ski the track in the direction that, if my perception was accurate, would lead to Woodland Bell and thence to the parking lot. Five minutes later, I glimpsed a signpost at the top of the next rise. My heart was pounding more with apprehension than exertion: my stay in Urda had left me in excellent shape. But I was determined not to conclude anything about where I was until I could read the directional markers on the post. Sure enough, they proclaimed *Woodland Bell* and under that *To Parking Lot*.

From here the route out became double-tracked, testament to

Woodland Bell's heavy use by beginners. The parking area was fifteen minutes away. I lifted my left wrist and brushed aside my sleeve to check the time; my watch read twelve noon. But the date startled me. My watch had either been damaged when I landed, or had reverted to the exact Wednesday in January when I had fallen to Urda.

Had I looped through time? If my car was at the warming hut, if a paper I could buy at the convenience store at the foot of the mountain gave me news of issues current in the media when I left, described the world I remembered, then I was home as if I had never been absent.

Yet, if I was back, that meant Munin was lost to me, held fast by another universe. My heart constricted, and I coasted to a stop. Grief welled up. I saw Munin's beautiful face, watched her body float toward me in the firelit evening hall. I heard her beloved voice, her laugh. My fingers remembered the silkiness of her hair, and her skin. Chance, time, or whatever elements separated parallel worlds had erected a pitiless wall between us.

If I was truly returned to my old life, I could try skiing the trail from which I had fallen, in the hope I might break through to Urda again. Yet based on how few visitors from this existence appeared below, I doubted the opportunity to cross over readily occurred. Nels would report my ascent. Munin would feel the agony, the obliterated chance for joy that wracked me now. I would in time be transformed into a memory for her, and she would be only a memory for me.

The prospect of never again holding her, kissing her, speaking with her, was devastating. My limbs were too heavy to function. The icy wind lifted once more through the highest branches of the firs. I heard in the sound no answer to my anguish. Yet I knew I couldn't remain indefinitely here in the snow, blubbering. I had to pick up my life where it had been suspended. In the hours and days ahead I could attempt to deal with my sorrow at lost love.

I managed to heave myself forward, arms and legs functioning mechanically. I slid along Woodland Bell, trying to organize the whirl of feelings that clanged and clashed within me. My pack was lost in Urda, too, hanging on its peg in the vestibule to Hrolf's hall. I mentally inventoried what I would have to repurchase: parka, thermos, spare ski tip, waxes. My wallet and key case were stored in my sleeping-compartment. They and their contents—driver's licence, credit cards, house key, car key—would also need to be replaced.

Two elderly skiers shuffled into sight, approaching along the level track. As I neared them, my mouth automatically formed the greeting-words I had learned in Urda. The elderly couple responded loudly and distinctly, "Hi there," as one does to foreigners.

Minutes later, gliding around another curve, I observed the warming hut in the distance, with about two dozen vehicles in the mainly empty parking area. Four or five people clutching skis and poles straggled from a SUV over the plowed and sanded white expanse toward the hut. If I was really back at the same moment and place from which I had fallen, I would have to phone my office. Cancel the afternoon's appointments. Ask someone to pick me up. I recalled the joys of a hot shower. A cup of coffee.

I braced myself for phoning Erin, for what I now needed to say to her. But before I contacted anybody, I had to confirm I had, incredibly, lived almost six weeks in mere minutes. I could see my station wagon. At the end of the track I removed my skis, gathered them up, and stepped onto the cleared lot.

# LOVE IN THE AFTERLIFE

Squirrels were everywhere in Toronto. Dennis was seated at a patio table in Pasta-chio's, an Italian-themed café along Bloor. He counted four of the treeborne rodents juddering in turn down the trunk of a curbside oak and scurrying across a tiny patch of May grass between sidewalk and street. Their frantic jerk-and-freeze motion resembled in Dennis' eyes the stop-frame animation of early films. The backyard where he was house-sitting north of St. Clair Avenue hosted two or three resident gangs of squirrels, involving ten or twelve of the rat-like creatures. When he took a lawn chair out behind the house to read in the strengthening sun, the squirrel factions squabbled madly on the ground, in the trees and along the power or telephone wire which was strung parallel to the lane. Even at Elizabeth's apartment, six blocks from the café in the Annex district, hordes of the rodents constantly darted across the street and over the miniature lawns that flanked the walks leading up to porches.

Dennis found the constant presence of the squirrels creepy. "Why do people in Toronto think rats are horrible and squirrels are cute?" he asked Elizabeth once.

She had laughed at him. "Come on, Dennis, you have squirrels in Vancouver, too."

"They don't overrun the place. We keep them mostly penned up in Stanley Park."

She laughed again. "Squirrels are part of the natural environment. Toronto is a city of ravines and river-valleys. Ideal habitat for squirrels. Vancouver isn't the *only* city in the world where people live close to nature."

He glanced into the interior of the café, and saw Elizabeth standing talking to two men seated at a table. She had spotted them when they first entered. And she had urged Dennis to accompany her when—their own intense conversation over—she had stopped squeezing his hand and stood up to *just go over and say hello.* That was her standard description for schmoozing.

He had declined.

"How does it hurt if they get to know you better?" she had insisted. This exchange was a familiar argument between them.

"I want my writing to stand on its own, to be judged according to its accomplishments or its failures—not praised or promoted because of who I know, whose ass I kiss." He'd given a version of this speech about 100 times in the nine months they had been going out.

Elizabeth's eyes had sparked anger. "They're just people. When you're not friendly, they think you don't like them."

"I *don't* like them, for one. For two, why are they so insecure? How is it they need another friend so badly?"

"They're friends of *mine.* Since you and I are involved, they naturally want to get to know you."

"They're not friends of yours. They're *business* acquaintances. There's a difference."

"They're part of the arts community, the writing community. Like you are. Like I am. We share goals in common, so we're friends."

Dennis had taken a sip from his rapidly cooling after-lunch cappuccino. "One of them is the host of a pretentious arts report on CBC Radio. The other spasms out an insufferably opinionated arts column for the *Star.* You, on the other hand, cobble together an honest living writing book reviews for whoever pays, freelancing articles for *Flare* and *Canadian Living*, plus researching for that awful TV talk show your pal Janey is a producer on. *And* you scarf up whatever crumbs of interview work people like Mr. Ed over there deign to toss your way."

She had shot to her feet, all five-foot-one of her, her fierce disapproval rattling the designer dishes and cutlery on the table. "While you sit on your big fat Canada Council grant and judge the rest of us, is that it? They're part of *my* community, even if they're not part of yours. Stay here and stew in your own self-righteousness, if you want." Her face was rigid with fury.

He reached to wrap his right hand around her left hand, where she had compressed it, like its twin, into a fist that pushed down against the white linen tablecloth. "Please. Please sit."

"No. You always think you're right. You think you know more than anybody."

"Elizabeth, that's not it. Please." He hadn't meant their disagreement to spin this far out of control. "Please sit down. Please."

She tugged her hand from his grip. "I'm going over to talk to my friends."

"Please listen to me." He could hear the urgency in his voice. Why was he so afraid of her withdrawal? If he was back in some East Vancouver bar entertaining his friend Wayne with this scenario, describing her insistence on paying court to—brown-nosing, that's what they'd agree it was—these two self-important, puffed-up Toronto cultural capos, he and Wayne would be hooting with laughter at the silliness of it. But looking up at Elizabeth, his arm stretched toward her across the table in a café on Bloor near Spadina, he felt only a ballooning anxiety.

He had stood too, his legs weak. "Elizabeth, I don't want us to fight."

Obviously he proclaimed his wish too loudly. At the next table, a woman angled her face toward them.

"I love you," Dennis had continued, trying to pitch his voice lower. "I was sitting here revelling in what you'd just told me. I was enjoying being with you, like I always enjoy being with you. But this moment was extra special. Because of all you just said about Mark. I'm more in love with you than ever, if that's possible. Suddenly you want to dash off and hobnob with ... with—"

"—with a couple of insufferable people," she had finished his sentence. But her tone and face were transformed, softened with pleasure. "Oh, you," she purred. She stepped around the table toward him, and as he rotated to meet her they had embraced tightly. Her lips pressed hotly up to his. Her tongue flickered inside his mouth, exciting him. When they broke apart, he could see her eyes were filled with equal parts of mischievousness and desire. She tightened the fingers of her right hand around those of his left and they continued to hold hands while they manoeuvred to sit down across from each other again.

A heavy bubble of happiness expanded in his chest. He couldn't speak.

She looked fondly at him, then leaned forward. "I love you, too. I just wish you weren't so ... contrary." She laughed, but squeezed his hand at the same time. "We've got the rest of today and all night to spend together. Can't I take a few minutes to talk to my—" her eyes flashed with delight "—*pretentious* friends?"

He found his voice. "Yeah," he croaked. "Sure. Okay."

"Thank you." She bent across the table and kissed the tip of his nose.

"I just want to mention—" he had kept his voice light "—the American poet Robert Bly distinguishes between a community and a network."

She tilted her head to the right, her habit when she meant to tease him. "He does, does he?"

"Yeah."

"What's that got to do with anything?"

"You said Mr. Ed and Mr. Red over there were part of the writing *community*. Bly says a community involves people of all ages and opinions, from the village idiot to the wise old crone. What people call a community, he claims, is actually a network, something very different: a group of equals, peers."

Her hand recoiled from his. Her head straightened to the vertical as her face started to close, eyebrows descending toward her eyes: the commencement, he knew, of her angry squint. Her mouth arched into a scowl. Experience told him he better act fast to repair the mood. He angled forward to kiss her. She jerked back, out of reach. "I only thought you'd want to know," he blurted, then tried desperately to generate a humorous comment to restore the atmosphere he had clumsily ruined. "Hey, now I think of it," he babbled, "you frequently say I behave like an idiot. Maybe I'm the *village* idiot. That would mean you are entirely right: this *is* a community and not a network."

Her face had relaxed. She inclined forward, her eyes again dancing. Relief flooded through him.

"Let me get this straight. Now you're telling me I'm a wise *old crone*, is that it?" she said, her tone jokey.

He raised his left hand, palm outward, as though attesting to some legal declaration. "Wise, yes. Old, never." He lowered his open hand, palm up, to rest on the table. She had restored her hand to it.

"Seems to me I've heard of this Bly," she pretended to muse. "Ah, I remember. Janey had me prepare a background on a guy from Ottawa they wanted to interview who used to be big in the men's movement. Wasn't your Robert Bly a grand pooh-bah of that nonsense in the States? Wasn't Bly's idea that you men should spend your weekends naked together in the woods, drumming and chanting?"

He kept her game going. "Yup. That's where you'll find me, any weekend you don't find me naked and chanting with you."

She had laughed and angled closer to kiss his nose another time. Then she had extricated her hand, stood, and walked over to connect with the two arts gurus.

Dennis pushed back against the chair and stretched out his legs. He felt drained by the past few minutes' mercurial shifts between emotional highs and lows. In Elizabeth's absence, he became aware of the warmth projected onto his forehead and cheeks by the patio heaters secured to the building wall above him. He tried a sip of his coffee, but it tasted cold. Catching the eye of a distant waiter, Dennis beckoned, pointing at his cup. The man nodded and disappeared in the opposite direction.

Beyond the patio railing, three of the squirrels on the grass strip beside the sidewalk were engaged in a discussion over a piece of pizza crust nestled amid candy wrappers, a pen top, a dog turd and shreds of unidentifiable paper. Dennis' eyes shifted to scan the café again: a chair had been located for Elizabeth. He watched her head lift back as if she were laughing merrily over some witticism uttered by her tablemates. A steamy pleasing scent of coffee and bread, the clinking of the gleaming tableware, and a muted hum of nearby tables' conversation enveloped Dennis. The strain that had stiffened his body slowly dissipated. As the details of the just-concluded tiff faded, Dennis realized he was recovering the ecstatic sensation Elizabeth's earlier words concerning Mark Gould had created.

A waiter materialized beside the table, proffering a coffee pot. Dennis nodded, and a half-minute later the rich brown heat of the beverage swirled down his throat to augment the delight suffusing him as his mind replayed and savoured Elizabeth's speech.

From somewhere in the depths of Pasta-chio's he heard the bellow of a wheezy, snorting laugh momentarily eclipse the ambient sound. Three jarringly loud, breathy hee-haws. Mr. Ed. Because of the man's disturbing laugh, Dennis had decided to name him after the talking horse of the 1950s movies he remembered as a child watching on a kids' TV program specializing in golden oldies. The bizarre laugh had amazed him the first time he heard it, crowded around a dinner table at the Kaufflers'.

He had met Paul Kauffler and his future wife Simone Rosten a dozen years before at the University of BC when they were second year Honours English students in a Chaucer class. The three of them had achieved AS despite the Chaucer prof's eccentricities, and had stayed friends. Paul came from a wealthy family, a good catch, and he and Simone moved to Toronto soon after graduation. She was a literary officer with the Ontario Arts Council now, very much a presence in the Toronto book scene. After abandoning a U of T master's in English, Paul had achieved considerable prowess as a Bay Street stockbroker.

Dennis enjoyed the Kaufflers' company. Simone had phoned to invite him to dinner when Dennis' first collection of stories had been published, and he had written to say he would be coming to Toronto for some promotional readings and interviews. She and Paul had greeted him warmly at the door when the taxi dropped him off a little early. His hosts seemed eager to catch up on what Dennis' life was like in Vancouver, and on his breakup with Angie after five years. Dennis was impressed at how Paul let his wife shine at the literary soirée she had organized. Paul worked hard in the kitchen before the meal, letting Simone circulate and chat with the invited as they arrived. He was clearly intent that the evening be a success, that their guests mingle, feel at ease.

A large portion of the before-dinner conversation centred on a new deck opening off the kitchen through glass doors. Simone had arranged to have it built as her birthday gift to Paul, who in warmer months liked to sit out in their garden and work with his laptop.

"He claims the industrious activity of our squirrels inspires him," Simone said, laughing. "Personally, I think he just likes to watch them scuttle aimlessly up and down our trees. Reminds him of the stock market." One by one, and in clumps, the guests were taken into the cool evening to tour the deck, illuminated by floodlights recessed in flower boxes.

At this meal, Dennis had met a female book reviewer for the daily *Toronto Star*, a female editor at the Toronto branch of a New York publishing house, a male novelist whose first book had been the talk of the town two years ago, and the male long-time editor of a national arts-and-current-affairs monthly. The guests, who also included a couple of spouses, had to pry any discussion of mutual funds or corporate mergers out of Paul. He let his wife be the focus of the evening; he seemed content to listen to the lively banter around the table, or reminisce with Dennis about smoking grass on Wreck Beach below the university when they were younger. There was no sign from Paul that his book on investing, *Dancing with Bulls*, had been a non-fiction bestseller for fourteen weeks when it appeared three years previously. Nor that the volume was reissued annually in an updated version, and had probably already sold more copies this year than would most of the season's new books being dissected over the penne with chicken, asparagus and pine nuts.

Dennis admired Paul's reticence to engage the other guests on literary or publishing matters. Once the Chardonnay had gone around a couple of times over the cold cucumber soup and a melon appetizer, a quick wordplay began that left Dennis feeling provincial, decidedly no match for these people in a contest of wit.

"Penne!" the book editor had exclaimed when Paul brought the main dish in from the kitchen. "Simone, as I've always said, 'Penne's from heaven.'"

A general groan greeted the comment. "A penne is the lowest form of humour," remarked the magazine editor.

"Now that was a lame one," the novelist's wife said, accepting the heavy dish as it was passed to her. "I guess we'd have to call it a penne lame."

More groans and laughter.

"Penne port in a storm," the editor ventured in reply.

"Yes, penne are called but few are chosen," Simone declared.

"Okay, but a penne saved is a penne earned," the *Star* reviewer said, dabbing her lips with a napkin. A chorus of derisive "oooh"s sounded, ending with chortling and a buzz of side-conversation.

"This really tastes great, Simone," Dennis broke in. "You've outdone yourself."

Other voices echoed his compliment. Encouraged, he continued. "I always remember you as a good cook. This is a whole level of magnitude higher than the old days. You've obviously gotten worlds more knowledgeable about cooking."

"Maybe she has," the novelist said, "but she better beware: penne wise, pound foolish."

"What do you say to that, Simone?" the *Star* reviewer wanted to know. "Penne for your thoughts?"

After the meal, Dennis had lingered to help Paul wash up. Simone and the *Star* reviewer, who had also stayed late, had settled on the living room rug in front of a fire, brandy snifters in hand, gossiping about affairs between people Dennis hadn't heard of. From time to time Simone would appear in the kitchen to urge Paul and Dennis to join them, to leave the dishes for the cleaning woman to cope with in the morning. Dennis took his cue from Paul, however, and the two continued to tidy up. As they transferred leftovers into containers, prepared bowls and cups for the dishwasher, and handwashed wineglasses, Paul's droll assessments of the night's guests was astonishing to Dennis. Several times he had to chuckle over a comment by Paul skewering some pronouncement on culture or politics that had been proclaimed above the tomato and onion salad like a divine edict. Evidently Paul in private did not rate the Toronto literary scene at its own assessment.

Simone had hosted a second event in Dennis' honour after his story collection, *Who Are These People And What Are They Doing In My Life?*, had surprisingly, thrillingly, been nominated for that year's Governor-General's literary prize for fiction. The phone call from the award organizers in Ottawa had been entirely unexpected: the book had received far more negative reviews than positive ones. "Dennis Benson has an adequate eye for detail in providing setting and generating mood," the *Star* reviewer he had met at Simone's and Paul's had written. "Yet many of his characters come across as sketchy, only roughed-in. We might well ask, 'Who are these people?' A few more drafts, Mr. Benson?" Back home, the *Vancouver Sun* reviewer had displayed, as far as Dennis was concerned, an appalling lack of exposure to contemporary short fiction. "Benson's stories mostly seem like the start of novels. Is that what he was intending? One wonders."

Then Dennis was shortlisted for the national honour, and his publisher arranged another series of interviews and a couple of public readings. Even his former partner, Angie, phoned to congratulate him. Dennis assured her, as he did all his friends, that he had no chance of actually winning. He reminded well-wishers of the dismissive tone of the majority of the book's reviews. But a tiny drop of hope bubbled to the surface. He bought and read the other books nominated for the fiction prize, and the droplet of hope became a thinly flowing stream.

The competing books were dreadfully written, he had explained to his friend Wayne one night over brews at the Commercial Drive pub they sometimes favoured. A novel written by a middle-aged woman, formerly known as a poet, was ridiculously syrupy. Every scene was interrupted by overwritten descriptive passages comparing everything to something else. And a rival collection of stories relied for its literary impact on a continually repeated trick: vital information about the main character was withheld by the author until three-quarters through the story, when the reader finally was told the protagonist was wheelchair-bound, or had murdered her children, or was narrating from the other side of the grave. "When I read this junk, Wayne, I start to feel I'm a shoe-in," Dennis confessed.

Wayne was amused. He was the proprietor of a small new-and-used bookshop on West Broadway he had purchased with his parents' help after graduation from UBC. A careful reader, he considered himself an astute judge of artistic merit in contemporary literature.

"It's been my observation, Dennis, that the more poorly realized anything is, the more likely its chances to receive a prize," Wayne declared. "Which public buildings in Vancouver are the worst to find your way around in? Which are the complete worst to work in, according to the people who have to endure them daily? Which are famous for leaks and all sorts of architectural flaws? Right! Simon Fraser University and the Robson Square Courthouse. Doesn't the architect of these win every award going?" Wayne tilted his glass for another sip of honey lager. "How many bad, no, I mean *really* bad actors or actresses are handed prizes for best performance, whether stage or screen?"

"This is true," Dennis concurred.

"It's no different with literary awards," Wayne went on. What did you think of last year's Governor-General's fiction winner?"

"Crap," Dennis exploded. "That guy wouldn't know a plot if it—"

"My point exactly," Wayne said. "You may be no great shakes as a writer, Dennis. But I don't think you're quite bad enough yet to win the Gee-Gee. Someday, perhaps, but not with *this* book. Cheer up," he added, seeing Dennis' face darken. "You're young yet. Plenty of time for your writing to deteriorate into prizewinning quality."

Wayne's prediction had proven true. Dennis had been informed by the award organizers that he would be contacted at the end of October to arrange travel to Ottawa if he was the nominee who actually won. The last days of the month arrived and departed in silence. He had been in Toronto for a reading during those final hours, checking his home phone for messages several times a day; the award was given to the poet-turned-novelist. When he went for supper at Simone's and Paul's place a day after the announcement of the winner, his hosts were full of condolences, as were the other guests. Yet his nomination seemed to have increased his status among his tablemates at the Kaufflers' more than his failure to win had diminished it. He was seated beside the editor-in-chief of one of the city's main literary quarterlies, a magazine that had rejected his work consistently. The editor, a woman in her late thirties, expressed detailed interest in Dennis' writing plans. Afterwards, he concluded he had talked too much about himself to her, even sketching the outline for the novel he wanted to try. Nothing was said by either of them about her magazine's steadfast refusal to publish any of Dennis' stories.

However, as everyone was fumbling into coats late in the evening, she offhandedly suggested that Dennis send her some of his newer work. At home in Vancouver again, he mailed off a sort of allegorical piece he had recently finished, about a man delayed by weather on a flight to the BC Interior who discovers that the region where the airliner is temporarily grounded has two main habitations, a lakeside resort village named Poetry and a mountainside mining and smelter town called Prose. A woman he sits beside on the plane turns out to be a native of the area, and offers to be his guide during the holdover. She has a home in each settlement, but she seduces the hero in Poetry. The story was accepted by return mail.

This occurrence was just one more Toronto experience Dennis had gleefully mocked in conversation with Wayne and his other Vancouver friends. Yet the idea that an extended stay in Toronto might be a boost for his career started to take shape in Dennis' mind. Simone had originally planted the seed, urging him on his two prior visits—and by letter on his return home—to try a few months in what she termed "like it or not, the literary capital of this country." She spoke of her migration there with Paul, and the opportunities they unearthed that would not have been available in Vancouver, "much as we love that city." When Dennis tore open with shaking fingers the envelope from the Canada Council that contained the wonderful news that his application for a year's support to write had been approved, Simone was the first person he phoned. Within days she had located a ten-month house-sit starting in September. The house was that of a sabbatical-bound English professor she and Paul had become friends with during Paul's abortive master's program.

Dennis handed in his notice at his apartment and at the part-time job he had held the past two years—a marker in the English department of a south Vancouver high school. This work, a support union rather than a teaching position, had meant he was home by three in the afternoon. His day consisted of six hours in the school's library where, along with his Social Studies counterpart, he read and graded student writing as a means of lightening the teachers' loads. He arrived back at his apartment with more energy left for his fiction than when he had delivered prescriptions for a pharmacy, was dispatched from a day labour office, or was employed as an assemblyman at a cable manufacturing factory. Stints of unemployment insurance between manual jobs had provided Dennis previously with uninterrupted periods to apply himself to his writing. But the Canada Council grant meant, as well as time to write, recognition by his peers—or at least, the grant selection committee. As Dennis' departure date neared, he hauled most of his books and household goods to the basement of Wayne's rented house for storage.

At a dinner party Simone convened during his second week in Toronto, he had first met Elizabeth. Also Mr. Ed, whose wheezy bellow continued to issue from the table in Pasta-chio's where Dennis could spy Elizabeth continuing to speak earnestly with the two men. That same September evening at the Kaufflers' he had been introduced to Mark Gould, as well.

"I've invited someone I think you'll really like," Simone had told Dennis. She winked at him. He had arrived on time, although a half-hour before any of the other guests. Dennis was sipping a single-malt Scotch that Paul had provided. He and Simone were standing beside the kitchen island, while Paul mixed up a salad dressing in a large blender near the sink.

Somewhere in Simone's orbits through the book scene she had encountered Elizabeth. The two had become acquaintances and then, after they discovered both had signed up for the same early-morning exercise class at the neighbourhood community centre, friends. Elizabeth had been raised in Winnipeg, and had moved to Toronto after university with her first husband, now a local radio personality Dennis had never listened to. Simone had seated Dennis beside Elizabeth at the table. Despite the awkwardness he felt at Simone's obvious matchmaking, he found himself enormously attracted to Elizabeth as they chatted over the medallions of lamb and creamed spinach and almonds. The litheness of her small frame mesmerized him; Simone had told him that as a girl Elizabeth had been a gymnast of near-Olympic-team accomplishment. She still walked and sat exhibiting a grace and poise that registered with Dennis in the Merlot and candlelight of Simone's dinner table as highly erotic.

Even then he was aware, though, of the fierce bestowing and withholding of her attention. One moment she was turned to reply to a comment Dennis uttered, or to ask him a question, her beautiful face framing eyes alight with intelligence and wry humour. The next second the same gift of her total concern had been directed toward another of their table companions. Her body seemed to quiver from the intensity with which she fastened on a person. Dennis later decided there was something squirrel-like in her abrupt shifts of total absorption in now one direction, now another. At Simone's, what had struck him, besides the rush he felt when Elizabeth projected her concentrated intelligence his way, was how perfectly at ease she was with the people seated around them. She could banter with them as if they had all been best friends for years.

Dennis was astounded when early in the dinner he had comprehended exactly who Mr. Ed was. The introduction had occurred in the midst of a blur of before-dinner jabber; Dennis only realized as table conversation was crescendoing that this person was *the* CBC national radio arts fixture. The broadcaster's program had been one Dennis often had spoken of scornfully: the man seemed to make a special effort to focus on non-Canadian writers, musicians, artists, and museum and gallery shows. "Today in the first half-hour we'll be looking at southwest Brazilian pottery shards, currently being exhibited in the Los Angeles County Museum of Art," Dennis had imitated Mr. Ed's tones one evening when Wayne and he had been castigating the state of the CBC. Wayne had seconded Dennis' assessment: "That man will search out *anything* anywhere else in the world rather than present what's happening here." Mr. Ed's preponderance of interviews with foreign authors especially infuriated Dennis. He raved to Wayne about how the CBC had sent Mr. Ed to Europe to prepare a series on the new German novelists and poets, but would never conceive of having him travel to Saskatoon or Lethbridge or Vancouver to introduce Canadians to new talent in their own country.

At the Kaufflers', though, the most salient impression Dennis had of Mr. Ed was his incredible laugh. The man acted unaware of his distressing affliction, or its irritating effect on others. In the decade Dennis had listened to that voice over the radio, he couldn't remember ever experiencing the signature breathy snorting. "They edit it out," Paul had told him later as they cleared away the supper dishes. "Like a lot of things in life, what on air appears as spontaneous is actually the result of painstaking work."

"Why would they hire him in the first place, with that goofy laugh?" Dennis asked, placing a load of salad bowls on the tiled counter next to the dishwasher. "His hee-haw practically qualifies as a disability."

Paul restocked the cutlery drawer with unused coffee spoons.

"Strange things are done 'neath the Toronto sun," he chanted, misquoting Robert Service. Then: "We may never understand."

Mark Gould and his wife had proved as adept as the other dinner guests at the witty repartee that swirled around the table from the moment the guests seated themselves under Simone's direction. The fast-paced puns and turns of phrase lasted until an hour or two after Paul placed three different liqueur bottles on the tablecloth beside the residue of the chai cheesecake and invited the company to serve themselves.

For Dennis, Mark Gould was difficult to like. Dennis knew vaguely that Gould was a well-regarded poet, although he had never read any of his work. Gould, a few years older than him, had a sour, permanently frowning mouth. Slitted eyes peered guardedly through thick glasses, which formed the baseline of a forehead extending far back onto his balding skull. Gould's comments were usually acerbic. He was spending the academic year as writer-in-residence at the University of Guelph, an institution he categorized as staffed by petty and inept professors, who displayed widespread ignorance of contemporary literature. To the general amusement of the Kaufflers' guests, he told of a cocktail party in his honour when he first took up his appointment. Speaking with the university president, Gould had used the term "Orwellian" in connection with a policy or practice of the institution's library to which Gould had taken offense. He insisted the term had been a mystery to the president, who had been CEO of an insurance firm, and later a college vice-president in Alberta. When the poet explained that the designation was a reference to the English novelist George Orwell, the president's face had lit up. "Orwell, Orwell, let's see," Gould claimed the president had uttered, snapping his fingers in a slow rhythm as mental gears and shafts rotated. "I know, I know: got it. Yeah: the *animal* guy."

But Gould's disparagement of the university head scarcely indicated the boundaries of his belittling manner. He viewed his own position in the institution as equally absurd. "They've given me the office of a CanLit prof who's on leave this year. I sit at my desk in his office, writing on my laptop, and look around at book after book of CanLit criticism on the guy's shelves. I get paid to write stuff. Then guys like him get paid to critique it and teach it. Those activities generate enough money so they can hire me to write more of the same, so they can have additional material to critique and teach. When I'm writing in that office I feel I have two tubes in my arm, one in and one out; I'm simultaneously getting a transfusion and donating blood."

Listening to the poet over the course of the evening, Dennis' aversion to the man grew. He couldn't understand why Elizabeth spoke with him so animatedly now and then, and seemed to find his sneering outlook entertaining. Gould not only complained about his appointment in Guelph and derided the very idea of anyone being a writer-in-residence. He also did a long riff on the failure of the literary mandarins at the University of Toronto to recognize his obvious talents and select him for their annual writer-in-residence job. He observed that such a post would mean less domestic disruption for himself and his wife and two children. As it was, he lived in a pied-à-terre apartment near the campus in Guelph four days a week, and was back home in Toronto the other three.

Dennis' sole attempt to engage Gould in conversation had been a failure. After the meal, Dennis was helping Paul scrape and stack plates in the kitchen preparatory to washing them, when Gould entered. He was in search of a previously declined refill for his cognac, which he and a number of late-staying guests had been sipping in front of the fire. "Are you by any chance related to *Glenn* Gould?" Dennis had asked. He meant the question about the pianist as small talk while he sought, following Paul's directions, the cognac bottle which had already been restored to an upper kitchen cabinet.

"No, I'm not related to Glenn Gould," the poet had snapped at Dennis. "Are *you*?"

Dennis let the taunt pass. Since he was in an excited daze at having met Elizabeth, and looking forward to joining her and the others around the Kaufflers' living room hearth, he tried to ignore Gould's reply. When the kitchen chores were mainly complete, Paul sent Dennis away. He discovered Elizabeth talking to Gould's wife, Cindy.

Cindy had raised Dennis' ire at dinner with her remarks about Vancouver. From the ebb and flow of talk Dennis had deduced she had spent several years living in the city with her first husband, who had been a transit executive. "I mean no disrespect to our honoured guest," Cindy had said, nodding in Dennis' direction between shovelling forkfuls of the arugula, cilantro, and bean salad between lips perfectly shaped by flesh-coloured lipstick. "Mmmmm. This is divine, Simone. But I just can't stand *stucco*. What a hideous building product. Acres and acres of houses all done in stucco. *Yuck*. What sort of person would *live* in a house coated with stucco?"

Dennis felt roused to defend Vancouver's ubiquitous outside wall surfacing. "Actually, it's waterproof, relatively cheap, and durable. I've lived—"

"That's what I was constantly told, dear," Cindy cut him off. "But, frankly, I was so relieved to get back to TO and inhabit a house built of *brick* once again."

When Dennis, brandy snifter in hand, had sat beside Cindy and Elizabeth on the Kaufflers' rug, Gould's wife was in the midst of complaining about the cost and shortcomings of the Filipino nanny she and her husband employed to tend the couple's two young daughters while Cindy worked. She was currently a senior programmer for CBC television's children's shows. Dennis gathered from her monologue, throughout which Elizabeth provided sympathetic comments, that the Goulds had run through a series of childcare employees, none of whom measured up to Cindy's standards. She was of the opinion that one of her priorities as a mother should be to monitor, and to increase the parenting skills of, immigrants employed to tend her children.

"Esmerelda provided excellent references from Louise Hagan," Cindy said, referring to the wife of a wealthy owner of a chain of electronics stores. "But in practice, Esmerelda was totally inadequate in caring for Sophie and Julie. Of course, our kids are spoiled rotten by Mark's parents, who have showered them with toys since the instant they were born. They're quite rich. The parents, I mean."

Dennis' irritation with Cindy Gould was more than compensated for by his nearness to Elizabeth. Next morning he phoned Simone to thank her for the party, and obtained Elizabeth's phone number after enduring some teasing from his hostess. When he had called Elizabeth that evening, she informed him she had already been well briefed by Simone. They laughed at that, before agreeing to meet for supper the following Friday night.

For their first date, he had planned to conduct her to a downtown restaurant where he had been treated to lunch once by a Toronto promotions woman hired by his publisher. The restaurant, in the Yorkville district a couple of blocks north of Bloor, was in a courtyard lined with shops set between some tall office buildings. Dennis had felt very sophisticated, eating amid a flock of stylishly dressed women and expensively suited men. His choice from the menu had been essentially a chicken wrap, but cost his publisher the equivalent of, back in Vancouver, a gourmet salmon steak entrée plus glass of wine.

When Dennis had arrived at Elizabeth's apartment, she suggested a substitute agenda. She lived on Kendal Avenue, south of Dupont, an easy walk from the Spadina subway stop. Her apartment occupied the second floor of an old house, set amid three tall maple trees. While Elizabeth finished getting ready to leave, Dennis stepped from her living room onto a covered porch extending across the entire front of the second storey. From this vantage, with the leaves just starting to adopt their fall colours, he had a squirrel's-eye view of the creatures as they leaped through the foliage from branch to branch. "It's great in summer, when I practically live on the porch," Elizabeth said, appearing in a stunning jumper-like dress that to Dennis emphasized her shapely body. "It's not insulated, though. In winter I shut all the doors and just use the porch to keep wine cool if I'm having people for dinner."

Elizabeth's idea for their meal, which Dennis readily acceded to, was that the café he proposed was fine for lunch but overpriced for supper. Before they ate, she wanted in any event to drop off an article on window shutter design she had sold to a home decorating magazine. Following that, they could eat around the corner at an interesting restaurant she knew. After a short cab ride, Dennis had found himself seated in the waiting area of a suite of editorial offices on the fourteenth floor of a downtown high-rise. Elizabeth had disappeared into the nearly deserted premises of the magazine, going over her article with her editor, who was working late.

This was the first of Dennis' many such waits for Elizabeth. Wherever they were bound, for whatever purposes, he often would be parked in some anteroom of a book publisher, newspaper, or arts organization, or in the cafeteria in the CBC building, while she negotiated some aspect of her freelance work. Often she would bring an editor or producer or administrator out to meet Dennis, if she thought the contact would be advantageous for his career.

Dennis felt embarrassed at shaking hands with men and women whose names and roles he quickly forgot. He tried gently at first, then more firmly, to discourage Elizabeth from the practice. "I know you're busy with deadlines and such that I don't have," he told her. "I don't mind killing time while you're in there meeting with these people. But please don't drag anybody out here to the waiting room and make me go through a 'shake-a-paw' routine. Half the editors or producers you introduce me to are the ones you tell me you hate working with, regard as incompetent manglers of your writing, and generally despise."

"When they meet you, you're no longer a name, but a person," Elizabeth responded. "That could be important for your fiction, down the road."

Dennis vehemently disagreed, but continued to politely converse on cue whenever Elizabeth reappeared with her latest selection of who he should be exposed to. Yet once the boredom of riffling through old issues of magazines was over, along with the intermittent stupidity of having to interact with people he would never set eyes on again, Dennis was delighted to be with Elizabeth. Those moments she turned the full force of her mind in his direction, he was lost in the appeal of her focussed interest in him, of her bright, quick intelligence, and in speculations about her alluring form: what making love with her might be like.

She seemed happy to show him her city. Their first time out she had taken him to a restaurant of a type he had not even known existed. The space was furnished with groupings of stuffed chairs, sofas, and low coffee tables. Patrons ordered and picked up their rather expensive meals at a counter, and ate with their plates on their laps, as though seated in someone's living room. On their second date, the following week, she led him to a restaurant whose tables were arranged far below an immense glass roof. They watched the sky darken into night as they ate and drank and chatted.

Now and then they went to parties at the apartments or houses of her friends. Here Dennis invariably encountered someone he had met at the Kaufflers'. To Dennis' surprise, the partygoer always acted pleased to see him. As at the Kaufflers', the talk at these gatherings was high-speed, ricocheting from the latest books and movies and television productions to insiders' gossip about corporate decisions and individual career moves at the city's book and magazine publishers, newspaper editorial departments, and the CBC or TV Ontario. Also offered for analysis were the love lives of people and couples Dennis didn't know. He mostly listened, and later queried Elizabeth for background information on the disastrous career manoeuvres, affairs, and domestic breakups that had been the mainstay of a party's conversation.

While Elizabeth was providing Dennis with an expanded knowledge of cultural and culinary Toronto, their hours together also had been his opportunity to learn much more about her. One Wednesday he idled in her living room before taking her for lunch, their fourth date. She was closeted in the extra bedroom she used as a study, finishing the final corrections to a book review the *Toronto Star* had commissioned. Restless, he began leafing through a copy of a London, Ontario literary quarterly that had topped a stack of magazines on her coffee table. In the quarterly were a group of three poems under her name. He read them attentively, impressed by their skill with language, surety of tone. Two were landscape pieces, and one was a sardonic farewell to a lover.

As they walked to lunch through the newly crisp fall weather, he began to question her about the poems. This first cool September day boasted summer-blue skies but with an autumn thinness to the light. The change of season had driven the squirrels along her street into a frenzy. With more than their normal energy, the creatures dashed through and over the piles of leaves Elizabeth's neighbours had raked.

All down the sidewalk, and throughout their meal of French onion soup and house salad at the Brown Cow, Elizabeth responded to Dennis' probing about her poetry: her models and compositional strategies, her other literary publications, and her plan eventually to assemble a first book of poems. He wanted to ask her who the poem about the lover referred to, but restricted his questions to professional issues. She kept their lunch fairly short; she had to begin setting up interviews for a 1000-word article she had successfully pitched to *Maclean's* on innovative educational toys that would be on sale at Christmas. When they returned to her apartment, before sending Dennis off, she printed out a dozen additional poems of hers for him to read at home.

Six of the poems, a suite which dealt with the heartbreak of a terminated romance, were unbearably poignant to Dennis. Thinking of Elizabeth's sprightly, enthusiastic engagement with the world, he found the concept of her being trampled emotionally by an oaf painful to endure. Dennis was effusive in his praise for her poetry when he next saw her, after she telephoned the following afternoon with an invitation to stroll in the Rosedale ravine park.

She accepted his compliments with only a few demurring comments, though he could tell she was flattered. They were drinking a cup of herbal tea at her kitchen table, preparatory to their walk. He had just praised her for her evocation of an image he had attempted in his own writing—light sparkling on the waves of a lake—that he felt she had handled much better than he. The reference reminded him she had never responded to his stories. He had presented her with a copy of *Who Are These People* on their first date.

To his amazement, her face clouded when he asked her directly what she thought of his writing. She hesitated a few seconds.

"In lots of ways your stories are lovely, Dennis," she began. "I like what you do with metaphors, and I laughed out loud a few times."

"Great."

Elizabeth took a breath. "But they also made me feel ... I felt ... so *mad* reading them." She shoved her chair back from the table, hoisted a foot booted in readiness for their outing, and slammed the sole into the wall a half-metre above the floor.

Dennis was amazed at her outburst. He stared at her, struggling to concoct a response. "What ... what about my fiction gave you—"

"There's no place for *women* in your stories," Elizabeth nearly shouted.

Differing emotions surged and collided in Dennis' stomach. He was momentarily nauseous. Remorse gripped him that he could have caused Elizabeth to be this upset. Opposing this sense of shame was a wave of indignation. His stories, he was convinced, *did* take women's lives into account. His ex, Angie, had berated him enough over the years about what she categorized as his reprehensible attitudes toward women. As a result, Dennis was ultracareful in everything he wrote concerning a female narrator or character.

Dennis broke the silence that echoed following Elizabeth's kick at the wall. Speaking as calmly as he could, he drew her attention to his story "Yesterday's Beans," in which the character Sally resolves everything in her favour and not that of the more reasonable-sounding boyfriend. "Furthermore, if you look at my story 'Petition For—'"

"I'm sorry, Dennis, I shouldn't have said what I did," Elizabeth interrupted. "It's just your women are always acted *upon*. They're never actors themselves. I don't mean to hurt your feelings. You asked me what I thought."

Dennis' head was whirling. "No, no. It's okay."

She leaned across and poured more tea into his cup. "In what you write, women never are fully realized *beings*, is what I mean. I hate that, because otherwise I think you're a *wonderful* writer. Technically, descriptively, in every other way, including the male characters, you've got so much going for you."

Dennis had tried not to be sulky as they deposited their cups in her sink, trooped down the stairs and out to the street. Her critique didn't seem fair to him. Not only because his writing *was* consciously aware of how it portrayed women. He also had been so laudatory about her scribblings. *Then she hands me this?* he thought. Yet it's probably to her credit, he reasoned, that she speaks her mind. Most women would simply go along with whatever man they were with, saying what they figured he wanted to hear. No question Elizabeth is one of a kind, he concluded. But maybe a kind that's better to admire from afar.

They had descended the zigzag trail to the bottom of the ravine, and started along the wider footpath there side by side. Suddenly Elizabeth reached over and took his hand. Dennis was surprised and thrilled by the soft pressure of her palm against his. Blood pounded in his head. He felt slightly dizzy at this implied promise of a physical aspect to their friendship. Yet tiny flickers of resentment continued to blaze in him: *she dumps on my work, and then thinks she can make it all better with a little hand-holding?* He knew, after his years with Angie, that he should not let a residue of anger at Elizabeth spoil this moment he ought to cherish. He reminded himself sternly that the intention of her gesture was to compensate for her words' effect on his ego. As they swung hand in hand along the path through the wooded valley, overtaken by joggers and passing slower strollers, his tenseness eased. At the end of the afternoon, back at the door to her apartment, they kissed goodbye for the first time.

Henceforth, this was the new dimension to their dates. They would hug briefly when Dennis showed up, and spend a little more time holding each other and kissing at the very end of the evening. Dennis realized he was unsure what Elizabeth expected or wanted in regard to initiating more intimate contact. Afraid of a misstep, he decided a cautious inaction was best, to see if she provided any clues as to what might occur next between them.

They continued to see each other two or three times a week. Plays, authors' readings, book launches, a movie, and sometimes in the afternoon, art galleries or museum exhibits. Dennis scoured the newspapers for events he might invite her to. Frequently she declined his ideas but proposed an alternative she said she planned to attend anyway. He didn't mind the change. Anywhere he went with her was new to him, stimulating.

One such suggestion of Elizabeth's had been a gallery opening at which Dennis initially met the arts columnist ensconced now inside Pasta-chio's with Elizabeth and Mr. Ed. Dennis had been in an ecstatic mood when he picked her up. A glowing feature on him had just appeared in *Pen & Platen*, a book industry trade monthly. Elizabeth was gratified, too: her relentless introducing of Dennis had led directly to the article, which would be read by hundreds of librarians and booksellers across the country.

Three weeks before, dropping off a review that *Pen & Platen* had asked her to write of six new first books of poetry, she had brought out her editor to meet Dennis. The woman had never heard of Dennis' collection. But she had been intrigued with what she learned of his origins in the West, plus his Governor-General's award nomination—which she was unaware of—and his current Canada Council grant. "We've been catching flak from some quarters about being too Ontario-biased," she mused. "Would you be willing, Dennis, if we assigned one of our freelancers to interview you? No promises. But if the piece is interesting, we'll probably use it right away." She smiled. "I'd ask Elizabeth to write it, but I have an idea that's a conflict of interest."

Dennis had subsequently spent an afternoon being asked questions by Debby, a friend of Elizabeth's and Simone's. Like Elizabeth, Debby wrote and published poems as well as scrabbling a living by freelancing. He had agreed to rendezvous with her at a Bloor Street café, Dooney's, that featured, besides the standard range of European coffee drinks, a selection of desserts: lavish helpings of various cream cheeses, tortes, chocolate-laden cakes, fruit pies, and enormous cookies. In

Dooney's the week before with Elizabeth, Dennis had been introduced to a couple of TV Ontario producers she knew who were seated at an adjoining table. She had also pointed out to Dennis the author of a series of short stories, about a suburban family, that was broadcast nationally on radio to a sizable and devoted audience. When Dennis the previous year had forced himself to read a published collection of these yarns, he had judged them terminally insipid in plot and character. But with the Toronto media types seated so close, he saved his airing of his opinion for when he and Elizabeth were en route back to her place.

Dennis enjoyed being interviewed by Debby. She was similar in build to Elizabeth, although with a more conventionally beautiful face, and fetchingly dressed in a tight white sweater and jeans. Her manner was more relaxed, more playful, too. Dennis flirted with her a little.

He managed to discover she intended to abandon freelancing soon to return to university for an advanced degree. "I just don't have Elizabeth's single-minded drive," Debby confessed. "I envy her, but I'm glad I'm not her." Dennis was fascinated by this perspective on Elizabeth. And from Debby's comments on the Toronto scene, Dennis ascertained she was less accepting than Elizabeth of the personalities who comprised it. Although Debby was born and raised in the city, her opinion was that too many of the "Toronto culturati," as she called them, had an unwarranted belief in their own importance. "Let's face it; they're not that great," Debby concluded. Dennis applauded her idea.

He found her very attractive, and guessed she also felt drawn toward him. He learned he could easily elicit her laughter, and idly wondered if she was involved with anybody. Yet as he rode the subway home, he decided she was probably a less substantial person than Elizabeth, lacking her depth of character as well as that unflinching resolve to succeed on Toronto's terms.

Dennis had brought the new issue of the magazine with Debby's interview to show Elizabeth when he arrived to accompany her to the art opening. But Debby had already dropped off a copy. Elizabeth teased him about his unbending resistance to the schmoozing process which in this case had paid dividends for him. They climbed the stairs to the gallery just off Queen Street West in mutual good humour.

As they had entered the glaringly track-lit space, Dennis heard Mr. Ed's horselaugh above the vibrant murmur of the crowd. After securing a glass of wine for Elizabeth and himself, Dennis made a rapid tour of the gallery walls. Elizabeth had attached herself immediately to one of the clusters of people speaking animatedly together near the centre of the room.

The paintings didn't do much for Dennis. They were composites of black-and-white photos of individuals and locations that looked like they had been torn from magazines, overpainted in part by streaks of colour that extended into empty areas of the canvas. Enigmatic phrases had been stencilled onto the pictures as well. SHE SPEAKS one artwork proclaimed above news photos of a guided missile battery, streaked with red and yellow paint. Underneath the photos read the cryptic phrase, BUT SHE DOESN'T ROW. The construction boasted a red sticker to indicate it had already been sold. Dennis angled forward to read the price: a third of his year-long Canada Council grant. He stepped back and re-examined the painting, searching for its appeal.

He gave up, and decided to locate Elizabeth. She was part of a group that included, to Dennis' dismay, both Mr. Ed and the less-than-friend-ly poet from Dennis' most recent dinner at Simone's and Paul's, Mark Gould. Wineglasses in hand, Gould and Elizabeth were deep in conver-sation about a Swedish poet unfamiliar to Dennis. Others around them were either listening, or absorbed in their own discussions. Dennis stood by patiently. Elizabeth and Gould eventually wound down, and Dennis was re-introduced to the poet and to Mr. Ed—who produced a succession of jovial snorted wheezes in recognition.

Elizabeth, Gould, Mr. Ed and some others were about to depart to inspect the gallery's offerings, and he was invited to accompany them. One of the men in the circle had, like Dennis, already done his duty. In a moment, the two faced each other alone.

"I'm glad to meet the man of the hour," Dennis' companion had sighed, extending his hand. They exchanged names. Dennis had recognized him from his picture in the *Star* over his three-times-a-week column on the arts. The face resembled Gould's in featuring a high-rise forehead. But whereas the poet's eyes were slitted with suspicion, the eyes looking at Dennis now were hooded with sorrow: a bloodhound's rather than a pit bull's. All the columnist needed was floppy ears,

Dennis decided, and his visage would resemble A.A. Milne's Eeyore, the perpetually gloomy donkey of the Christopher Robin series Dennis had had read to him as a child.

Although the man's column dealt mainly with twists and turns of federal and Ontario arts policy, his portion of the entertainment page occasionally reviewed books, theatre, dance performances or fine arts exhibits—invariably from the perspective of social utility. The writer was evidently the newspaper's token left-winger; Dennis had come to regard him as Mr. Red. Art was always to be in the service of humanity. As a critic, Mr. Red was dismissive of any experiment for form's sake or of any other difficult-to-interpret productions. Dennis silently cheered the column's occasional dismantling on political grounds of some widely praised fiction writers like Findley or Ondaatje or Munro. Nevertheless, Dennis was uneasily certain his own writing would be as savaged by Mr. Red should his stories ever be the subject of the column's scrutiny.

"Man of the hour?" Dennis had been modestly puzzled. "Oh, you mean the *Pen & Platen* article? That just—"

"*Pen & Platen?*"

"I thought you were referring to the profile in the current—"

"Did they do a squib on you? Congratulations. I assume it was their usual puff piece."

"Their interviews are usually...? I wasn't aware. I don't often get to see—"

"Of course. They're selling books, aren't they? Look who funds them. Actually, I was referring to your liaison, or whatever it is, with our Lizzy."

Dennis had never heard Elizabeth referred to by that name. Her personality seemed remote from his mental picture of a *Lizzy*. "You mean Elizabeth?"

"That's what she insists we call her these days," Mr. Red replied. "When I first met her, she was Lizzy. After she flamed out last year with that playwright, what was his name, Jonathan something, she insisted she would only respond to *Elizabeth*. We've all had to humour her."

"I didn't ever hear ... she didn't say...," Dennis stammered. His mind balked at how much of her history was a blank to him. "We haven't ... we're still getting to know one another."

"Don't get me wrong. It's to your credit she's interested in you. Jonathan Seagull, or whoever he was, won the Chalmers prize that year for his tedious two-acter about his navel. *You'll* probably win the Gee-Gee."

"No chance of that," Dennis said, recalling his dashed hopes the previous autumn. "I'm not even sure Elizabeth likes my stories. In fact, she's pretty scornful of some of them."

"She's probably just being PC. If she really didn't believe you were about to go places as a writer, she wouldn't spend a minute with you. We have a saying about our Lizzy: 'If *he's* hot, *she's* hot.'"

"She's been ... she's been involved with other men, I mean, other writers? Besides the playwright?" Dennis wanted to kick himself for appearing so naive.

Mr. Red sounded weary of the subject. "These are post-modern times, I'm told. Not just *men*. Do you remember the so-called critic, Valerie Post?"

"No," Dennis lied. He and Wayne used to chortle over Valerie Post's slash-and-burn approach to Canadian writing. For more than three years, her reviews and opinion pieces in the national edition of the *Globe and Mail* were always available to provide a contrary take on any famous-for-a-season or canonical Canadian novel or story collection. Contemporary poetry, she decreed, was beneath her dignity to assess. Dennis admired her refusal to endorse the received judgment of the literary media on the newest trendy writer, and of academia's enshrined national literary icons. But he had been rather intimidated by the breadth and depth of her literary references. English-born and educated, she was capable of providing examples of fiction from many national literatures and languages in aid of demolishing some rising Canadian talent.

"Valerie terrorized authors around Toronto," Mr. Red was explaining. "She didn't like anybody. Her wretched hatchet jobs flailed about in so many directions she was bound to hit somebody in the head." His expression brightened for a moment, then faded. "Last year she got religion. She disappeared to Arizona to save the world by sitting at the feet of the latest perfect spiritual master."

"You mentioned her in connection with Elizabeth," Dennis reminded the columnist. "Did she attack some of Elizabeth's writing?"

"Valerie and Lizzy were an item."

Dennis realized his face was flushed. "You ... you mean they...?"

"Only for a month or two. Of course, Lizzy wasn't much longer with that Jonathan ... uh ... Jonathan Duvall. I *think* his name was Duvall."

Dennis wondered if Mr. Red was pulling his leg about Elizabeth. She hardly seemed the type. Yet he'd read that women did sometimes experiment with other women. "No offence, but that's hard for me to believe. How do you know that she...?"

"Why don't you ask her?"

And, weeks later, after Elizabeth and Dennis had begun sleeping together, he did. Elizabeth gaped at him.

They had been lazing away a Sunday afternoon by cruising the crowded antiques market at the lake front. Elizabeth was vaguely searching for a birthday gift for Simone, who had started a collection of pre-World-War-I Ontario glass. He and Elizabeth had paused for a coffee at a small stand near the market, speculating why a person might want to acquire objects for which somebody else feels no attraction whatever. The conversation mutated toward people's secret desires, secret lives.

"He is *such* an old lady," Elizabeth declared, in response to Dennis' cautiously phrased query about Mr. Red's revelation.

"But *did* you?"

"I'm not sure it's any of your business. Any more than it is his. Have you ever slept with a man?"

"No. I haven't. And you don't have to answer my question. You're right; it's really no concern of mine. I just ... it's a facet of you that I.... Let's talk about something else."

Elizabeth took a pull from her latte. "It's not something to be ashamed of." She fiddled with the handle of her coffee cup. "Valerie and I had become fairly good friends. One night we had been to a reading of women's erotica. A women-only event. She asked if I had ever made love with a woman, and didn't I feel this was an experience I wanted to try? She said I owed it to myself as an emergent writer."

"I can understand that, I guess," Dennis said. "My ex, Angie, used to say men are so clueless about women's bodies, it's no wonder many women prefer to—"

"She should speak for herself," Elizabeth shot back. "I don't think you're clueless about *my* body. I like what we do together. No, this was something else." She hesitated. "Sort of, I don't know, an idea. That was in the air. Have you read the French critical theorists? Luce Irigaray?"

"Not her. Though I think I understand what—"

Her eyes blazed. "You *don't* understand. With Valerie, it was awful."

Dennis registered a sense of relief, though he wasn't sure if he should. "Awful?"

"She had false teeth." Elizabeth gave a self-deprecating laugh. "I know I'm terrible. I just can't *stand* anybody with missing parts. It's probably not right. But I'm totally repelled if a man has a toupee or a prosthetic limb. Or false teeth. She wanted to take them out when we.... You don't want the gory details. Believe me."

"No, no," Dennis hastened to assure her. "We've all had bad—"

"Not like this." Elizabeth gave a little shudder. "If I had any leanings in that direction, she was such a turnoff."

Dennis and Elizabeth had first made love on Hallowe'en. Her friend Janey, the television producer, had hosted a costume party. Elizabeth chose to go as a ballerina, "a childhood fantasy," she told Dennis. He decided to appear as Chewbacca, the bipedal lion-like creature from the *Star Wars* movie trilogy. "That'll make us beauty and the beast," Dennis had joked. The realization dawned on him during their discussion about costumes that Elizabeth had only the haziest idea who Chewbacca was. She said she had watched portions of the *Star Wars* movies, but had never managed to endure an entire one of them. "Science fiction just doesn't interest me," she shrugged. "I hate to use a cliché, but it must be a guy thing."

Dennis was glad to be behind the mask at the jammed and noisy party. Unlike his customary sense of being out of his element at social occasions he attended with Elizabeth, in his rented outfit he didn't care that he didn't know most of the people present. Two Darth Vaders wandered around, but he was the sole Wookiee. He did recognize Simone and Paul, since the effort they had made at disguises was minimal: Paul came as a cowboy and Simone wore an East Indian sari she had acquired on a trip to Nepal the couple had taken several years earlier. After identifying himself, Dennis chatted with them. He had brought along a straw and was able to drink without taking off the mask, congratulating himself on his forethought.

When dancing got underway in a room adjacent to the living room, he sought out Elizabeth and led her into the middle of the heaving and swaying pack of bodies. As Chewbacca he was expected to be clumsy, so for once Dennis wasn't self-conscious about his efforts on the dance floor. After two songs, Elizabeth headed back into the talk in the other room. Dennis stayed on. He started dancing by himself, but found himself joined by a succession of partners. One of them, wearing a Little Bo Peep dress and with a sheep mask, leaned close to him between songs and identified herself as Debby. She asked him how he liked the *Pen & Platen* interview.

"Awesome," he said. Then he remembered Mr. Red's comment on the publication's mission. "Is it true, though, *Pen & Platen* only runs positive articles?"

"What?" The music had started again.

"I was knocked out by your interview. Thank you for it." Dennis strained to be heard over the pounding rhythm. "Yet this guy I met told me the magazine only ever prints good stuff about authors."

"Not true," the sheep yelled. Conversation was obviously going to be difficult.

"How'd you know Chewbacca was me?" Dennis shouted.

"Elizabeth. She said you were a dancing fool."

"Say again?"

"Elizabeth said you were a dancing fool. Not in those words exactly."

He and Debby were partners through another song. Then more tunes. Dennis thought she moved with far more fluid grace than Elizabeth, who, despite her normal poise, tended to a jerky dance step. Finally, winded and sweaty inside his costume, and feeling guilty at his absence from Elizabeth, he explained to Debby he was going to take a break.

Elizabeth made room for him on the couch where she was talking with Simone and a person encased in what Dennis thought was a rat costume. The rat proved to be their hostess, Janey. During a lull in the conversation, he complimented her on her ratishness. Janey protested she was actually a squirrel. "See the bushy tail? What rat has a gorgeous tail like this?"

"Dennis has a thing about squirrels," Elizabeth said, her voice mischievous.

"Chewbacca *devours* squirrels. Gourmet item on the Wookiee planet," Dennis contributed.

Elizabeth, amid the others' laughter, reached for and held his hand.

When they returned to her apartment, she invited Dennis in for tea, as had become standard with them. They talked about the party; both had enjoyed it. Dennis slipped out of his costume and washed away some of the sweat from his arms and chest in her bathroom while the tea was steeping. At Elizabeth's suggestion, instead of drinking the tea at her kitchen table as usual, they shifted into the living room. They lowered themselves side by side on her couch, Dennis a little rattled by the change in routine.

Somehow they began kissing. After a time, his hands stroked along her legs and back, and then daringly near and then directly on her breasts. Half an hour later, after considerable exertions to discover how Elizabeth's ballerina costume was fastened, his fingers were travelling across bare skin in places.

Eventually Elizabeth murmured, "We should go into the bedroom." A fragmented conversation ensued as they ascertained both had tested negatively for AIDS since splitting up with their previous partners, and that Elizabeth was fitted with an IUD.

When they were naked, Dennis' kisses continued their exploration of her face. Elizabeth's expression was blissful as his lips landed everywhere across her forehead, nose, cheeks, before settling on her mouth again. Later his hands and tongue journeyed further afield. Her muscular thighs still bore evidence of her childhood successes as a gymnast. She had a repertoire of small squeals and groans of pleasure when his fingers or lips or tongue encountered particularly erogenous regions, protuberances, concavities.

He had penetrated her, and was submerged in rapturous sensations, when she suddenly announced, "Let's try it the other way."

"Huh?"

She scrambled up from underneath him, rotated and knelt, presenting herself to him. In a second he had entered her again and resumed thrusting. Her hand reached back and caught the shaft of his penis and directed it higher, placing the glans against her anus.

Dennis was stunned. Clearly she was requesting anal intercourse, which he had never attempted. Anxiety about his ability to properly proceed flooded through him. He ineffectually pushed forward a couple of times, and felt himself soften with nervousness.

"Wait," Elizabeth said. She disappeared off the bed into the bathroom, and returned with a jar of lubricant. She applied the contents to herself, then rubbed it on Dennis, stiffening him. When they resumed their former posture, he was able to ease a little distance inside her.

He tried to concentrate on the delight he was aware he should be feeling from this position. But his mind kept reviewing the little he had read about anal penetration. What had *The Joy of Sex* said about the source of women's pleasure, if any, during this act? When he pressed forward, Elizabeth let loose an unsettling wail that he was unable to interpret. Pain? Extreme gratification? Elizabeth's possession of the required lubricant meant, Dennis decided, that she was prepared for, used to, this type of intercourse. With whom? Dennis imagined her performing with other partners far more skilled than himself in such situations. If so, she was probably weighing his performance now and finding him deficient. And what about his coming, which he knew would be accompanied by vigorous motion? Was that the right or the wrong procedure in the anal approach?

Finally he withdrew, rapidly reinserted himself in more familiar territory, and brought matters to a conclusion. They toppled forward, and she lay in his arms for a few minutes. He rolled her over and kissed her face and breasts. Then, uncertain whether she had achieved orgasm, he applied himself manually between her legs. Her outcries indicated she reached a series of peaks of excitement, until her hand stopped his.

She rearranged their bodies for sleeping. She liked them back in a spoon configuration, with him on the outside, his palms flattening her breasts. When her even breathing indicated she was asleep, he removed his arm from beneath her. It was tingling from lack of circulation.

Being sexually intimate established a new pattern between them. Dates now meant sex at the end of the evening, most often at her apartment, although two or three times she had stayed over at his house-sit. They never talked about the sex they were engaged in. He tried to interpret her likes and dislikes from her responses, and she did not question him about his preferences. He became more adept at anal penetration, but had remained unsure about reaching climax in such a position and inevitably withdrew before that state had been reached.

Elizabeth behaved a little more tenderly toward him, taking his arm when they walked together, and providing an unexpected kiss outdoors or in. She opened up about her interior life: her considerable emotional distance from her parents in Winnipeg, where her father was the chief financial officer of an agri-marketing corporation that controlled a string of grain elevators. Elizabeth also described her worry about an older sister in Brandon who was dissatisfied with her marriage but unable either to end or repair the relationship.

For Dennis, inaugurating a sexual connection with Elizabeth raised questions about their future. Did he want to live with her, stay in Toronto, return with her to Vancouver? Marry her? She was now more desirable to him than ever: not simply sexually, though he cherished their activities in bed. Rather, he saw how she had opened a place for him in her fierce pursuit of her life. He was awed that a creature so energetic and determined would honour him in this manner. They still argued strongly about whether Dennis was using his literary gifts effectively, and taking maximum advantage of the opportunities Toronto provided. But once she had agreed to join him in the act of love, some vulnerability was permitted to be shown him.

He had penetrated her vagina from behind one evening, kneeling with his hands cupped on her shoulders while he pushed deep and then partially pulled back in an exquisitely slow rhythm. Suddenly she lifted her left hand up to caress his right hand. At the same time she twisted her body and neck enough that she could look back at him. Her expression so mingled delight and gratefulness that for a moment he was overwhelmed by a love for her as powerful and urgent as his desire. He came seconds afterwards with a shout. They collapsed sideways onto the bed; he held her close for a long while, wrapped in the bliss of a oneness with her. He couldn't speak. When their bodies had cooled enough, she wriggled free to pull a sheet over them. They resumed an embrace, and he said to her for the first time: "I love you." She kissed his face repeatedly, without words.

Such occurrences were contrasted, though, with incidents that reminded Dennis how emotionally distinct in many ways he and Elizabeth remained. In early December, he had been scheduled to read at a downtown library branch. The invitation had arrived the previous winter after Dennis' nomination for the Governor-General's prize, and Dennis had been elated. The library's reading series, held in a large auditorium that was part of a complex of municipal buildings, was regarded as prestigious, intermittently featuring international literary celebrities.

Elizabeth reminded him that she had never heard him read. "You sure you want to go?" he had asked. They were speaking on the phone from their respective houses one evening, comparing time commitments for the next few days. "You don't like my stories, remember."

"I never said that."

"I thought you told me there was no place for women in them?"

"Dennis, that doesn't mean I don't like them. Would you rather I didn't go? Is that it?"

"No, no." He could feel sweat forming on the skin over his ribs. "It's great that you want to be there. I just don't want you to have to listen to something you hate."

"I don't hate your stories."

"Okay, dislike."

"Dennis, if you don't want me to be there, just say so. I admire your work. I've never been to one of your readings. I thought it would be a nice idea."

"No, no. It is."

"You don't sound like you think so."

"I do. Should we go for dinner afterwards? I never eat too much before a reading."

"Alright. As long as you're sure my being there won't detract from your performance."

"The thing starts at 7:30. I can pick you up at 6:45," he offered.

"I'll meet you at the reading."

Elizabeth wasn't in the auditorium when he arrived, but he was early and only a handful of people were seated in the rows of chairs. Then he was swept up in introducing himself to his host, Elmer Berry, and arranging to have the copies of his books he had brought with him displayed for sale.

Berry proved to be everything Elizabeth had predicted. "Abrasive is his middle name," she had warned Dennis the day before his reading, while they ate lunch at a new café on Front Street she'd heard about. "He thinks he's God's gift to literature, whereas in fact he's a librarian who happens to run a reading series. He's tenacious about publicity. Over the years, he has gotten a lot of coverage for the readings he organizes. He confuses this with importance."

"Sounds as if you don't like him," Dennis had teased.

"I don't. Nobody does. But everybody is pleasant to his face, because they want to be invited to read there."

"I can't imagine you being pleasant to anybody you didn't like."

She stretched across the table and swatted him on the arm. "Oh, you."

"Just kidding."

She beamed at him. They held hands across the table.

"Anyhow," Dennis added, "I don't even know him and he invited me."

"He probably invited all the Governor-General nominees. That way he was covered: he invited the star, whoever won."

"Maybe. But, as you say, he sure generates publicity." Besides ads for Dennis' reading placed in the two Toronto dailies and a couple of weekly entertainment papers, he had been interviewed both by the local CBC radio station's arts program and by somebody from a technological institute's TV channel.

At the auditorium, Berry had wasted no time in deflecting Dennis' effusive praise for his promotion of the reading. "I'm the best at what I do," Berry stated. "Most people in the literary world are incompetent. I don't suffer fools."

The man was short and grotesquely overweight, as Elizabeth had indicated he would be. He rocked back and forth on his feet, his eyes measuring Dennis. "You have forty minutes, max. Not a second more. I've concluded that's all a reading audience can take. I hope you're not one of these *artistes* who, as soon as they get behind a microphone, lose the ability to tell time. Because if you are, I intervene pretty decisively to stop you."

"Your letter mentioned I'd have forty minutes to read," Dennis said mildly.

Berry swiped at his hairless head with a handkerchief. "As long as you know what the rules are."

"Definitely," Dennis replied. "And I want to thank you for inviting me. I appreciate it that you—"

"I don't consider you all that good a writer," Berry interrupted. "To be frank, I was dumbfounded when they nominated you for a Gee-Gee. Your endings are pretty weak, wouldn't you agree?"

Dennis was staggered that the man would insult a reader he had invited. "I ... uh ... To me, the ... uh ... closure strategies in my stories are—"

"You do have promise," Berry continued. "One of the obligations I've set myself is to make space in my reading series for people who might one day amount to something. My audiences should be exposed to authors like that, even if right now your writing doesn't cut it. You have forty minutes, remember."

Dennis had stood at the podium with his mind whirling. But the familiar passages of his stories he had chosen to read steadied him. Overall, he thought, his reading went very well. Berry's advertising had brought in a crowd: the room was nearly full. Dennis could see Elizabeth seated near the back.

He had tried not to be intimidated by Berry into checking his wristwatch too often while he spoke. After thirty-five minutes, he stopped reading in the middle of a scene, paraphrased the balance of that story's plot, and stepped away from the podium to the auditorium's applause. After the audience waited through a long announcement by Berry extolling the virtues of the next few writers set to appear, people had clustered around the book table. Dennis was kept busy making change and answering questions. The book buyers seemed to have responded favourably to the reading; Dennis basked in their appreciative comments. He glanced around for Elizabeth several times between book-signings. She was speaking to somebody near the rear doors of the room. At one point, Berry elbowed to the front of the clump of people at the table, and asked Dennis if he wanted to go for a drink.

Exuberant that Berry had witnessed the audience's keen interest in his writing, Dennis explained he had dinner plans with his girlfriend, Elizabeth. Maybe Berry could join them?

Berry asked for Elizabeth's last name. "Lizzy!" he said when Dennis told him. "Yeah, I noticed her here. I'll tell her we'll be a few minutes. You finish up."

Dennis was still radiant when he disentangled himself from the final book purchaser, an elderly woman who wanted to know if she could hire Dennis to write her memoirs. As gently as possible, he advised her he had several projects of his own in progress. She at last wandered off. Elizabeth was by this time standing talking to Berry, who efficiently flicked the auditorium lights out as they left.

Berry insisted they accompany him to a Portuguese tapas bar a couple of blocks over. Most of the meal he talked about himself: how a California-based Nobel laureate he had hosted had praised Berry's poems. He also mentioned a New York literary magazine that had been grateful to publish his writings, and a national arts prize he was about to receive in recognition of his years of organizing the library's readings. He also disparaged several established novelists and poets, his comments arising out of a recent stint on a City of Toronto book prize committee and on a couple of Canada Council literary juries.

Dennis, pleasantly drained by the reading and the scramble afterwards of meeting people and selling his book, was content to contribute the requisite approving monosyllables intended to communicate the awe due Berry for his accomplishments. Berry offered several suggestions to Dennis about how he might improve his writing skills and advance his career, all of which Dennis assured him he would consider.

Elizabeth tried to engage the rotund librarian in conversation, mildly challenging a few of his pronouncements on authors, books, and the path to literary success. Berry responded to many of Elizabeth's ideas by restating his own beliefs in a louder voice. Elizabeth would not concede, but she did not argue her opinion in the manner Dennis expected from his own past disagreements with her. Berry also continually addressed her as "Lizzy." She, every bit as determinedly, corrected him each time: "My name is Elizabeth." Dennis realized Berry was intent on needling her. Yet Dennis was uncertain how to intervene to end Berry's supposed forgetfulness about her preferred name.

Not long after their post-supper coffees had been brought, Elizabeth declared she had to be up early because of deadlines she faced the next day. Berry ostentatiously picked up the cheque, insisting he would arrange to have the library cover their meals. At the door to the restaurant they all shook hands, and Berry waddled off down the sidewalk toward the library.

He had travelled less than half a block when Elizabeth erupted. "That's the last, the absolute last time I ever go to a reading of yours." Dennis, worried Berry might have overheard, cast an anxious glance down the street.

Elizabeth caught his look. "Never mind about that fat, arrogant—"

"Shhh—"

"And don't tell me to be quiet. I came to your reading and you *completely* ignored me. Then we have to go out with that ridiculous, stupid, opinionated—"

"Look, I'm sorry the evening ended so badly. I didn't much want to eat with him either. But you're always saying I should make more of an effort to—"

"So this is *my* fault! He isn't the issue, anyway. You *ignored* me. We're supposed to be together and—"

"How did I ignore you?" They were striding toward the subway now. "You met me at the reading as we had agreed. I read, sold books, then Mr. Porky asked me if I wanted to go for a drink and I told him you and I had plans. We—"

"You treated me like I didn't count. Like I wasn't with you."

He desperately tried to review his behaviour over the evening. *Had* he slighted her? He couldn't think how, and said so.

Elizabeth raged at him, or was moodily silent, until they reached her place. They exchanged frosty goodnights, and on the subway home, his mind continued to churn through the sequence of events at the reading and after. A dark hypothesis formed: she was angry or jealous because, for once, he was the centre of attention rather than she when they were out in public in Toronto. He dismissed the concept as unfair to her, unworthy of their relationship. But he could not otherwise account for her reaction to the evening.

He phoned her the next day. Both of them were cautious and a little remorseful. She let him take her out for dinner and apologize repeatedly. She had returned to a more affectionate mood when they wound up back at her apartment. His lovemaking was less mindful of her responses than previously, a little rougher. She didn't appear to object.

But she had held fast to her promise not to attend another reading of his. After Christmas he was invited to replace an author who had cancelled out of an appearance at a bookstore in the Beaches district east of downtown. Elizabeth refused to accompany him, and they argued about the reasons for her stance. For a couple of days after this fight, he felt a little queasy each time he thought about the dispute. What kind of a partnership was it when one person won't support what is important to the other? How could he even think of living together, marriage, if she insisted she would never be present at any of his public performances as a writer?

In the end, he had decided her ability to identify and avoid problem areas between them was a strength, not a weakness, in their relationship. After all, he told himself, he might have had an old grandmother who loved him but who he wouldn't want at one of his readings because of the language and subject matter of some of his stories. Such a grandmother wouldn't love him the less because she didn't ever watch him perform.

And despite the edge to being involved with Elizabeth—that ability of hers to unexpectedly withhold her regard—he found joy in most of their times together. He especially delighted in their slow Sundays.

They would wake late in her double bed, since on Sunday Elizabeth permitted herself a respite from her freelance assignments. She brewed coffee and they would drink it while talking propped on pillows, after which they would make languorous love. When they got up, they ordinarily sauntered down to Bloor and Spadina, even in the slushy winter months, for bagels and eggs and more coffee at a favourite café. Elizabeth would buy a copy of the *New York Times*, and the rest of the day would pass in her living room as they pored over the paper's sections, stopping for lunch or sometimes a walk, depending on the weather and how energetic they decided they were.

The perusal of the *Times* was a new undertaking for Dennis; he had never read the publication before Elizabeth introduced him to it. If he was engrossed in a novel or somebody's collection of stories, he would skim the paper and return to his book. But Elizabeth frequently tore out articles that gave her story ideas to propose to her editors. And she wasn't the only one mining the *Times*. Dennis often recognized items or panel discussion topics on CBC Radio the following week based on features he had scanned at Elizabeth's.

These special Sundays, or occasionally a midweek candlelight dinner she cooked, were nevertheless only islands in a sea that could turn stormy without warning. Elizabeth was convinced Dennis ought to remain in Toronto over Christmas. She had been invited to a round of parties and at-homes and believed they should appear at them as a couple. He had planned to spend the holiday season back in Vancouver. Wayne had a spare bedroom where he could stay, and although the Christmas period was a frenzied time for Wayne at his store, Dennis intended to socialize with as many old friends as he could. He anticipated they would be eager to hear of his Toronto adventures; he had a mental list of amusing anecdotes to relate. On Christmas Eve he would take the bus to Vancouver Island, to visit his parents in Comox. His sister, settled now in Victoria, was going to drive up on Boxing Day with her husband and their four-year-old daughter.

Elizabeth was adamant that he should remain in Toronto. "Aren't we supposed to be going out? Don't you want to spend time with me during the holidays?"

"Of course I do," Dennis maintained. "These are plans I'd made long before we started seeing each other. I love you and want to be with you. We're talking ten days here."

During the week in December before Dennis left, the disagreement over his plans hung between them. Elizabeth had acted cooler toward him, her kisses more perfunctory except when they made love. After he flew to Vancouver, she was short with him when he phoned her, as he did every day. He had to prompt her to tell him about the status of a couple of articles she was writing, what else she had been doing, who she had run into. If, when he dialled, he connected with her voice mail, he always left a message assuring her he loved her and missed her.

Yet he was jubilant to be back in Vancouver. He delighted in the crisp sea air and the line of North Shore mountains already displaying winter's first coating of snow on their summits. He even gloried in four straight days of rain: a seasonal coastal storm. Walking through the downpour along West Broadway toward Wayne's store to meet him for lunch reawakened Dennis' happy memories of growing up in the city. He experienced a warm contentment at being out of the heavy rain, too, sitting snug and dry with his friends in a neighbourhood pub. He had a shared history of university or jobs with the people he phoned to arrange a rendezvous for meals or drinks. The hours exchanging talk with men and women who were not literary, although some of them read a little, were a relief to him. In the bars, he relaxed over pints of Granville Island Pale Ale, his old favourite. He and the others brought each other up to date on their lives, and reminisced about an overnight hike they made once to Garibaldi Provincial Park north of the city, or a mutual acquaintance who had endless trouble with his prized car, an ancient Jaguar. Conversation around the table included getting and keeping employment, incidents and troublesome personalities at the worksite, the vagaries and scandals of the province's political arena and labour movement. A couple of Dennis' friends recently had become active in the carpenters' union, running for election as vice-president and business agent, respectively. Dennis relished hearing again gossip about the back-room manoeuvring, personal shortcomings and career successes and failures in the BC trade union milieu.

When Dennis admitted he had begun a relationship with a woman in Toronto, he had been greeted with jeers and predictions that now he would never return when his grant was up, that he would be lost in the East forever. Dennis was troubled himself by that worry. He tried to imagine introducing Elizabeth to his circle in Vancouver. Except for Wayne, with whom she could talk about books and writing, he guessed she would have no time for the people he liked to hang out with. Few of the women he knew were serious about a particular career. Female friends, or women he had been introduced to as someone's girlfriend or partner, were usually ambivalent about their jobs. When they spoke, their conversational topics, like their ambitions, were vastly different from those of the women Elizabeth considered her peers. Among both genders in Dennis' circle, the topics readily described and debated were mainly, besides anecdotes related to employment, the sports they participated in or followed, television programs they admired or disliked, vacation travel plans and holiday memories, problems with parents or siblings, great deals obtained while shopping.

Dennis saw he spanned two worlds, and not just Toronto and Vancouver. In the West, he could pursue his writing without being as removed as he was in the East from ordinary working lives. The sphere he was increasingly integrated with in Toronto was more narrow in scope, even if many people who inhabited it exuded a self-confidence concerning their local or national importance.

Elizabeth would reject this view of her world, he acknowledged. But, back home, he was aware she would feel uncomfortable, out of her element, in his setting. He loved her, and, as he repeatedly assured her on the phone, longed to be with her. Yet he understood now that he also missed being included in a circle that encompassed many different personal solutions to life's puzzles. His daily interactions with his Vancouver friends he formerly had accepted without much reflection. Now he was not certain that gaining a permanent relationship with Elizabeth was worth losing the texture of daily existence that was available to him in Vancouver.

Wayne was unperturbed when Dennis had outlined his problem at Wayne's kitchen table one evening. They were savouring some blended Scotch after Wayne returned from his nine PM closing, worn out by a non-stop day of waiting on irritable Christmas shoppers.

"I have observed—" Wayne began.

"Boy, does that sound pompous."

"Shut up and drink. I have observed that bright young people in the arts, wherever in this great country of ours they live, youngsters like you—"

"You're younger than I am."

"But wiser, much wiser," Wayne continued. "Now, listen. Once you young people have achieved in the arts, even if what you have done is only an indication of potential, you are visited with an overwhelming urge to go to Toronto. It's biological, or something."

"Biological?"

Wayne clambered to his feet, and carried Dennis' empty glass and his own to the counter for a refill. "It's biological," he affirmed. "Like salmon heading upstream to mate and die. At least, in this country it's biological. If you're good in the arts, you have to go to Toronto."

"Biology is destiny, is that what you're saying?"

"Say what?"

"You know, Wayne, despite yourself, you might be onto something. Lots of the people I met in TO who are movers and shakers are not from there. Even Elizabeth is from Winnipeg. Went to U of M before—"

Wayne stood beside the table clutching two fresh Scotch on the rocks. "You, Dennis, are confronting the standard dilemma of this migration of talent. Should you go home again? Or should you stay? The fact that you've gotten tangled up with a fast Toronto woman just puts a human face on the question."

"A good-looking face, too. Wish I'd thought to bring a photo. She resembles—"

Wayne sat and handed Dennis a glass. "Mere details. What you have to concentrate on resolving is: what happens to you if you stay? What happens if you come home?"

"I know, I know," Dennis muttered, staring down into his glass as he listlessly swished his drink around its container. "I'm chewing over exactly those questions."

"Consider this, then: are people better writers in Toronto?"

"Better writers?"

"That's what I asked. Are they more accomplished than writers anyplace else in the country."

"They're more famous."

"Not the same thing. Are they better?"

"No. And, you're right: some of the most famous are the least deserving, by any objective—"

"Would you say *you* write better in Toronto than here?"

Dennis mentally reviewed his output during the fall. Two stories completed to his satisfaction, and two others drafted, although one of these revealed more weaknesses in characterization every time he reread it. "I'm not sure. I think I've been writing okay there. But when I read something three or four months later, I notice that—"

Wayne had aimed a forefinger at Dennis. "Just answer the question, Mr. Benson. Is there any evidence you write better in Toronto?"

"No ... Not really."

"Bingo."

"Bingo?"

"Bingo. Toronto is just the place you go after you've accomplished something elsewhere. It's the Afterlife, for poor schmucks like you. People say the Afterlife is either Heaven or Hell. I don't believe that. I favour the Greek idea: Limbo. Grey shades drifting around bumping into each other. They may be noisy shades, or shades with a ludicrously exaggerated sense of themselves. Some may even tell you they appreciate the scene or the scenery in Limbo. But most souls, given a choice, would rather be alive: be safely back where they came from, no matter how out of the limelight."

Dennis had admitted Wayne's notion might contain a germ of truth. But Dennis also had to account for his strong feelings for Elizabeth. When, on his return to Toronto, he caught sight of her again in the open doorway of her apartment, smiling at him, eyes alight, he was aware how intensely he loved her, loved the firm body he wrapped his arms around as though he would hug her forever. She seemed a little bemused by the energy of his devotion. They resumed the patterns of their pre-Christmas life as if he had never been away.

Yet eventually he had to insinuate into a conversation, with as much casualness as he could, that he would be returning to Vancouver in February to give a number of readings. Anticipating an uncomfortable scene, he had delayed informing Elizabeth until his departure date was only a couple of weeks off. A day of sunshine had interrupted the overcast winter weather, and he and Elizabeth had hiked down the Moore Park ravine toward the woods around the old Don Valley brickworks. The warmer January afternoon had brought the squirrels out of hibernation, and they were darting over mounds of snow at the feet of the barren trees, searching for their caches of food.

Dennis had stressed that his impending trip was, like his Christmas excursion, pre-arranged before he moved east. Besides two readings, he had lined up a four-day writer-in-residency at Douglas College in New Westminster, where he would meet with students individually, appear in classes to read, and offer a talk at a symposium.

Elizabeth had trudged on in silence when he finished. They were traversing a slushy section of the trail: other pedestrians before them had trampled a path, now melting in the bright day. But the route here was single file. He had addressed most of his explanation to the back of Elizabeth's coat.

They paced forward. All at once she stopped and spun about, face tight. "Sooner or later you're going to have to choose: Vancouver, or me."

Blood rushed to his cheeks. "What do you mean?"

"You're not back three weeks and already you're off again."

"I told you. These are obligations I'd taken on before I even met you."

"How is it you never mentioned them before?"

Dennis stared at a bridge that lifted a surface street across the ravine in the distance. He shifted his gaze once more to where her small form bristled. "I guess I was a little afraid of you, after what we went through at Christmas."

"Hah."

"If I had to go to Montreal, or to Hamilton, to give readings, you wouldn't be upset. You'd be pleased."

"I would?"

"This is good for my career. You're always urging me to meet this person or that because it'll be good for my—"

"I don't think this is about readings, or your career, Dennis. I think this is about Vancouver."

"Vancouver? This was planned—"

"You told me how much you liked being back at Christmas. Now you're heading out there again."

He tried to keep the exasperation out of his voice. "I promised way last *spring* to do these readings. Do you want me to cancel them now? Why is it so wrong for me to go?"

She reached out and tugged at a waist-high tuft of dried grass that rose from a snowbank. "Dennis, in a few months you have to give up your house here. What are you going to do?"

"What? I've got until *June*. That's *five* more months."

"Okay, five months. But then are you ... are you going to find another place to live?"

"In Toronto?"

"Yes. Or are you moving back west?"

"I ... uh ..."

"I need to know where I fit in your plans, Dennis."

His eyes scanned the high ravine banks on either side, covered with clumps of lifeless trees. He felt caught, blocked, confined. "I ... I love you, Elizabeth. But I...."

"Yes?"

His qualms about the future weighted his tongue. The heavy organ in his mouth was suddenly difficult to budge, to shift into the shapes necessary to produce the sounds of words. "I ... uh ... I ... I'm not sure ... what the right thing for me to do is. I know I love you. I hadn't really thought ... thought a whole lot further than that. I ... We ... Maybe we have to talk about some of this."

"We certainly do."

They stood rigidly, staring at each other, until she relented, stepped forward and embraced him. "I care for you, Dennis," she said as he relievedly hugged her in return. "I don't mean to make your life a misery."

"You don't ... make my life a misery. I love you. I—" The swirl of emotion choked his throat.

"I wonder what's going to happen to us, is all," she stated.

As at Christmas, Elizabeth made no secret of her disapproval of his impending absence during the time immediately before he left. In the cabin of the westbound jet, Dennis had tried to concentrate on sorting out the future he wanted. He removed a pad of paper from his carry-on bag, intending to list pros and cons of staying in Toronto, an exercise he had been ordering himself for days to undertake but had postponed repeatedly. He had duly inscribed his categories' titles on the pad when the in-flight movie screens descended. His evaluation project was temporarily put aside; the scheduled film was one he had always meant to catch. He knew he'd have plenty of downtime during the balance of the trip to focus on the issue.

Two days later, when he had made his daily call to Elizabeth, she told him she couldn't talk long. "Mark's here."

"Mark?" His mind had gone blank.

"Mark Gould."

"Oh yeah, the poet of sweetness and light. What's he doing there?"

"He stopped by. I really can't speak now. We'll talk tomorrow."

Other phone conversations with her during Christmas had been nearly as brief if one of her friends was over for tea or for supper. But Dennis had regarded the poet and his wife as only remote acquaintances of Elizabeth's. He could not recollect her speaking about them much, except after he and Elizabeth had bumped into them at literary occasions or parties. In dismissing his present call, her voice had an extra brusque quality that he also could not remember.

The next day, she explained. "Mark was pretty upset. I didn't want to leave him alone for more than a minute."

"Upset?"

"You're not to tell this to anyone. Cindy wants a divorce."

"I'm not surprised. He's not the most charming person I've met."

"You have to keep this secret. About him and Cindy. No one else knows. All this is happening right when Mark's new book is coming out. They're launching it in Guelph on the weekend, and in Toronto on Tuesday."

"Guelph?" Dennis' mind was on a more significant question he wanted to pose.

"Mark is writer-in-residence at Guelph this year. You know that."

"But—" Dennis' mouth produced the question before he could stop it "—why was Mark over to see *you*?"

"He was upset, as I said."

"But of all the people he must know, why you? I wasn't aware you guys were such friends. Doesn't he have other ... closer ... people that he—"

"I've been friends with Mark and his wife for years," Elizabeth said quickly. "I'm flattered he sought me out. Remember, this is a *secret*, though. Cindy and he have had their troubles for quite a while. It's finally come to a head."

*If she and the Goulds are such longstanding friends, how is it in the time I've known her she's scarcely mentioned them?* Dennis thought. He kept the question to himself. "I don't run with anybody in Vancouver who even knows who Mark Gould is. Or cares. Why is it such a secret?"

"I'm not sure. But Mark asked me to keep it quiet, and I respect that. I probably shouldn't even have told you. I think it's got to do with their families."

That Friday, when Dennis phoned, Elizabeth said she was going to Guelph the next day for the launch of Gould's new book, so she wouldn't be home until late. Because of the three-hour time difference she could still call Dennis, but likely she'd be tired out from the trip. They would talk on Sunday.

He responded with anger. "I thought you said there was a Toronto launch next week."

"There is. On Tuesday." Dennis thought he heard a defensive note, something he had never detected in her voice before. "Mark asked me to go to the one in Guelph. He's really emotional about Cindy leaving. He said he wanted at least one friendly face at the Guelph launch."

"Let me get this straight. You won't go to any reading of *mine*. But instead of simply going downtown Tuesday to support poor Mark, you're travelling all the way to Guelph."

"Guelph isn't far," Elizabeth flared back at him. "An hour on the bus, less by train. You're mixing up two wildly different things. You and I are in a *relationship*. That affects certain things we do. This Guelph trip is just a request from a friend for help, help I can give."

"If I asked you to attend another reading of mine because it would *help* me, would you do it?"

"That's ridiculous," Elizabeth hissed. "I'm not going to keep talking to you if you're going to be so selfish. A person I know, a friend of mine, is in trouble. If I can help him, I will."

Dennis didn't attempt to hide the disapproval in his voice. "Alright. Have it your way."

"I most certainly will."

When they next spoke, on Sunday, Dennis had asked how the launch had gone. "Fine. Great, in fact. Lots of students were there. Faculty, too. Everybody was very complimentary and Mark sold out the books he had. Thirty-five of them."

Dennis couldn't resist. "You didn't feel neglected?"

"Dennis, don't talk like that."

"Okay, okay. So what time did you get back last night?"

Her voice rang strange to him, meek. "I... I came back this morning, actually. There was a reception for Mark after the reading. By the time that was done I'd ... missed the last train. I didn't feel like taking the late bus, so I stayed overnight. I caught a ride back with Mark today."

Dennis was aware of a clammy sensation across his face. His mind sketched and rejected the unthinkable. "Did you—" he tried to keep his speech jaunty "—pick up any juicy details on the divorce?"

"I can't talk now, Dennis." Her voice was unusually low. "Mark is here."

The penny dropped for Dennis. "Oh. I see." Silence flowed down the line. His legs felt quivery. He didn't trust himself to continue to produce normal-sounding conversation. He also experienced an urgent need not to communicate that what she had just revealed had affected him. "Uh ... uh, goodbye."

"Goodbye, Dennis. We'll talk tomorrow." He thought he perceived relief in her tone.

Dennis was awake much of the night, debating whether he had inferred correctly that she had started an affair with Gould. His mind had ricocheted between a resolve not to call her the next day, or ever, and a wish to have what he feared confirmed. Or declared false. The next morning was a blur. His body ached, but he cheered himself in the afternoon with a brisk walk around the Stanley Park seawall, pacing through a light drizzle. He both yearned to phone Elizabeth and at the same time was determined not to make the first move to reestablish contact. He would fly back to Toronto when his last obligation in Vancouver was fulfilled, concentrate on his writing, have no communication with her, and return to Vancouver in June as originally planned.

On Tuesday, while Dennis was en route from Wayne's to an ATM to replenish his cash, Elizabeth phoned. He read her name and number on his cell's call display, and didn't answer. After listening to her short message, he went into a coffee shop, and thought about what best to do while he sipped a cappuccino. He had walked outside and punched in the numbers.

Their conversation had been strained, punctuated with immense empty moments. She wanted to know why he hadn't been in touch the day before. He told her he and Wayne had been out socializing. She accepted his explanation, although he guessed she was aware he had lied.

She asked what he had been up to. Their pattern had been the reverse: he inquiring about her days, and she questioning him about his Vancouver doings, if at all, only as an afterthought, late in the exchange. Now he was abrupt in reply. "Not much. How about you?" He couldn't keep a sarcastic edge out of his voice.

"Dennis, we need to talk."

He took a deep breath. "We'll talk when I get back. It's less than a week now. I think I do better with you in person."

"If that's what you want."

"Yes, it is." He hoped she'd counter with a firm denial of the conclusion they both knew he had jumped to with regard to Gould. He wanted her to tell him he was being silly in breaking off contact, that he was acting petulant, that she was firm in her commitment to him.

"So you'll phone when you get back?" she asked. Her voice had gone meek again.

"Yes."

"Promise?"

"Yes."

"I love you, Dennis."

He was astounded by her utterance. She had never before directly stated this. "I ... I love you, too, Elizabeth. I—" In spite of himself, his voice failed.

"We'll talk soon," she said hurriedly. "'Bye."

"Goodbye."

His plane from Vancouver had arrived in the late afternoon, local time, and discarding his resolve not to call her until the next morning, he spoke with her as soon as he completed a quick grocery shopping. She informed him that tonight was not a good evening for them to meet, but they should get together for dinner the following day. He agreed and hung up. His body was numb.

After a largely sleepless night, his head felt dizzy all day. He tried to resume work on a story he had been crafting before he left for Vancouver. The tale was an end-of-innocence account of a girl's visit to a mall, where she experiences a not-yet-specified example of evil. At two o'clock he gave up, and went for an extended walk through the neighbourhood.

When he met Elizabeth at her apartment, her face displayed a grim determination. She had kissed him hello, however. His response had been wooden.

During supper at a Malaysian-Thai restaurant they both liked, she had spelled it out to him. She assured Dennis she loved him very much. But she and Mark had become lovers.

Dennis felt the table swirl, and tilt away from him. Despite his earlier suspicion, even assumption, that Elizabeth had begun something with Gould, hearing her acknowledge the event conferred a finality on her betrayal. He grabbed for the edge of the table to steady it. Around him the cheerful clatter of eating utensils and conversation pulsed louder and quieter and louder again, like waves striking a shore.

"How did you...? What were...?" he managed.

"Let me finish," she commanded. She had always admired Mark, but she had no idea, due to his outwardly caustic personality, he was taken with her, too. He was so sweet and vulnerable when he showed up at her apartment after Cindy announced she was leaving and taking the kids.

Dennis winced at the word *sweet*. "But that didn't mean you and he had to—"

"It just happened." She was blushing, Dennis noticed. "He ... needed me."

"I need you, too." Nullifying a wish to conceal his reaction, his tone was whiny.

"You *don't*," Elizabeth snapped. "You've got your writing and you've got Vancouver. I'm only a diversion. A girl in every port, that's you, Dennis."

"That's not true," he protested. "I've never even thought about—"

"You're right." She took two deep breaths. "I'm trying to stay calm. This is hard for me, too."

"Not as hard as it is for me."

She did not respond. Dennis clutched at what floated past. "Isn't he a lot older than us?"

"He's *five* years older, thirty-four," she barked. She breathed again a few times. Then, her voice more subdued, she continued: "Things aren't all that clear with Mark. Cindy has made the grand gesture. But couples like them who have been together for years often take a long time to really separate. Especially when there's kids."

Her words reached Dennis through the throbbing clamour of the restaurant. He sensed at this moment she was talking to herself as well as to him.

"People aren't all that stable at times like this," she went on. "I know I wasn't when Alan and I split up. I thought I was totally in control and making rational decisions. I look back now and realize I was more or less mad." She uttered a brief, self-deprecating laugh.

Dennis recalled with a start that Elizabeth had been married before. She seemed so young, so fresh to him that he had put out of his mind that she had made an early marriage. What had she said about her and Alan's divorce? Dennis knew she and he had discussed it when they were comparing past relationships. The separation had not been her idea, he remembered. Had she said Alan had begun an affair?

Elizabeth was still talking. "A couple can also reconcile and decide to work on their differences." She breathed deeply. "Probably becoming lovers with Mark so fast was not very bright. I know Simone thinks it wasn't."

A wispy tendril of hope had broken out of black soil within Dennis. Simultaneously, a weed-like shoot of resentment sprang up. How could she have already discussed with Simone what she had done, what affected him, what reduced him to the pitiful status of rejected suitor?

Elizabeth was smiling at him now. "Simone considers me crazy to risk losing you, Dennis. She regards you as excellent husband potential. She's one of your biggest fans."

He attempted to humorously elevate his diction. "I have always considered Simone to be a young woman of uncommon good sense."

"Me, too." Elizabeth was grinning at him. Then the grin faded. "Here's what I'd like us to do."

Dennis immediately noted her use of the word *us*. Maybe they weren't through as a couple? They were interrupted by the arrival of a waiter flourishing their meals: a Singapore chicken salad for Dennis and a satay concoction for Elizabeth. Dennis automatically lifted a forkful to his .mouth. The peanutty chicken and lettuce leaves tasted like sawdust. He put his fork down. She took a sip of water. Neither of them had touched the glass of house white they each had ordered.

Elizabeth looked intently at Dennis. "I want to continue seeing both of you." She breathed out.

Dennis' mind stalled. "Both?"

"I love you, Dennis. But I'm also tremendously attracted to Mark. I'm asking that we give the situation time."

Dennis' hands played with his cutlery on the tablecloth. His fingers were shaking. He was aware of blood hammering at his temples. He absently rubbed at them. Then he returned to arranging and rearranging his knife, fork, spoon.

Elizabeth's hand reached across the space between them and touched his forearm. Her face looked anguished.

"Oh, Dennis," she whispered. In a moment she was out of her seat, and around the table, kneeling by his chair. She put her arms around his waist and hugged his torso to her. He looked down at the top of her hair. He felt like crying.

"I'm so sorry," Elizabeth mumbled, her face pushed against his side. "I'm so, so sorry."

His voice wasn't there. Then some of it was. "Me, too."

She looked up at him. Her arm rose and she brushed water from under his eyes. "Let's go home."

She stood up. "Come." She tugged on his arm.

His legs were trembling but they lifted him. He reflexively reached for his wallet, but she stopped his arm. "My treat," she said. This, too, was a departure from their custom. He paid for their meals out, in return, they had agreed, for the meals she cooked for them at her place.

Her arm around his waist, she guided him to the door. His body was heavier than it ever had been: he was a hard-hat diver, festooned with lead weights, lurching step after step along the ocean floor that was Bloor Street.

She helped him navigate the stairs to her apartment, and through her hallway to the bedroom. He undressed mechanically. Naked, they kissed for a long time. Each in turn cried while the other held and caressed and whispered to them about how much they were adored. Finally, they made love. Some time after they both had climaxed and Dennis was stroking the softness of her skin, he fell asleep. Then the room was washed by February morning sunlight.

But he awoke into a new world. Despite her tenderness the night before, her request stood. She wanted to be lovers with both of them. He knew the next move was his. He had asked for a day to decide. Yet his mind veered from the puzzle as though from comprehending the origins of the universe. His brain invariably froze at trying to assimilate the concept that everything once had been compressed infinitesimally, and that this speck was itself all that could ever exist and was not a particle that floated within some larger entity.

Back at his house, Dennis sat at his desk. Dust and crumbs had sifted between the keys of his keyboard, and the moment seemed opportune to remove the accumulated material. Wayne would advise him to cut his losses; he was certain of that. He couldn't think who else he could seek counsel from. Simone was as much Elizabeth's friend as his, and he had the impression anything he said to Simone would eventually be relayed to Elizabeth's ears.

If he did nothing, the dilemma would resolve itself either in his favour or Gould's. If he broke off with Elizabeth now, she was Gould's. On the other hand, he remained unsure of the future he wanted with Elizabeth, assuming he won her, and if living with her meant abandoning Vancouver. Of course, he had never asked her directly if she would relocate with him. To terminate their relationship would curtail that possibility, remote as it was.

Thus he had chosen inertia. He would continue on and evaluate what occurred. Elizabeth heard the news without evident emotion, although she said she was glad.

Arrangements to meet each other, however, became much more complex. Besides her work, there was his rival. Gould had his apartment in Guelph, but his wife kept their Toronto home. Whenever he was in the big city to visit his children, he stayed at Elizabeth's.

Often when Dennis suggested he and Elizabeth take in a play or movie, he would be informed she had already been to it with Gould. Yet, as previously, she invited Dennis to parties hosted by her friends, and to gallery openings and museum shows she was interested in. The lazy Sunday mornings with her that Dennis so treasured were still available to him, if not so often. He had decided not to ask her anything about Gould, about the state of Gould's and Elizabeth's connection or about the poet's with his wife. Sometimes he gleaned data from Elizabeth during the process of scheduling time together. She was free to meet Dennis on a Wednesday night because Mark had to cancel a date; he had consented to a session with Cindy and a relationship counsellor. Dennis was elated. Elizabeth couldn't go out with Dennis at all this coming weekend because Mark had invited her to his parents' cottage near Haliburton. Dennis was dejected.

Yet when he was with Elizabeth, she behaved as lovingly toward him as before. Her affection was no less subject to sudden wrath, though, if some behaviour of his displeased her. He had read Gould's new book of poems, and judged the content pathetic. Most poems were bald statements formed of chopped-up prose, without visible artifice. The gist of many of them was how much more intelligent the narrator was than the losers he encountered, how much more filled he was with decent impulses or environmental awareness or historical perspective. A series of love poems labelled "To Cindy" focussed entirely on the beloved's effect on the oh-so-sensitive speaker in the poetry. They could have been addressed to anyone.

Elizabeth was livid when he critiqued Gould's collection. In the course of their ensuing argument, he had tried to appeal to her own skill as a poet. "You're talking about my lover," she had lashed out when he had suggested that the prevailing ambience of the poems indicated a lack of emotional engagement with other people.

Their disagreements were not more numerous than they had been. But for Dennis the shadow of Elizabeth's dual attachment now hovered over their fights. As the weeks passed, her frustration with negotiating the terrain all three of them now inhabited became more evident.

"Neither of you really wants to commit to me," she raged at Dennis in the midst of a dispute that began with him complaining about how much more of her time she was allotting to Gould than to him. "Each of you has a backup. He's got Cindy and you've got Vancouver. How do you think that makes me feel?"

Some of the details of manoeuvring among two relationships Dennis found humiliating. He became aware from Elizabeth's offhand comments about her activities with Gould that the poet was now driving an old Nissan light pickup. Cindy had retained the family van for chauffeuring the children. The pickup had twice proven problematic on trips Elizabeth and Gould had made: once on a return from Guelph and once headed to the Haliburton cottage. Walking along Kendal Avenue to meet Elizabeth on a blustery March afternoon, Dennis had been stunned to observe such a vehicle parked by the curb outside her place. Had he mistaken their agreed-upon day or time? Maybe the vehicle wasn't Gould's. He peered in the cab. A paperback of a recent Atwood novel was cracked open face down on the passenger's seat. Many people read her books, of course. On the dash were a number of faded envelopes. Bending closer, Dennis could determine they included a bulk-mailed credit card application, and subscription solicitations for the *Times Literary Supplement* and *Maclean's*. He could read the addressee on a couple of them: "Joseph Mark Gould."

He doubled back to Bloor Street and called Elizabeth on his cell.

The date and hour for their meeting were indeed correct. Mark had left his truck with her while he flew out to Edmonton for a reading. Dennis retraced his steps to her door.

The arrival of Toronto's spring, interrupted only by a freak snowstorm in mid-April, changed nothing between the three of them. Gould was as vacillating as ever about his marriage. Dennis had finally seized his chance and asked Elizabeth if she would consider moving to Vancouver. He was at pains to qualify the question as a hypothetical one, since, as he stressed, he was aware that at the moment she was involved with somebody else besides him.

Her answer was as expected. Her life was in Toronto. This was where she had the contacts that enabled her to function as a freelance writer. Her friends were here.

Wayne had observed during a phone call that Elizabeth's confirmation of what Dennis had predicted didn't clarify much. "In a couple of months you've got to give up your house. Before she got involved with that idiot—"

"That *other* idiot, you mean," Dennis said ruefully.

"Okay, that other idiot. Your problem was simply whether to find another place and carry on with Elizabeth, or return home to sanity and the bosom of your friends."

"She has nicer bosoms than any of you."

"I'll take your word for it. Now, though, if you rent a place in TO, you can't even be sure you'll achieve your only purpose for staying. You could decide to hang in, she could select Mr. Poet as her eternal love, and, bam: you're a million miles from civilization for no discernible reason. In any case, how are you going to live? What kind of job can you get? And how soon does your grant expire? September?"

Dennis' writing had continued to be an uphill effort. His mind wandered off from any difficulty with a paragraph to reexamine yet again what his best course of action should be. He scheduled dates with Elizabeth, and tried not to dwell on what she was doing when she was unavailable. Twice he leafed through the apartments-for-rent section of the *Star*, but went no further.

He thought of calling Simone to ask if she had any insider's advice concerning jobs she thought he might be suited for. But once more he feared this request would wend its way to Elizabeth. He did not want her to know if he resolved to take concrete steps to remain in the city. She avoided questioning him about his future plans, and he did not broach the subject. Withholding information from her had begun to represent his only means to have some control over his predicament. Every other decision was in her hands. A few times when she phoned to ask if he wanted to meet for dinner, he was tempted to tell her he was busy that night. To be inexplicably unavailable. But he sensed she would recognize his claim as a transparent ploy. Also, if he rejected her invitation, that would be one less period of time to spend with her.

He knew he was drifting. Yet when all was smooth between them, he loved their talk together, their exploration of ideas and art and music and writing. He loved walking with her, eating with her, entering a party or a bookshop or a museum together. He loved them together in bed. He hated the threatening cloud of her relationship with Gould that darkened the hours during which he was permitted to be with her.

Then, on the patio at Pasta-chio's, their first time eating outside that year, she had announced: "I have to tell you what I think you'll want to hear. I don't want you to read more into this than what I say. But I want to say it."

"How mysterious," he had kidded her, but he saw in her face the solemnity that he thoroughly understood by now indicated he was not to trifle with what she was about to declare.

She had told him that, as he knew, she had driven with Mark on the weekend to the cottage at Haliburton. But she had a terrible time. Mark's constant mockery of everything and everybody finally got to her. They had quarrelled. Of course, they had often fought and reconciled, but this was another level of conflict. In some town en route back to Toronto, when they stopped for gas she had refused to travel any further with him. There had been a scene at the service station. He had thrown her suitcase out of the pickup bed and peeled off, leaving her stranded. She had been forced to take the bus back to the city.

Dennis realized he was tense, hardly breathing as he listened to her. "Sounds serious. Were you all right?"

"Getting dumped in Minden isn't the important thing—" she continued.

"It's not? I figure that—"

"Will you *listen?* The important thing is that all weekend I was only thinking about you. I was wishing I was with you. That never happened before. I wanted to be with you. Not him."

Dennis was unable to speak. He felt a grin expand across his face.

She mock-scowled, and wagged a finger toward him. "Don't get any big ideas," she cautioned, her tone jocular. "I'm not saying it's significant. It's just what happened."

Dennis found his voice. "Okay, it's not significant. I think it's pretty wonderful, though. I think *you're* pretty wonderful."

She beamed at him. Jubilation surged through his body. He had made the right choice, after all: he had persevered, and he had won. Or as good as. Things at least were going his way. "There must have been *something* positive about the weekend," he teased.

"I got ideas for a couple of poems," she laughed.

"I'll bet," he said. They held hands across the table and talked about her writing for a while, and how his latest story was unfolding. Then she had wanted to speak with Mr. Ed and Mr. Red inside the café.

Basking in the resurrected afterglow of Elizabeth's account of her weekend, Dennis caught in his peripheral vision a motion along the restaurant's patio tiles. One of the boulevard squirrels, more brazen than the others, twitched nearer and nearer to a couple of French-fried potatoes evidently fallen from the plate of a previous occupant of Dennis' table. The food debris was less than half a metre from Dennis' right shoe.

The rodent peered up at Dennis and their eyes met for a second. The squirrel hastily retreated to the patio edge and paused, before restarting its spasmodic advance toward its goal. Every few steps it would appraise Dennis, appraise the intended meal, consider, and forge on. The animal evidently was attempting to balance the threat of Dennis' presence against the lure of the edibles under the table.

The creature reached to within a metre of its objective, before again precipitously withdrawing. On the third attempt, closer than ever to the French fries, it did an about-face, sped back to the sidewalk, and vanished behind a tree trunk.

Dennis resumed meditating on what felt like victory, with the glorious-tasting coffee refill adding to his contentedness. He slipped into a daydream of Elizabeth telling him next that she had resolved to end things entirely with Gould. That would call for celebration, champagne. He saw Elizabeth and him eating by candlelight at her place, exchanging loving and lustful glances, giggling at the champagne bubbles ascending into their noses. Maybe that would be the moment to seal the deal and even propose to her. He'd need a ring. She'd expect it to be a high quality one.

But then what? Dennis' mood evaporated as the old anxiety gripped him. She had insisted she wouldn't move to Vancouver. That condemned him to life here in, he had to face it, her shadow. Every time they had a spat, would he be wishing he had returned to the West instead of living with her? He tried to picture himself phoning Wayne to tell him of the decision to remain in Toronto with Elizabeth.

The waiter halted Dennis' uneasy thoughts by depositing a small plastic tray displaying the bill. Dennis dug out his wallet. If he stayed on the patio until Elizabeth finished schmoozing inside, he knew he'd continue obsessing about his future. If she and he were to move in together, she probably would not want to shift camp. In that case, he would not have to hunt for an apartment. On the other hand, maybe she would decree her place was inadequate for the two of them. They would need to find new, mutually acceptable accommodation.

Wasn't he getting too far ahead of himself? She hadn't stopped seeing Gould. They had a quarrel. He'd had plenty with her himself. He had never stomped off and left her stranded, but he had definitely thought about it a few times. After everybody cooled off, she and Gould would probably revert to being nice to each other. Maybe that's all this dramatic moment at the gas station was: an incident she and Gould would laugh about, later.

Except she told him she wanted to be with him, not Gould. Surely that counted. If it did, however, he was back to the same hassle. Should he start searching for an apartment? Not to mention a job. Doing what? And did he really, really, wish to be in Toronto, even for Elizabeth? This time of year in Vancouver the neighbourhoods were gorgeous with the giant rhodos in bloom, and tulips and daffodils had been out for months. The winter rains were done and the sea wind was softer with the new season, lush. Dennis got to his feet.

He didn't want to keep thrashing this over. Mr. Ed's intrusive laugh caught his ear. Dennis checked inside the building. Elizabeth didn't seem in any hurry to end her visit. He decided to join their table, to try to extricate her.

The café was much warmer indoors. As Dennis threaded through the noisy customers, Elizabeth was bent forward in her chair toward the two men, earnestly communicating some point. Mr. Ed happened to look up, noticed him, and beckoned. Dennis observed him speaking to the others, but couldn't hear.

Elizabeth and Mr. Red also raised their eyes in his direction. The thought came to Dennis that the threesome had been talking about him. Who knew how much of her life Elizabeth was willing to share if she thought it might be to her benefit?

Only a few steps from where she sat, Dennis perceived with a jolt that her expression was identical to that of the squirrel a few minutes ago beside his table. Her gaze, like the creature's, was wary and preoccupied, as if he were an impediment to her possession of something she very much desired.